Busted. Thi ***d at all.***

"What are you d
due to all the blo

"Actually, I think that's my line," he said, unsmiling. "This is my bedroom, after all."

She began backing away from him and the nightstand, hoping for a clear shot toward the door.

Instead, he moved with her. His hand shot out and gripped her wrist, tightly.

"You're not going anywhere," he growled.

Alarmed, at first, she froze again. He was breathing harshly, his eyes glittering in the dim light. A slow heat began deep in her belly and she realized she was incredibly, unbelievably, turned on.

The thought just barely crossed her mind when he made a sound low in his throat, a cross between a curse and a groan. Then, while she was trying to process what this meant, he yanked her to him, and slanted his mouth over hers....

Dear Reader,

Everyone wants to be a millionaire, right? It's fun to fantasize about how so much money could change our lives. That's exactly what happens to Matt Landeta. He is given so much, and then what truly matters is taken away. Skylar McLain has also lost everything and only cares about her job as an ATF agent. When she's sent undercover to work with the millionaire cowboy, she sees beyond what's on the surface. But identifying and bonding with the target of a federal investigation is never a good thing and, in this case, can prove dangerous.

Family and loss have long been themes I've been interested in exploring. What keeps people going after the most profound loss of all? For some, it's faith. For others, it's revenge. Both my hero and heroine—Matt and Skylar—have lost everything. They both dealt with this in different ways. And when two battered and broken souls come together in a crisis, each wanting opposing resolutions, can a common ground of healing be reached? And with healing, can there be love?

I hope you enjoy the ranch, the horses and, most of all, getting to know Matt and Skylar. I thoroughly enjoyed writing their story!

Karen Whiddon

KAREN WHIDDON

*The Millionaire
Cowboy's Secret*

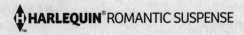

HARLEQUIN®ROMANTIC SUSPENSE

Recycling programs
for this product may
not exist in your area.

ISBN-13: 978-0-373-27822-0

THE MILLIONAIRE COWBOY'S SECRET

Copyright © 2013 by Karen Whiddon

Printed in U.S.A.

Books by Karen Whiddon

Harlequin Romantic Suspense

The CEO's Secret Baby #1662
The Cop's Missing Child #1719
The Millionaire Cowboy's Secret #1752

Silhouette Romantic Suspense

★One Eye Open #1301
★One Eye Closed #1365
★Secrets of the Wolf #1397
The Princess's Secret Scandal #1416
Bulletproof Marriage #1484
★★Black Sheep P.I. #1513
★★The Perfect Soldier #1557
★★Profile for Seduction #1629
Colton's Christmas Baby #1636

Harlequin Nocturne

★Wolf Whisperer #128
★The Wolf Princess #146
★The Wolf Prince #157

Silhouette Nocturne

★Cry of the Wolf #7
★Touch of the Wolf #12

★Dance of the Wolf #45
★Wild Wolf #67
★Lone Wolf #103

★The Pack
★★The Cordasic Legacy

Other titles by this author
available in ebook format.

KAREN WHIDDON

started weaving fanciful tales for her younger brothers at the age of eleven. Amidst the Catskill Mountains of New York, then the Rocky Mountains of Colorado, she fueled her imagination with the natural beauty that surrounded her. Karen now lives in north Texas, where she shares her life with her very own hero of a husband and three doting dogs. Also an entrepreneur, she divides her time between the business she started and writing. You can email Karen at KWhiddon1@aol.com or write to her at P.O. Box 820807, Fort Worth, TX 76182. Fans of her writing can also check out her website, www.karenwhiddon.com.

After nearly 35 books, I think I might have thanked everyone—and then some. So as usual, I want to thank my beloved husband of 25 years—my soul mate. And my best friend and occasional critique partner Anna Adams, who talked me down from the ledge when I accidentally overwrote (and deleted) the last two chapters of this book mere days before it was due to the publisher. She checked on me, cheered with me and commiserated as I locked myself in my office over a holiday weekend and completely rewrote 40-plus pages. Cheers to you, my friend! And thanks, of course. Always thanks for being there for me!

Chapter 1

Restless, Skylar McLain changed her stance. She let her body settle, with her weight distributed evenly and her feet planted in the earth. *Arms steady.* She used the two-handed stance since she was so petite. *Sight.* The target was now centered in her line of vision. *Squeeze the trigger and shoot. Then shoot again.*

"Bull's-eye," she muttered under her breath, taking small satisfaction in the achievement. Since she went to the shooting range at least three times a week, such accuracy was to be expected. She'd always been a good shot—now she was an excellent one.

She just wished she could exorcise the ghosts. According to her shrink, with whom she'd continued therapy after the mandatory Bureau psych evaluation, until she stopped blaming herself, punishing herself, she'd never be fully healed.

Blah, blah, blah. As if she'd ever be normal again.

Shrink talk. Mentally cursing, she pressed the button for a new paper target and began the sequence again.

The ghosts still taunted her, dancing just out of reach of her bullets. Though they'd caught the guy who'd robbed the bank and gunned down her husband and son, his lifetime prison sentence hadn't helped ease the grief. Even his death wouldn't bring back her family.

Finally finished, she clicked her safety on and holstered her Glock. Removing her eye and ear protection, she turned and exited.

The shrink had been right about one thing. The pain had sort of faded over time. Gradually over the past five years, the agonizing vise grip on her heart had been replaced with numbness. She'd welcomed the lack of sensation, of feeling. It allowed her to focus her attention, laser-sharp, on her job. Only her job mattered anymore. She might as well be good at it.

After she headed home, she dressed and packed her bag. Sensing something was up, her border collie, Talia, twirled in circles around the bedroom.

Smiling, Skylar reached out to ruffle Talia's furry head. "Yes, sweetheart. I'm going undercover, so you'll be staying at the kennel." She hated to leave her beloved pet—Talia had been her son's new puppy, only six months old when he'd been killed.

But then, did she really have to leave her? Her new assignment would be on a horse ranch, after all. What better place for a dog?

"Would you like to go with me, girl?" Skylar asked.

Talia barked, as if to answer in the affirmative.

Before she had time to reconsider, Skylar picked up the phone and called the kennel, canceling the reservation. Talia would go with her. Who knew—a dog with herding instincts just might come in handy around large animals.

She instantly felt the knot in her stomach ease. In a few hours, she'd be going undercover. From everything she'd read, Matt Landeta loved animals. He shouldn't have a problem with one hyperactive border collie.

Once everything was packed, including Talia's dog food, favorite toys and bed, Skylar got out the asignment file folder and flipped through it one last time.

Here. Her target. Studying his picture, she speculated, trying to figure out what it was about Matt Landeta that drew her in. He was a tall man with a ruggedly handsome face and muscular build. The peculiar blue shade of his eyes, sapphire mixed with summer-sky, was striking in his tanned face. Idly, she wondered if they really were that color or if he wore contacts. She'd be finding out soon enough.

Today, she'd begin an intricate game of cat and mouse with Matt Landeta. Wealthy and good-looking, he was a local celebrity due to the massive ranch he'd built on the outskirts of town and the beautiful show horses he raised.

She just had to remember not to act as if she worked in law enforcement. Over the years, this had become her biggest challenge, especially since she pretty much lived and breathed her job.

Ostensibly, she'd come to write an article on his Arabian horses for *Today's Arabian Horse* magazine. This was her cover. In truth, she had to discover if the millionaire had gotten rich because he was illegally selling ammunition to Mexican drug cartels. If so, she would take him down.

Once she had her rental car packed, she whistled for Talia. Since there was nothing the dog loved more—

except playing ball—she came running and jumped into the backseat.

Now Skylar had everything that mattered to her. According to her records, her destination—Matt's ranch—was about a half hour west of town. Her entire body vibrating with anticipation, she settled in the driver's seat and started the car.

Usually when she went undercover, she drove a department-issued vehicle. This time she'd left the Ford Taurus behind and rented a snazzy little Volkswagen Bug. Her boss should have seen that this car was more realistic to her journalist persona.

As she navigated the country roads, her beloved dog happily panting in the backseat, she couldn't help but feel confident. She'd thoroughly prepared herself with every video, every article about Matt. She knew how this first meeting would go. He'd be charming and arrogant, just a touch condescending, confident that his darkly sexy looks would make her willing to cut the next notch on his headboard herself.

She hadn't yet decided how she'd react to him. She had two choices—she could go for professional and detached, which would be more natural, or the blushing, tongue-tied pseudo virgin, which would undoubtedly appeal to him more. Now that she thought about it, she'd have to react on the fly and go with her gut, once she discovered the type of woman he found attractive.

She relaxed and looked at the passing landscape with interest. Though she'd grown up here in Anniversary, Texas, it had been years since she'd bothered to drive out here from her home north of Dallas. Her family had moved to Anniversary her junior year of high school and any friendships she'd forged in those days had long since died out.

Amazing how not much ever changed in small towns. The shops on Main Street had been renovated and were apparently now thriving in this lakeside community. She saw two martial-arts studios, several cafés, bars, clothing shops and even a general store. People strolled the sidewalks and shopped and ate at small outside tables.

Pushing down the weird sense of longing the sights brought, she continued to drive past the city limits, over the long bridge that crossed the lake. There were a couple of marinas here, with bait shops and lakeside bars, frequented by the locals who drove up in their boats.

As she stared at the sparkling blue water, the unexpected ache in her throat made her furious. Once, this was the sort of place she might have brought her family. Now that opportunity was long gone.

Giving herself a mental shake, she gripped her steering wheel and drove on. Sentimentality was not compatible with her life or her job. She'd returned here for a reason, one that had nothing to do with her personally.

She'd do best to remember that. Finally she turned from the paved two-lane road to the single-track gravel one that, according to the map she'd been given, led to Matt's impressive spread.

After a series of left and right turns, she pulled up to an immense black wrought-iron gate. Closed, of course. As she coasted to a stop in front of it, she stared, wondering if its resemblance to a biblical entrance to heaven was intentional.

If so, the irony wasn't lost on her.

Rolling down her window, she spoke into the call box next to the gate, identifying herself. A moment later, the imposing barricade swung slowly open.

As she proceeded up the drive, she craned her neck, looking for a glimpse of the ranch house. No such luck;

the first buildings were barns and sheds. She counted three outdoor riding areas, a large arena and then a huge building that had to be an enclosed arena next to a square place with a large sign that said Ranch Office. On the far side of the parking lot, away from everything else, was a lovely old barn made of stone and wood. Exuding a sense of age and history, it looked as if it had sat on this land long before anything else was built.

There were several horses, wearing light blankets to protect their coats from the sun, grazing in various green pastures. She even saw one fenced-off field full of cattle.

And still no house.

Then, as she drove around the side of the indoor arena, she saw it, slowing her speed to a crawl so she could take it all in.

The red-tiled roof gleamed softly in the afternoon sun, perfectly complementing the creamy stucco walls. Low-slung and elegant, the house blended with the landscape, managing to look as though it had sprung from the earth decades ago. Even though she knew from her research the hacienda was a mere four years old, the structure had a weathered, peaceful look that would have made a lesser woman melt inside.

Parking, she reflected on how lucky it was that she was not that woman.

Killing the engine, Skylar inhaled deeply. She took her time getting out and leashing Talia, mentally rehearsing her cover story for perhaps the tenth time.

Talia happily began investigating a host of interesting smells. Then, raising her head, she looked past Skylar and let out a single woof as a warning.

Registering the sound of footsteps behind her, Skylar took a deep breath. *Showtime*. Steeling herself, she slowly turned. Despite her hours of preparation, her first glimpse of him brought her a jolt.

As expected, he was tall, dark and boldly—devilishly—handsome. This she already knew from the photos she'd pored over. Muscular, fit and tanned. Check.

But she hadn't been prepared for the blatant masculinity radiating from every inch of Matt Landeta's body. Or the restless energy laced with power exuding from him as he strode toward her. The mere fact that he'd shaken her out of her inertia enough to even register such a thing shocked her.

Though she'd sort of decided to go with overawed girlishness, her defenses immediately came up. She straightened her shoulders and became an ice maiden instead.

Talia, however, had no such reservations. She greeted Matt with the same affectionate joy she bestowed on everyone. Plumed tail wagging, her entire body wiggled as he petted her.

"Nice dog. You must be Skylar," he drawled, straightening and holding out a tanned hand. "Pleased to meet you."

When Skylar took it, she noted the calluses, so at odds with the elegance of his long fingers. As she met his gaze, she couldn't help but study him, her law-enforcement-trained eyes missing nothing.

He carried himself with an air of self-confidence. Though he was virile and masculine, genuine pleasure softened his stubborn, arrogant face, as if he were actually glad to see her. Despite the perfection of his granite-like features, there were touches of humor around his eyes, and his generous mouth appeared as though he were always on the verge of smiling.

Interesting. Did he truly enjoy his work so much?

"I hope you don't mind my bringing her," she said, really not caring what he thought. "She's well trained and usually accompanies me on assignments. I promise she won't be any trouble."

"I don't mind." He glanced around. "I'm sure we'll all become great friends while you're here."

His hair, exactly like the pictures she'd studied, was thick and black, tapering neatly to his collar. The shadow of a beard gave him an even more masculine appearance.

Damn. She shivered.

"Are you all right?" Pausing in the act of scratching behind Talia's ears, he peered up at her with a concerned expression.

Somehow, she found her voice. "I'm fine." Attempting a smile, she tried to figure out how in real life a person could look completely different than photographs. Hell, she was a photographer herself and knew there'd be minor incongruities, but this...this was unreal.

Despite his surface air of approachability, Matt Landeta looked tough, lean and sinewy. She could sense the danger lurking right underneath his innocuous appearance, like a wild animal biding time until it struck viciously.

Fitting, considering he was allegedly a criminal.

But worse, at least to her, despite everything she'd made herself into, she somehow found him as sexy as hell. Which felt as if she was committing the worst kind of betrayal. She felt this knowledge like the sharp stab of a knife.

Ruthlessly, she pushed all emotions away. All that was for another place, another time. Not now. She had a job to do. Luckily she'd developed nerves of steel. Keeping her expression friendly, she continued to let her gaze roam over him, exactly as any other red-blooded woman would.

"Wow," she drawled. "You don't look like any horse breeder I've ever met."

He grinned back, the beauty in his smile making it difficult for her to keep up the flirtatious act. In fact, the longer she studied him, the more unsettled she became. Rather than making her uncomfortable, this pissed her off. Seriously.

Not good. Not good at all. Her job depended on her getting to know this man, but she couldn't allow personal feelings to factor in.

"And you don't look like any journalist I've ever met, pretty lady." Cocking his head, eyes molten, he gazed at her as if she were the most beautiful thing he'd ever seen. Her fake smile froze on her face. Again, she had to suppress a surge of anger, which threw her off her game.

His gaze sharpened at her lack of response and he leaned closer, bringing with him the scent of coffee and the outdoors.

"Who knew *Today's Arabian Horse* magazine hired such gorgeous journalists?" Even his voice, deep and as rich as chocolate, stirred unwanted desires inside her, despite the blatant B.S. he was spouting.

Damn. Somehow she managed to smile back, at the same time tugging her hand free. She decided to ignore the fact that he'd held her hand a bit longer than was normal, especially since he was well-known as a player.

She blushed on purpose as his gaze swept over her, growing more confident as she regained her focus. After all, she had years of field experience behind her. She wouldn't falter just because this one guy had movie-star good looks and sinful bedroom eyes.

She could do this. She would do this. Nothing would

destroy her 100 percent success rate. Just like with all the others, she'd get to the truth. Eventually.

After all, she could refocus. Glancing down at her dog, her *son's* dog, who had taken a seat on Matt's foot and had her eyes closed in bliss while he petted her, Skylar simply remembered the life she'd lost, and boom, she was back on track.

With that sobering thought, she straightened her spine, looked him in the eye, and let her smile widen. "Looks like you've got a fan there," she said, gesturing at Talia. "I hope she isn't bothering you."

He shrugged, apparently not in the least bothered. "In case you hadn't noticed, I'm a dog person."

She nodded. "I'm glad. Thank you so much for allowing me this opportunity," she said, managing to sound just on the edge of gushing. To distract herself, she reached down and scratched Talia just below the collar, which was her favorite spot.

A comfortable silence fell. When she finally looked up, she was surprised to find something hungry, something sharp, in his warm gaze. Perfect. As soon as she noticed, his expression changed, becoming the amused, flirtatious one from before. Ah, so she wasn't the only one playing a role.

Interesting.

"Let me show you where you'll be staying," he said, the resonance of his voice still trying to pull her out of her nice, safe numbness. "Are your bags in your car?"

"Nope. Just Talia's food and bed." She hefted her backpack. "I travel light."

His warm smile told her he approved. Reaching in for the dog bed and the sack of dry food, he snagged both and then straightened.

"Follow me." Turning, he strode off, apparently trusting she could keep up. For a moment, she caught herself admiring the view—well-worn Wrangler jeans and what had to be the perfect male butt—before collecting herself and hurrying after him, Talia happily trotting along at her side.

He led her to a small camper parked under a towering tree. Surprised, she looked around. "A bit isolated, isn't it?" she said, aware most women would be a bit apprehensive staying alone.

"No worries." Placing a casual hand on her shoulder, he lightly squeezed. His touch felt hot, even through the thin material of her T-shirt. "This camper is where my foreman's wife stayed while they were separated. They got back together, so now this is where I put temporary ranch hands and other assorted visitors."

Nodding, she tried not to show her disappointment. Glancing back at the magnificent showpiece of a home, she sighed. "I so wanted to stay there." The better to keep an eye on things.

Now she'd lobbed the ball squarely into his court. In real life she'd never have been so pushy, but for this job, she had to take any advantages she could. Even those that hadn't been offered. Especially those.

He frowned, giving her what she'd have sworn was a passable imitation of a confused look. "I promise this is a nice trailer. It's clean and private and better for your dog. You'll be close enough to still do your job, but not underfoot. I'm sorry, Ms. McLain. I do value my privacy."

She'd bet he did. It might be difficult organizing and running a massive illegal-export empire with a snoopy journalist underfoot. *Well played, Matt Landeta,* she thought. *Well played.* Of course, she'd expected no less.

"I understand." She didn't have to feign her disappointment.

"Go ahead, have a look inside." He opened the door, motioning for her to precede him. "After this, I'll take you on a tour of the house."

Humor colored his smoky voice once more. A quick glance at him confirmed her suspicion that he was laughing at her. For a heartbeat, she felt a flicker of unease— did he suspect?—before she managed to make herself chuckle along with him.

The interior of the camper was surprisingly neat. A slide-out in the living area widened the space, giving the impression of more room that the exterior had hinted at.

Talia close at her side, she wandered from the compact kitchen to the living area and checked out the tiny bathroom along the way before dropping her backpack on the full-size bed.

"Very nice," she said, meaning it. "I used to camp as a kid, so this brings back memories." This was actually true. The closer she stuck to the truth while undercover, the easier things generally went.

"I'm glad." His broad shoulders made the tiny space seem even smaller. He dropped Talia's bed in the perfect spot next to the compact couch and placed the bag of dog food on the kitchen table.

For a moment they stood in a sort of awkward silence. Finally, he gave her what she was beginning to think of as his trademark smile. "Ready to see the house? Do you think your dog will be all right here? The air-conditioning works just fine."

She nodded. Fishing her camera out of her pack, she also grabbed a small notepad and pen.

Still smiling, he held out his hand to help her out of the camper. The moment she slipped her fingers into his, sensation once again slammed into her. It took every ounce of her self-control to keep from yanking her fingers from his.

Gritting her teeth, she kept her expression pleasant. As soon as she'd descended the three metal steps and had her feet firmly on the ground, she nonchalantly pulled her hand free.

She'd barely taken a step when she heard the sharp crack of a gunshot. Instinctively dropping, she rolled, intending to take cover behind the nearest bush, managing to snag hold of Matt's arm on the way so she could drag him with her as she pulled her weapon.

Chapter 2

What the... Jerking his arm away, Matt stared at Skylar. He'd expected to find her a bit intense, given what he knew she actually did for a living, but this? It had never occurred to him that she might be skirting the edge of crazy.

"Get over here," she whispered. To his shock he realized she'd drawn a pistol, a wicked-looking Glock.

He didn't move. "That was my farm tractor, the one my hands use to clean out the barn. It backfired. Are you all right?" He held out his hand to help her up. Confusion flashed across her aristocratic features, warring with embarrassment and then relief. Finally, ignoring his gesture, she climbed to her feet, holstered her gun and dusted her hands off on her jeans.

"Sorry," she drawled, her face flushed. "I could've sworn that was a gunshot."

"Obviously." Debating, he gave her a long look. "Do you always carry a pistol?"

She cocked her head. "Always," she said firmly, surprising him. "I got my concealed-handgun license the first year they came out. I'm a firm believer in self-defense for women."

"I agree." Smiling at her, he kept the conversation banal. "Are you a fairly good shot?"

"I'm an excellent shot. I practice whenever I can. It's a hobby of mine, second only to the shooting I do with my camera." Holding up her camera, she smiled back, the first genuine expression she'd used since she'd arrived.

Her smile stunned him. He'd noticed her beauty before, but now she looked…radiant, with the kind of unconscious sensual appeal that begged exploration.

Damn. He slammed the lid down on his errant thoughts. No way was he planning to go there. He had enough on his plate as it was.

"I also have a CHL," he told her, his voice sounding a bit huskier than he'd have liked. "But, no offense, you seem jumpy. I don't like the idea of you waving around a gun."

Meeting his gaze straight on, she considered his statement. "You're right," she finally said, surprising the hell out of him. "I promise you it won't happen again."

He noted she didn't offer to turn in her weapon. Of course, as an undercover ATF agent, she really couldn't.

Studying her, he considered his options. He could send her away and wait for the Feds to drum up another ridiculous excuse to send someone else. Or he could let her do her job while unwittingly serving his purpose and helping him get to the people he wanted—the Mexican drug cartel.

She'd do, he decided. Plus, it didn't hurt that she was easy on the eyes. "All right," he finally said. "You can stay. You say you've taken all the courses and are well aware of the responsibilities that come with carrying a loaded gun?'

"Yes." Her mouth tightened. Pushing her, he knew, but he hadn't been the one overreacting to the sound of an engine backfiring. Were all ATF agents this jumpy? Or did this one have a particular reason to be?

When he didn't immediately respond, she opened her mouth as though she meant to argue her case, but then closed it, apparently deciding against saying anything that might give her away.

"Fine." He decided to let it pass. "Come on. I'll take you to see the horses."

He turned and strode off in the direction of the barn, knowing she'd have to hurry to catch up. Which she did easily and without comment.

As they crossed the parking lot, passing by the tack building and the ranch office on the way to his large barn, she looked around and whistled. "Nice."

Allowing a slight grin, he nodded. "Thanks."

"I've heard your horses are beautiful."

Of all the creatures on this earth, Matt loved horses the best. Especially his. The purebred Arabians were grace, elegance and intelligence combined.

Instead of taking Skylar directly to the barn, he led her to the indoor riding arena to which the stalls were attached. His trainers were working two of his newest mares now.

Taking Skylar's arm, he stopped at the edge of the arena to watch. He glanced at her, knowing her reaction would tell him if she truly was a horse person at heart or pretending to be one because of her assignment.

To his surprise, she had her chin in the air, eyes

closed. The expression on her face was one of rapt wonder.

"What are you doing?"

One corner of her mouth curled up. "Inhaling the scent. There's nothing like the smell of a horse barn."

Curious, he continued to study her. "Most people don't like it, especially the manure."

Shaking her head, she grinned at him. "Well, I do. I like it a lot."

He didn't know her enough to know if she was faking. For him, the scent of horses and hay and leather and sawdust were as heady as the finest perfume. No, better.

When she turned her attention to the two horses being lunged at each end of the ring, he waited expectantly. If she'd done her research, she'd know that these two animals were among the finest examples of the purebred Arabian horse breed.

"They're beautiful," she breathed. Raising her fancy camera, she snapped shot after shot.

Idly, he wondered if she even knew how to take decent photographs. One way to find out. "Let me see." He held out his hand for the camera.

Slowly, she handed over the expensive piece of equipment. "Please be careful with it," she said.

He'd already located the button that would display the digital images. Calling them up on to the display, he viewed them one by one.

They were first-rate. Professional quality. She'd truly done his horses justice.

Surprised and impressed, he handed the camera back.

"They're good," he said. "Very good."

She gave a nonchalant shrug and turned away. "That's my job."

"How's your dog around horses?" he asked. The last thing he needed was a crazed dog frightening his stock.

"She's good." Her easy smile told him she once again spoke truth. "I used to have a couple of my own. She came with me to the stables every day. I promise she won't be a problem."

"That'll work." If the dog couldn't handle it, he'd simply ask her to keep it in the trailer.

His cell phone buzzed, indicating a text message. Digging it out of his pocket, he saw it was from José. I have news, it said.

"I've got to go," he told Skylar. "Feel free to take a look around the barn and talk to my employees. I'll see you up at the house later, if you'd like to eat with us."

Her eyes widened, as though she hadn't been expecting the invitation. Finally, she nodded. "Sounds good," she said, then turned away.

Matt hurried up to the house.

José had apparently watched everything from the kitchen window.

"That's her?"

Matt nodded. Skylar McLain hadn't been at all what he'd expected. The slender redhead looked strong and fit, as befitted a federal agent, yet she was lushly shaped. Her facial bones were delicate, showing off her full mouth and wide green eyes. Worst of all, she was beautiful, even with her silky straight hair scooped back in a careless ponytail.

"Wow!" José's grin showed his crooked teeth. "A looker, isn't she?"

"Not at all what I expected when you said the woman coming to do a story on me for the *Arabian Horse* magazine was going to be an undercover ATF agent. I still don't know how you found that out."

José's grin widened as he executed an exaggerated bow. "One of my many talents. I know people who know things."

Despite the worry that gnawed at his stomach, Matt forced himself to smile back. His friend had gone the extra mile, using his past prison experience and connections. Not only to place himself between the ATF and Matt, but with the Mexican drug cartel La Familia, as well.

"She's pretty damn hot for a federal agent."

"I agree." José briefly grinned, then frowned. "You can't let that distract you."

"You know better than that," Matt said, not bothering to try to hide his anger. José knew better than anyone else what he lived for.

Vengeance, plain and simple. And he didn't give a damn who or what he had to go through to get it.

"Take it easy, man." José cuffed him on the shoulder. "It's all gonna work out."

"Maybe. I'm still not sure why we don't just send her packing. If the cartel gets wind that we have an ATF agent here…"

"They will." José sounded confident. "We just have to make sure they learn about it when we want them to."

Elaborate plans. Even as a kid, José had always engineered complicated schemes that always seemed to work out. This time, he'd planned the most intricate of them all. Not only did they have to fool the ATF, but La Familia, as well. Good thing Matt trusted his friend implicitly. He wanted revenge, and that was what José promised he would get. With no collateral damage. This was important, too. Matt didn't want anyone else to get hurt.

Jamming his hands into his pockets, he stared out the

window at the ranch he'd developed from the ground up. Too late for his family to enjoy it.

"You're right, though. I'll have to be careful," he muttered, thinking out loud. "Since you're positive your plan is going to work, I've got to figure out a way to let Skylar McLain hang around without allowing her to find anything."

"At least until you want her to," José reminded him.

"Yeah." Matt gave a short laugh. Reaching deep inside to that dark, still place he carried with him always, he straightened, infusing the steel into his spine the way he'd learned in the army. "Let's hope it all works out the way we've planned. I'd hate to be the one responsible for getting someone else killed."

"Amigo, you need to stop." José cuffed his shoulder again. Matt braced himself to blow off the words he knew his friend was about to say. He ignored them at least once a month.

"None of this is your fault."

José always said this, like a litany, and by now Matt thought his friend truly believed it. Of the two of them, José had changed the least. Oh, prison had hardened him, shown him life was not all sunshine and roses, but José somehow managed to remain an eternal optimist, just like he'd been when they were kids. Most times, Matt envied that. Other times, he couldn't help but feel José was foolish, destined to get hurt.

Rubbing the back of his neck with a tired hand, he thought he'd been playing this game for far too long. He was more than ready for it to be over. Patience had never been his strongest trait, but in this he'd had no choice.

"These things take time," José said, correctly reading the expression on Matt's face.

"So you keep saying." Matt knew he sounded sour,

but didn't really care. "With your newfound serenity and all, you're starting to remind me of our old priest, Father Peter, from Wednesday night catechism."

José grinned, taking it as a compliment. Matt suspected José himself had once toyed with the idea of becoming a priest. Growing up, they'd both attended the same church, worshipped at the same masses. They even briefly served as altar boys together. Back then, the future had seemed rosy and bright. Neither had imagined what life would have in store for them, though they'd each been certain they were going to change the world.

After high school, though they'd remained best friends, they'd drifted apart. After all, they'd taken opposite paths after graduation. Matt had enlisted and had become a sharpshooter for the army. José had gone to work at his cousin's body shop. He'd gotten into trouble soon after that.

By the time Matt had completed his second tour of duty in Afghanistan and finally returned home, José had already been arrested and was doing time. Possession with intent to distribute.

José had done his time and emerged better for it. He'd cleaned up, gotten reformed and, when Matt picked him up outside prison the day José was released, he'd been ready to help his best friend get revenge for the brutal murder of his entire family. José was the only one who'd known Matt before the complete identity change, back when Matt's name had been Miguel Lopez. José knew about Matt's past and understood his future.

These days, Matt trusted no one. Except José.

Skylar waited until Matt's footsteps had faded into the distance before heading toward the barn. In a way, she was glad he'd taken off. She'd always loved horses and wanted to take her time examining his.

The instant she entered the barn, her chest felt tight. Enraptured, she saw nearly every stall was full. Matt's horses were the most magnificent animals she'd ever seen.

Walking down the barn's broad cement aisle, she inhaled the aroma of horse and straw, and grinned. Perfectly chiseled features, the classic arch to the neck, the flowing lines and ideal conformations told her she was among rarified specimens. Purebred Arabians, every single one of them. Expensive, finely cared-for animals. A dazzling bay mare in the first stall, two grays, a chestnut gelding with a huge white star on his forehead. All of them looked up at her approach, swinging their beautiful heads to eye her.

None seemed skittish. Petting their velvety noses, she found herself wondering which one Matt rode. Then, when she reached the big stall at the end of the aisle and saw the huge black stallion inside, she knew.

This would be his horse. She could envision him astride it now.

Blinking rapidly, she took a step back. What the hell was she doing? She'd known going in what she'd be facing—a rich, charming playboy with more money than sense. Why on earth she was letting someone like that get to her?

As she turned to exit the barn, her cell phone rang. Caller ID said it was a private call. Which meant it would be her boss, David Northrup.

"Checking your progress," her supervisor barked before Skylar even finished saying hello.

Quickly, she outlined what had happened since she'd arrived.

"Did you meet José Nivas?"

Matt Landeta's right-hand man. "No," she answered. "Matt hasn't actually introduced me to any of his employees."

"Be careful. He's dangerous."

Gripping her phone, Skylar grimaced. She'd reviewed the dossier front to back. "I know."

"Then you're aware that Nivas has been clean since he got out of prison. He works with Landeta at the ranch. We've had our eyes on him for a long time, but he's—to all appearances—stayed straight."

She sighed. "That was all included in the paperwork I was given."

"You have to befriend him."

"Matt invited me to dinner up at the big house tonight. Maybe he'll be there."

"Perfect." David cleared his throat, which meant Skylar wouldn't like whatever he was about to say next. "You know what you have to do. Turn up the charm. Landeta won't be able to resist a pretty lady like you. That's one of the reasons you got this assignment."

As if she needed to be reminded. Though she'd had numerous assignments in the past—all successful—she hadn't ever had one where she was actually *attracted* to the suspect. Maybe her coworkers were right and it was time for her to take a vacation.

After she wrapped up this case, that is. She'd go to Jamaica or Key West, lie around on a beach and sip fruity umbrella drinks.

"Are you there?"

Belatedly realizing her supervisor was waiting for a response, she sighed. "Yes, of course. I'll do whatever I can."

"Excellent. Report back to me if you learn anything. I'll expect regular status updates."

Pushing the button to end the call, Skylar wondered why she didn't want to seduce Matt Landeta. After all, she'd played the seductress role before, all in the line of duty. Yet this time, she sensed her own psyche would be in peril. Not good. The man was too damn sexy for her own peace of mind.

But she didn't have a choice. Ever since a drug-crazed junky had robbed the bank and shot her husband and son, she'd dedicated herself to her job. If Matt Landeta was enough of a bastard that he supplied the Mexican drug cartels with ammunition, he deserved what he got.

She straightened her spine, once again in the right frame of mind. All she had to do was think of Robbie and Bryan, standing in line at the bank where she should have been instead, and she could do anything.

Including seduce Matt Landeta.

Glancing out the window, Matt considered Skylar McLain. Something about her bugged him. It wasn't her beauty—hell, he had his pick of gorgeous women. Or the tough-girl exterior she tried to hide, instead wearing it like a shield.

Maybe it was the simple fact that she didn't react to him the way other women did. Especially when they wanted something from him, like this one did.

Not his problem. He had more important things to worry about. Like making sure this complicated plan didn't fall apart.

"So what's up?" he asked his friend.

"I got a phone call—" José sounded troubled "—from my contact down in Matamoros. La Familia just slaughtered twenty people and strung them up along the road leading back into Texas. It's a warning."

Matt swore. "Were any of them our guys?" By this he meant the ones wanting to buy his ammo.

"I don't know yet." José's frown deepened. "But I'm betting this will put a damper on them being so eager to try to form their own cartel."

Which meant they wouldn't need so much ammunition. Matt had been buying it for the past two years, both from online and various gun shops around the state.

Cursing, Matt dragged his hand through his hair. "Do you think they got word of what Diego and his men are trying to do?"

"I don't think so. If they did, Diego would be dead."

"And you're sure he's not?"

José snorted. "Amigo, I ain't sure of nothin'. The only thing I'm sure of is that, no matter what happens, somebody's gonna need ammunition."

With a sigh, Matt tapped the newspaper on the table in front of them. "True, and if we were really in the business of selling it, we'd make a small fortune."

"Hey, come on, man." José looked over at him hopefully. "Even if Diego can't buy it, we can still sell it, right?"

Since this question came up just about every day, Matt didn't respond. José already knew the answer. All of this, the stockpiling round after round of ammunition, putting out feelers in the dangerous world of the Mexican cartels, had been done for one reason only.

To lure Diego Rodriguez. Nothing more, nothing less.

Glaring at him, José finally shook his head. "Fine. Though it seems like a lot of trouble for nothing if it doesn't work out. We ought to be able to make some money someway."

"Right." Matt glared right back. "We've already got the ATF sniffing around here. First time you try anything like that you'll end up right back in prison. You know that."

Expression sullen, José looked down. He knew Matt was right. "So what did you think of the ATF lady pretending to be a magazine photographer?"

"She's okay." Matt didn't feel like elaborating. The last thing he wanted to do was discuss Skylar's obvious charms.

Instead, José grumbled to his hands, "I still don't get why the ATF had to send her anyway."

Matt wasn't sure, either. Before embarking on this monstrous undertaking, he'd researched the law. Texas had no laws about how much ammo a private citizen could stockpile. He'd been careful, too, ordering from various online sites, trying to order as much as he could without gathering too much attention. He had close to a quarter of a million rounds now. With more on order.

As long as he stopped there, he'd be good. Selling it to the Mexicans, however… That would put him in the realm of federal law breaking, not to mention what the Mexican government would do to him if they found out about it.

Lucky for him he had no plans to sell even a single round. He only wanted the cartel—or specifically, several specific members of the cartel—to believe he did.

Since José knew Matt wouldn't even discuss doing anything else with the ammo, he sniffed again and continued talking about Skylar. "I wonder who in the ATF came up with the horse-magazine reporter as a cover idea."

Matt grinned. "I have to say, it's brilliant." He was known for his love of his Arabian horses, and he had a full-time team who worked on showing them around the country. He had a second full-time team who stayed here at the ranch. They took care of breeding and training and all the other things that came with having a successful horse ranch.

Leaving Matt to focus on his overarching goal: vengeance. He let his grin slide off his face, replacing it with a frown.

"When this is all over, you know it won't bring them back," José said for what had to be the hundredth time.

"Are you taking up psychoanalysis?" Matt asked as he always did. "If so, stop."

José shook his head. "Fine. But what about the Fed? Are you letting her in the house for meals?"

"Sure, why not?" Matt shrugged. "I don't really have a problem with her. Plus, she'll be easier to keep an eye on if I keep her close."

José's knowing smile made Matt grimace. "And it doesn't hurt that she's easy on the eyes, does it?"

Refusing to dignify that remark with a reply, Matt snatched up his hat and stalked off to check on his barn. He'd hired several new barn helpers and wanted to make sure they stuck to the established schedule. Nothing upset a horse worse than a deviation from its normal routine.

It dawned on him that he'd become a lot like that, too.

Shaking his head, he realized it might be time to mix things up. Since he was planning for a big showdown to occur soon, he'd damn well better be ready.

After photographing the barn horses and the surrounding area for future reference, Skylar strolled outside toward the pasture. Twenty or thirty head of horses grazed lush grass under the cloudless sky. She took several more photographs, knowing when this investigation was over she'd be able to use some of these for her growing portfolio. Photography as a hobby brought her more enjoyment with each passing day. It was the only other thing besides her job that she could lose herself in for hours at a time.

She thought of Matt with his craggy features and easy-limbed grace. If possible, she'd like to sneak in a few shots of him, but only when he wasn't aware. She'd bet he'd make an interesting subject.

She snapped the pasture in all four directions, knowing she could enlarge the digital images later and study them for any anomalies.

"Are you still out here?"

Speak of the devil. Matt had come up behind her unnoticed. Either he was able to move with a lot of stealth, or she'd been way too involved with her camera.

Glad she hadn't jumped, she turned slowly. "I can't get enough of your beautiful horses," she said, meaning it.

He wore a black cowboy hat, putting much of his face in shadow. She felt heat begin a slow burn somewhere in her stomach.

The odd look he gave her told her he didn't believe her, as though he'd seen her taking additional shots of the pasture, barn and outbuildings. Ignoring the uneasy feeling tickling her spine, she leaned on the fence and busied herself snapping a few more photos. This time she made sure they were only of the horses.

"I'm surprised you didn't go get your dog," he said. "A dog like that would love running through the pasture, especially if you brought her a Frisbee."

Surprised, she glanced at him. "She does love her Frisbee."

He graced her with another one of his devastating smiles that sent her pulse into overdrive. "You did bring it, didn't you?"

Slowly, she shook her head. "No. I planned on taking her for a walk after dinner. On a leash, so I can get a feeling for how she's going to react."

"I thought you said she was used to horses."

"She is. Or rather, was." Fidgeting with her camera, she squinted up at him in the early-afternoon sun. "It's been a while since I owned them. I probably need to take it slowly with her."

As she stared at him, his smile slowly faded. He made her uneasy. And not for the usual reasons. It wasn't because he struck her as particularly dangerous—she'd been around a lot worse characters than this millionaire cowboy who apparently amused himself by dabbling in illegal ammunition sales.

No, it was more of a physical-appeal thing—she felt his presence like a punch in the gut, making it difficult for her to catch her breath. She didn't like this and needed to find a way to cope with it.

Oddly enough, she sensed Matt felt equally uncomfortable around her. Despite his brash self-confidence, she sensed this was as much an act as her pretend photojournalist job.

The next instant she nearly snorted out loud. She needed to stop overanalyzing him and do her job.

Making a show of glancing at her watch, she managed a fake smile of her own. "I'd better get going. I need to unpack, let Talia out and freshen up before dinner."

He nodded. "See you then."

Batting her eyelashes and hoping she wasn't overdoing it, she looked at the house, shadowed by the towering oak trees. "Will there be a lot of people at dinner?" She kept her tone deceptively casual.

"No." He tugged his hat lower, hiding his eyes. "Just me and my friend José, and of course a few of my staff."

His staff. She nearly shook her head. Unlike the rest of the world, the man was filthy rich, with *filthy* being the operative word. No one knew where he'd gotten his millions, but she had no doubt they hadn't been by ethical means.

"See you later." Turning away, he headed off. Unable to help herself, she once again watched him go. The inexplicable yearning she felt filled her with disgust as she headed back toward her little trailer.

Focus. On. The. Job.

So she would meet Matt's right-hand man. Good. She planned to watch José Nivas like a hawk. In fact, after meeting Matt and noting his laid-back manner, she wouldn't be surprised to learn José was behind the entire ammunition-smuggling operation. Once a criminal, always a criminal. Just like that thug who had robbed the bank and killed her husband, Robbie, and young son, Bryan.

Pushing the painful thought away, she grimaced. At least the shrink had been right about one thing. She'd taught herself coping mechanisms. These days, she considered herself fully functional—at least as a federal agent. As a woman, not so much. After all, how many women went around with a gaping hole where their heart used to be?

As she neared the trailer, Talia's enthusiastic barking told her the dog had heard her arrival. Opening the camper door, she let the border collie jump and whirl around her in greeting. Locating the leash, she took her pet outside.

Once that was done, they went back inside and Skylar unpacked. She fed Talia and made sure she had a bowl of fresh water.

"Matt invited me up to the house to eat, Tali," she said. Used to the one-sided conversations, Talia cocked her head and wagged her plumed tail.

"What do you think about that?" Skylar continued. Since the accident, she used her pet as a sounding board for everything and took comfort in hashing out her problems out loud. Another coping mechanism, she supposed. But it worked, so it was all good as far as she was concerned.

"I find the invitation suspect." She ruffled the dog's black-and-white fur. "But then, the fact that he's letting a reporter from an obscure horse magazine stay in his guest trailer for ten days is kind of weird, too. Come on, how long does it take to come up with an article?"

Talia woofed once, as if in agreement.

"I wonder if he suspects who I am. Especially since I had that embarrassing overreaction to the backfire. I thought it was a gunshot."

Talia whined, turning around three times before lying down. Skylar grimaced. Hell, even her dog knew this wasn't a normal reaction. "I guess I'm still not healthy," Skylar said, sighing. "As long as the ATF doesn't know that, we're okay."

Talia shook her head, almost as though disagreeing with her.

"You know what?" Skylar asked, grinning at her own foolishness. "You're right. When you're around a man suspected of smuggling ammo to the Mexican drug cartels, you sort of expect to hear gunshots...."

Turning to hang up her clothes, she sighed. She hadn't brought much to wear. In fact, she had two dresses, three pairs of jeans and maybe seven shirts, most of them T-shirts. How to dress for dinner was an interesting conundrum. Did she go for sexy siren or casual, artsy photographer girl?

She thought of Matt Landeta with his enigmatic smile and amazing blue eyes, and reached for the expensive sheath. Something in-between, she thought.

As she zipped up the formfitting pale green dress, she peered at herself in the small bathroom mirror and sighed. She supposed she looked okay, but she had trouble pulling off sexy, despite the amazing platform stilettos she'd packed. How could a woman manage to ooze sensuality when she felt all dried up inside?

This was the only part of her assignment that gave her trouble. She'd known what she was getting into before agreeing to take this on. She was supposed to seduce Matt Landeta and hopefully get him to reveal— during pillow talk—secrets about his alleged ammunition sales.

She supposed she looked passable. Ready, she sat down. Hard. Up until now, she'd pushed that part of her assignment away, hoping it wouldn't be necessary. Maybe she'd get lucky and it wouldn't be.

Yet she couldn't deny the way her pulse picked up at the thought of some face time with Matt.

Chapter 3

What was her problem? Skylar scowled. She'd per-
formed similar tasks, all under the guise of her job, in
the past several years. Of course, she hadn't slept with
any of her suspects—she would go only so far, even for
her precious job.

But, she admitted the truth to herself, none of them
had been as sexy as Matt Landeta.

Her sources had been right. She hadn't been prepared for the man in the flesh. She could only hope as
time went on she'd grow immune to his considerable
masculine charms. Considering the model/actress/cen-
terfold type of woman he usually attracted, he probably wouldn't even notice an ordinary woman like her.
Which meant she'd have to work that much harder.

Talia whined as though she understood. Leaning
down, Skylar kissed the top of her furry little head.
God, she loved that dog. She didn't know what she'd
do without her.

A sharp tap on her door startled her out of her pity party. Jumping to her feet, she slipped into the awesome shoes and smoothed down her skirt. Talia barked, only once in warning, before a hand signal from Skylar had her lying back down.

Willing her heartbeat to slow, Skylar took a deep breath and pasted on a friendly smile before she opened the door. But it wasn't Matt, and her stomach clenched. A man who had to be José Nivas stood there, his hard gaze sweeping over her as though he was undressing her with his eyes. And the look he gave her wasn't friendly. Definitely not friendly.

She stared right back. Short and stocky, he'd decorated his olive skin with multiple tattoos. He had the tough look of a man who'd spent time in prison and now didn't care what anyone thought of him.

One corner of his mouth lifted in a sneering sort of smile. "Hey," he said, crossing his arms.

Straightening her spine, she speared him with a look. "Yes? Can I help you?" Steel and ice rang in her tone, along with the tiniest tremor that she couldn't manage to suppress.

Worse, he noticed it. Shaking his head, he took a step back. "Calm down, lady. Matt sent me to bring you up to the house for supper."

What the hell was wrong with her? She'd never, ever had this much trouble with an assignment before. Refusing to allow herself to feel foolish, she nodded. "Just give me a second, okay?"

Without waiting for an answer, she pulled the door closed, shutting him out. Taking deep breaths, she rummaged in her jewelry bag for the chunky silver necklace and dangly earrings she usually wore with this particular dress.

Meanwhile, Talia continued to regard her curiously. José's appearance hadn't alarmed her pet, and the dog was a damn good judge of character.

Which, if she stopped to think about it, was odd. Talia shouldn't like either of the men.

Once she had her jewelry on, she grabbed her purse and her camera and opened the door again.

Holding on to the side rail, she made her way gingerly down the three metal steps, hoping her sky-high heels didn't trip her up. Watching her from the shade of a huge mesquite tree, José made no move to help her.

Nice guy.

"Be good, Talia," she murmured before closing the door.

They walked together in silence all the way to the house. Or rather, she trailed along behind him, noticing he made no move to slow his steps in allowance for her heels. That was okay, she told herself grimly, because she refused to hurry to try to keep pace with him.

By the time they reached the back patio, even though she knew his actions were deliberate, she had to tamp down her fury as José held open the door. The slight smirk on his face told her he expected a reaction. Clearly, the battle lines were drawn.

Summoning her fake bubbly persona, she beamed up at him. "Thank you so much for being kind enough to come get me." Then, without waiting for an answer, she swept past him, her head held high. She didn't bother to check to see if her refusal to let him antagonize her had registered.

The instant she stepped inside the house, the aroma of lasagna or spaghetti or something Italian made her mouth water and her stomach growl. She'd managed to forget to eat lunch with everything going on, and whatever Matt was serving for dinner smelled amazing.

Hmm. Maybe this assignment would have some culinary benefits, too? No doubt he had a full-time chef.

As she headed in the direction of the kitchen, she steeled herself for her reaction to him.

Matt looked up at her approach, his long-lashed eyes sweeping over her, approval shining in them. As she'd known she would, she felt his gaze like a punch in the gut.

"Is there anything I can do to help?" she asked softly.

"Nope." He offered her a confident grin. "Pour yourself a glass of wine and hang out, if you want."

Instead, she got out her camera. Even though she found she used it more like a crutch around him, she couldn't resist snapping a few photos.

"What are you doing?" Matt asked quietly after she'd taken a shot of his pasta boiling on the stove.

Despite the way she felt her face color, she managed a casual shrug. "You never know what other articles I can get out of these shots. With your permission, of course. A food magazine might want a short piece on dinner at Matt Landeta's, you know?"

"No, I don't know." Despite his noncommittal tone, she could swear she saw hurt flash across his face. "I'm not that well-known."

"Maybe not on a national level, you're not." She smiled. "But around here, you're sort of a legend. I'm thinking *D Magazine*."

"I didn't know you were freelance."

"Yep." She kept her smile steady. "Journalist and photographer for hire."

Again his gaze swept over her, as though he expected her to say something else. Like what?

When she didn't speak again, he appeared to lose interest, turning away to tend to his sauce.

Though she knew she shouldn't, she couldn't resist another push. "I'll need your recipe, if you don't mind."

"We'll see."

"You nervous?" José asked, pulling out a chair and sitting down. Apparently Matt must have asked him to keep Skylar entertained so he could focus all his attention on cooking.

"No, why?" she answered, lifting her chin as she met José's gaze.

"Your leg," he said, pointing. To her consternation, she realized she'd been jiggling her leg, a nervous habit she'd abolished years ago.

"Well, maybe a little," she confessed, glancing at Matt and then mentally cursing when she realized what she'd done.

When they were all seated in the dining room, Matt began passing around the bowls of food. "Spaghetti with clam sauce," he said, looking directly at Skylar. "My specialty."

There was also salad and garlic toast. After a tentative first bite, Skylar relaxed. It was good. More than good. Restaurant quality. "You can sure cook," she told Matt before twirling up another forkful of pasta. "This is marvelous!"

He dipped his chin in a nod, barely sparing her a glance. Again she felt a bit uneasy, though for no good reason she could fathom.

When they'd finished the meal, José jumped up and went into the kitchen, returning with a tiramisu that looked almost too good to eat.

"Don't tell me you made that, too," Skylar said, eyeing the cake and wondering how she could possibly eat another bite.

"Nope. I picked it up at the bakery." Unabashed, Matt grinned at her. Despite thinking she had her armor firmly in place, she felt the warmth of that grin all the way to her tailbone.

Which reminded her to straighten her spine. "None for me, thank you," she said, keeping her expression pleasant. "I'm already full, and if I eat anything else, I'm going to need a nap." Not to mention gain a couple of pounds.

Rather than press her, Matt simply began cutting slices from the cake and passing them out. Eyeing the three layers of sin, Skylar's mouth watered, but she managed to resist, pushing the piece of cake back into the middle of the table, where it sat, practically begging someone to eat it.

"Testing yourself?" Matt asked, one eyebrow raised.

Surprised at his perception, she almost nodded. But she caught herself just in time. "No, I'm just full."

The glint in his eyes practically calling her a liar, he dug in. She fiddled with her camera while he and José devoured the cake.

Ignoring José's glare, Skylar looked around, intrigued at this slice of Matt Landeta's ordinary world.

Finally, Matt pushed back his chair and stood. "Skylar, do you want to take a walk with me? We can sit outside on the patio and discuss the particulars of your photo shoot."

Her heart skipped a beat. He wanted to be alone with her? José's narrowed eyes and tight lips told her what he thought of the idea. As for her…well, she was supposed to try to seduce Matt, after all. She hadn't expected him to make it this easy.

"Follow me," he said, apparently taking her silence for consent.

Intrigued despite herself, she did. They went into the kitchen, then out the back door onto the patio. Immediately, the greenery and flowers, along with the warmth of the evening air, soothed nerves she hadn't even realized had become jangled.

Turning to face her, Matt jammed his hands into his jeans pockets. Despite her earlier resolution to begin her seduction attempts, she stood frozen. Maybe because he looked...vulnerable.

And devastatingly handsome both at the same time.

Reminding herself who and what he was, she decided he was a damn good actor. As she needed to be, if she was going to successfully close this case.

Swallowing hard, she tilted her head to look up at him. She knew how to flirt, knew to angle her pelvis just so or brush her breasts up against his chest.

The only problem she had was that she still couldn't force her body to cooperate. What she couldn't figure out was why not. She'd never had a problem detaching herself from her job. She did what needed to be done and wrapped things up.

Except now. She couldn't even flirt with the guy.

This angered her. She wasn't weak or helpless. She was a crack shot, a damn good ATF agent, and she needed to do her job.

"It's a beautiful night. Relax with me," he said.

Flirting, she reminded herself. Simple flirting. She could do this—she'd done it at least twenty times on her last assignment.

Closing her eyes, she breathed in deeply, striving to find her center and the calm resolve that resided there. Instead, she caught a whiff of his scent, spearmint and the outdoors, masculine and tantalizing and too damn sexy for her equilibrium.

Hurriedly, she opened them and looked around. A fat robin perched on the edge of the porch railing. Acting on instinct, she raised her camera and squeezed off a couple of shots. When she finally lowered the camera, he shook his head.

"You look like you're thinking about taking off and running away," he drawled, moving slightly closer.

Despite her instinctive desire to keep distance between them, she held her ground, gritting her teeth and trying like hell to look mildly interested. Scratch that—greatly interested.

"Not running." Her slightly breathless laugh had perfect timing, if she did say so herself. "But quite honestly, Matt, you're a bit out of my league. I'm just a reporter who—"

"Happens to be exquisitely lovely," he interrupted smoothly.

Despite knowing it was all an act, she couldn't help blushing all over. "Er, thanks." It should have helped that she knew the truth—she was passably pretty, but not even close to the level of women he usually had hanging on his elbow.

Only one man had ever found her beautiful, and he was dead. She crushed that train of thought, aware now would be the worst possible moment to wallow in grief.

Forcing herself to focus on Matt, she realized her reticence most likely was the very thing that made him want to pursue her. Men like him loved a challenge.

Now would be the perfect time to say something. Anything, but she couldn't seem to force words past her lips. Damn it. She couldn't help wondering why it felt as if this assignment was already beginning to spiral out of control.

The way he watched her with his head tilted just so told her he'd expected…more. Inwardly wincing, she knew she couldn't give it to him. Not yet. Not now. Maybe not ever.

Glancing at her watch, she knew she'd better go back to her trailer and figure out a plan of action. If doing this felt like retreating, then so be it. "I need to go. Thank you for dinner and everything, but tomorrow is going to be a big day with the photo shoot."

He raised his wineglass in a sort of farewell salute.

Then, moving far too slowly on her too-high heels, she fled.

"What the hell was that all about?" José asked, coming up behind Matt. Together, they watched Skylar pick her way across the grass as she headed toward her trailer.

Matt took a long drink of his wine before replying. "Damned if I know. She reminds me of one of those wild horses I picked up at auction."

José nodded, looking thoughtful. "I wonder if my information was correct. She sure doesn't act like a federal agent."

Staring at her wobbly retreating back, Matt had to agree. "Double-check, will you? Either she's really a photojournalist for that horse magazine or she's a damn good actress."

"Will do." José looked pensive, a rarity for him. "I've also tried three times to reach my buddy in Matamoros. He's not answering and he hasn't returned any of my calls. I'm worried about him."

With good reason. Anyone brave or foolish enough to go up against the largest of the Mexican drug cartels knew they were putting their life in danger. If they were caught, they would be lucky if they were merely killed. The usual modus operandi was brutal torture and a slow, agonizing death.

"Keep trying." Matt squeezed José's shoulder. "Maybe he's just busy."

"Maybe." But José didn't sound convinced. "He's the one who's been carrying messages back and forth between us and Diego Rodriguez."

Matt swore. "If he's been caught, we'll have to start all over."

"True." Looking glum, José turned away. "I'll let you know as soon as I find out something."

"Please do that."

After José left, Matt continued staring down at the little camper trailer where he'd put Skylar. The approaching sunset bathed the sky in a rosy-orange glow.

A moment later, the door opened and the black-and-white dog bounded out, nearly pulling Skylar after.

He noted she'd changed not only her high-heeled shoes, but she'd exchanged the dress for a pair of faded jeans and a T-shirt. Even from this distance, she still looked hauntingly lovely. Every nerve ending in his body came alive as he watched her.

Weird. While he wasn't sure why he reacted so strongly to her, the fact that he did intrigued him enough to make him want to explore the connection more deeply.

In the pasture, Skylar raised her arm and threw a red ball. Her dog joyously bounded after it, returning a moment later to drop it at Skylar's feet.

Matt grinned. There was nothing on earth like the happiness of a dog with one of its favorite toys. And when Skylar laughed, the musical sound carrying on the light breeze, he realized her uncomplicated joy equaled that of her pet's.

Taking another drink of wine, he debated joining her. He liked dogs, and even though he hadn't allowed himself another one since his beloved Rottweiler was killed in the massacre, he wasn't averse to spending time with hers.

He frowned. Usually he wasn't in the habit of lying to himself. He'd enjoy the dog, true. But it was the woman who fascinated him. It wasn't her beauty—hell, ever since he'd won the lottery and become a multimillionaire, he had his pick of gorgeous women.

Maybe, he mused, it could very well be the challenge of getting past her defenses that drew him to her. Either way, it had been a long time since he'd been attracted to any woman for any reason other than the occasional consensual sexual encounter.

Before he had time to reconsider, he moved across the patio and headed down the sloping lawn toward her.

The dog—Talia, he remembered—saw him first and came bounding across the grass to greet him. With one joyous bark and a series of acrobatic spins, the black-and-white fur ball launched into an elaborate greeting. He could swear the border collie wore a silly canine grin the entire time.

Skylar not so much. Expression wary, she eyed him with the same enthusiasm one might give a rattlesnake coiled in the grass. Her earlier carefree expression had been replaced by guarded curiosity.

Though he felt a twinge of remorse, he pretended not to notice.

"Mind if I join you?" he asked, aware she most probably did.

"No problem," she replied, her smooth voice and

pleasant expression giving away the lie, though he doubted she realized how transparent she was.

Though he'd originally intended to discuss his horses, giving credence to his pretense of believing her cover story, as he watched her with her dog, he chose silence instead.

After she realized he didn't intend to chat, she went back to playing with her pet, though she never completely relaxed.

Watching her, he tried to analyze why Skylar continued to fascinate him. She was pretty, though not his type. As a rule, he favored tall, leggy blondes rather than curvy redheads. Even ones who exuded an unconscious sex appeal, as she did.

No, he decided, it wasn't just physical. It had to be her inner vulnerability that fascinated him. He'd noticed the shattered expression flash across her face as she took in his home, his life. He'd seen the pain—from what?—that she'd tried so earnestly to hide.

In that, they were very much alike. He, too, had known his share of pain, of loss. He couldn't help but wonder what life events had wounded her. She intrigued him, even as he wondered why he cared. He never cared. Too much potential for hurt. He was safer living on the surface, keeping his focus on his goal.

With that, he realized standing here watching her was a colossal waste of his time. Dipping his chin in a brusque nod, he turned away and headed back to the house.

The instant he strode off, Skylar felt all the tension leave her in a whoosh. "Matt Landeta is weird," she told Talia, who dropped her ball at Skylar's feet and now watched intently for another throw.

They played for another fifteen minutes in the diminishing light before Skylar called it quits.

As soon as she crawled into bed, she fell into a deep and dreamless sleep.

In the morning, waking for once without the nightmares haunting her, she rose hours before dawn. Unable to sleep, she finally gave up and rose. She'd showered and dressed long before the sun began to color the eastern sky pink.

Checking over her camera, she briefly wished she truly was a photojournalist, then shook her head at her odd flight of fancy.

Prior to this assignment, she'd been given an intense photography class, so she knew at least the basics of operating the expensive, professional-looking camera. She'd taken several artistic landscape shots as part of her homework and discovered, rather to her surprise, that she enjoyed photography.

She'd even begun using her free time composing shots, learning her way around the different settings for action shots versus landscapes.

She couldn't wait to begin the official photo shoot later today.

In jeans and boots—yes, she'd brought a pair—she snapped a leash on Talia and walked down toward the barn area in the dark, hoping to beat the barn crew's morning feeding process. Instead, they were already there, much earlier than she would have guessed. A small tractor pulled a flatbed trailer heaped with hay and a huge bucket of grain. One stable hand doled out the hay and the other used a coffee can to scoop out grain, pouring it into each stall's feed trough.

All the horses, every single one of them, had their

heads out the stall doors, watching and waiting in the darkness for their early-morning meal.

With Talia sticking close to her side, Skylar sidled around the feed wagon, earning a few semi-curious glances, but no one questioned her. She supposed word had gotten around that she was here on behalf of the horse magazine and no one wanted to bother her.

Which was good, as she didn't want to be disturbed. Since she knew after the horses were fed they'd be left alone for at least an hour to digest their breakfast, she could take a few candid photos. Of course, she wouldn't bother to pretend these were for the magazine—true horse lovers wouldn't be interested in head shots; they'd want to see the entire animal so they could judge conformation and coat. But among horses, Arabians had the most chiseled features, aristocratic and regal. She always admired them from afar, though she'd never really gotten this close to them.

In addition to horse photos, she needed to do some snooping around and see if she could learn where Matt stored the ammo. She doubted he'd store something so explosive anywhere near his expensive livestock, but maybe she could pick up a few clues.

Gradually, the horses were fed and the barn emptied of people and went quiet. The only sound was the horses contentedly munching. Skylar wandered down the well-lit aisle, inhaling the familiar barn smell, feeling more at home here than she did anywhere else on his ranch.

Beside her, Talia whined.

"What's wrong, girl?" Reaching down, she ruffled her pet's fur. "Do you need to go for a walk?"

Though of course the border collie couldn't answer, Skylar left the barn and headed in the dark toward the empty field. There, she unclipped the lead and let her dog take care of business.

Once Talia had finished, Skylar whistled for her and headed back to her trailer to eat a breakfast bar and have a cup of coffee. She had several hours to kill until the promised photo shoot. Heck, she had at least an hour—maybe more—until sunrise.

Sitting on a chair outside the small trailer, sipping her Kona breakfast-blend coffee and waiting for the sun to come up, she debated phoning the office, but since no one would be there yet, plus she had nothing real to report yet, she decided against it. Other than Matt's single comment about being licensed to carry, she hadn't seen a single clue that might tell her if he really was planning to smuggle ammunition across the border.

They'd seen the receipts and knew he had it, but thus far she hadn't been successful in locating where he stored it.

Of course, she hadn't really expected to find it lying around out in the open, now, had she?

As she was about to get up for more coffee, Talia's bark had her stopping. She knew her dog's barks and this was the warning one. Expecting an intruder, she looked around her carefully and saw nothing.

A moment later, she smelled smoke. More than smelled it. The air was thick with it, the southern breeze carrying it low and thick, tendrils of gray against the darkness

The barn! Her first thought was immediately followed by another. Ammunition! If Matt's stockpile were to catch fire, the explosion could take out his entire ranch.

She took off running in the dark, heading in the direction of the smoke. The air smelled awful. In her limited experience, that meant some sort of toxic accelerant had been used. Running full-out, she grabbed the hem of her T-shirt and used it to cover her face so she could breathe.

The horses. She had to get to the horses. But she couldn't do it alone. She didn't know if the others had been alerted to the fire, so she yelled for help over and over as she ran toward the inferno.

Chapter 4

Even that effort left Skylar gasping for breath and coughing. She didn't dare waste any more energy.

Eyes watering, she hurried. Arriving at the barn, she saw it was ablaze. Rushing inside, despite the now-black smoke roiling off it, she heard the panicked screams of the horses.

Someone loomed up in front of her—Matt, leading one of his terrified horses. She jumped aside, grabbed a halter and entered the first occupied stall.

Inside, the panicked animal lashed out with her hooves.

"Don't halter her," Matt shouted. "Just release her and my men will herd them toward the door. Hurry."

His words made sense. Opening the stall door wide, Skylar used the halter to slap at the frightened mare's hindquarters. The horse bolted forward, eyes wide with terror.

Skylar didn't wait; she hurried to the next stall. Matt rushed past her, doing the same.

In the next few minutes, she lost track of time, focusing intently on saving the horses one by one. Soon all the stalls were empty except the stallion stall at the end of the barn.

And the fire had leaped across the aisle from the empty stalls, the hay in the feeding trough already ablaze.

The staccato sound of hooves pounding the wooden stall door mingled with the roar of the fire. This one, this one last horse, had to be freed. She would not let it roast alive.

Beside her, Matt's grimy face showed similar resolve.

Heedless of the danger, he ran to the stall and yanked the door open. Nothing but black smoke and the bright orange and red of the flames.

Skylar's heart skipped as she cursed. No way the horse could survive that conflagration. No way. Heart pounding, she rushed after Matt, whether to offer her assistance or try to drag him to safety, she didn't know.

A shape appeared out of the smoke. Burned and terrified, huge nostrils flaring, Matt's stallion nonetheless let Matt lead him to safety. The instant they were free of the stall, the horse bolted, nearly knocking Skylar out of the way.

"Come on, hurry," Matt shouted. "The roof's about to collapse. Get out!"

Side by side, they ran for the door. They'd barely cleared the opening when something inside the building exploded, sending them flying and knocking them to the ground.

Dazed, Skylar pushed herself up to a crouch. She'd

skinned her knee, and her elbow was bloody, but that appeared to be the extent of her injuries.

Squinting in the smoke, she tried to locate Matt.

José and several of the stable hands hurried over, helping Skylar up. Matt limped toward them. From his appearance, he had similarly minor scrapes and cuts.

Belatedly, she realized the stallion had disappeared. "The horse," she croaked. "Where's the horse?"

"Go find Saint," Matt ordered, his voice sharp with what sounded like fury. Two of the stable hands rushed off to do his bidding. He turned to his friend. "José, call the vet and get him out here pronto. Saint is burned and some of the others probably are, too. They all inhaled a lot of that smoke."

Nodding, José whipped out his cell phone and turned away to make the call.

Dusting herself off, Skylar coughed. Her legs felt shaky. "Don't you think you should call the police?" she asked quietly. "It seems pretty obvious that fire was deliberately set."

"Do you have proof?" He stared at her, his gaze narrow, his mouth a hard, thin line.

"I smelled something. Right before the explosion. Gasoline or kerosene—some kind of accelerant."

He turned away, the rigid set of his shoulders telling her he already knew. "We've already called the fire department. It's going to take them a while to get here, though—they're volunteers. I know they have one guy who specializes in that sort of thing. We'll see what they find out."

Though she knew she might be pushing it, she had to find out what had exploded in the barn. Surely he wasn't foolish enough to keep explosives around his precious horses?

"Matt, wait." Grabbing his arm, her heart still pumping with adrenaline, she took a deep breath to speak. Instead, she immediately began coughing.

To give him credit, Matt waited until the coughing fit had subsided.

"Something exploded there in the barn," she said, wiping at her stinging eyes with her fists. "Any idea what that might have been?"

Clearly exhausted, he dragged a hand across his face, smearing the soot. "No." His answer short and sweet, he seemed to sway as he stared at her. "Do you?"

Since she couldn't come right out and voice her suspicions, she slowly shook her head. "I have no idea."

"I thought not." To her surprise, he held out his hand. His fingers were black and filthy, exactly like her own. "Come on. By the time the fire department gets here, the barn will be nothing but embers. You can help me round up the horses so the vet can check them over."

Not sure how to react, she finally slid her hand into his. As his fingers closed around hers, she couldn't help but think how long it had been since she'd held a man's hand.

Five years or more. A lifetime.

Again she pushed the thoughts away, letting Matt tug her after him. This was different. This was a crisis, not a date.

Somehow, they managed to round up all the horses, chasing them into a large fenced arena across the parking lot and upwind a distance from the still-burning barn. All the horses were accounted for. All except one. The beautiful stallion he'd called Saint was nowhere in sight.

"The vet's on the way," José said. "Where the hell is

the fire truck?" About to say more, he apparently got a good look at Matt's face. "What's wrong?"

"Saint's missing."

"Is he badly hurt?"

"I'm worried," Matt muttered. "He looked like he had some pretty bad burns."

José clapped a hand on his shoulder. "Well, hell, you know this entire area is fenced. Even if he made it out of the barnyard and into one of the other pastures, it shouldn't be too hard to find him. He's got to be here somewhere."

Still, despite the reassuring words, worry continued to etch lines in Matt's face.

Rubbing the back of her neck, she turned a slow circle, searching. "There's no chance a gate could have been left open, right?"

José shot her a look heavy with annoyance. "Anything is possible. Whoever started this fire could have left a gate open. But all the pastures are divided up and fenced."

Biting back an instinctive retort, Skylar kept her gaze on Matt instead. She wouldn't allow José to bait her. Whatever his problem was with her, she wanted no part of it.

"Even if someone left a gate open, Saint couldn't have gone far." Matt's voice, weary and husky with worry and exhaustion, made her long to go to him and put her arms around him.

Since there was no way in hell *that* was going to happen, she clenched her hands into fists instead.

Behind them, there was a loud pop, then the crack of lumber as the barn's roof collapsed. Fire roared up into the sky, engulfing the remains of the building.

Matt nodded, gesturing toward the blaze. "Even if

the fire department shows up now, it's too late. The barn's a total loss."

At least the other buildings appeared to have been spared. One of them, she knew, was his office. Two men stood near that smaller building, continuously spraying it with hoses to make sure the fire didn't spread.

Matt sighed. "Skylar, you can go back to your trailer. Thanks again for all your help. I'm going out to find Saint."

"I can help search," José offered. "But it's pretty damn dark out there. You know it'll be easier to find him once the sun comes up."

"That's true." Matt set his jaw. "But he's hurt and scared and I can't leave him alone. I want to bring him back so the vet can take a look at his burns. We've got a couple more industrial-strength flashlights in the tack room."

With a nod, José hurried off to retrieve those.

"I'm going to look, too," Skylar said quietly. "And before you turn me down, think. You know you need all the help you can get."

Expression shuttered, Matt finally nodded.

José brought the flashlights. Matt took two from José and handed one to Skylar.

"I thought she was going back to her trailer," José protested, his voice dripping with dislike.

"Look," Skylar started, clamping down on a flash of anger, "I don't know what your problem is with me, but—"

Matt squeezed her shoulder in warning. "Easy, now. Both of you. It's been a rough couple of hours. Arguing isn't going to solve anything."

He was right. Just like that, she felt the urge to fight roll off her. José nodded. "Sorry."

"Apology accepted," she bit back, managing to soften her tone a little.

Apparently satisfied, Matt nodded. "Skylar, thanks for all your help. You saved several horses."

Keeping her chin up lest her own exhaustion show, she nodded. "Now we just need to find your stallion. Have you heard from the stable hands?"

"No." Matt checked his phone. "They know to call me if they locate him. They went in pairs. I sent one group to the north pastures and the other group went south. We probably should search separately."

"Agreed. I do think we should split up," José put in, his expression and his tone neutral. "We can cover a lot more ground separately."

Her heart skipped a beat while Matt considered. If he agreed, searching for the missing horse would be the perfect time to also conduct a search for the hidden ammo.

"Good idea," Matt finally said. "Skylar, do you want to go alone or with me?"

She pretended to consider. "I think José's right. We can cover a lot more ground if we go alone."

"José and I will take west, you go east."

She nodded, then watched as they vanished into the darkness. Now, while she helped search for the missing horse, she could also take a look around for a potential ammunition-storage site. They knew he'd purchased enough bullets to supply an army. Her job was to find out what he'd done with them.

Despite the mini explosion in the barn, she knew that hadn't been due to ammunition. According to the reports she'd been given, if a stockpile the size of Matt's blew, it would have left a crater.

Matt's devotion to his horses was obvious after this

morning. She knew he wouldn't do anything that might endanger them.

Ergo, he must have an outbuilding on another part of the ranch. No doubt far enough away from the livestock that it would never be a threat.

Hefting the heavy flashlight in one hand, she set out, glancing back over her shoulder to see if anyone was watching her. Flashing lights down the road indicated the arrival of the fire trucks. The still-burning barn illuminated the corral of agitated, frightened horses, the flickering light of the flames an eerie mix with the sour smell of smoke.

The acrid scent seemed to follow her as she set off. At the last moment, she decided to go the same way as Matt. She had a hunch. While she didn't doubt he was actually searching for his stallion, she knew if she were in Matt's position and someone had set fire to a barn, her next concern would be to check on the stored ammunition. In case that was his plan, her best bet would be to follow him while continuing to keep an eye out for the missing horse.

"That Skylar chick surprised me. She was really something," José mused, falling into step beside Matt.

Matt hid his grin. "Yes, she was. She's obviously a horse person. Without her, I'm not sure we could have gotten all the horses out."

"Yeah, we need to have a talk with the stable hands."

"I agree." Matt grimaced, the knot that had settled into his gut twisting. "They were so disorganized and in such a panic that they got in each other's way."

"You're also wondering if one of them might have had something to do with starting the fire," José guessed.

"Exactly. They said they'd already fed the horses. What were they doing feeding so early?"

"True. And why didn't they smell the smoke?"

Considering, Matt nodded. "Especially since Skylar did."

"True. Speaking of her…" José glanced back over his shoulder as if to make sure she hadn't followed. "Do you think she might have had something to do with this?"

"What?" Shocked, Matt stopped, staring at his friend. "Why would you think something like that?"

"To smoke out where the ammo is, of course."

"But to endanger all those valuable horses…" Matt's horror-filled voice trailed off.

José shrugged. "Just a thought."

"I think you're way off base with that one. You saw her this morning. She was obviously concerned for the horses."

"And that's it? That's the only reason you don't suspect her?"

"Isn't that enough? Plus, what would be her motive? The ammo thing doesn't really fly, as any idiot would know not to store explosive ammunition anywhere near horses." And, even though Matt didn't say it out loud to his friend, the simmering attraction he felt for the redhead also had something to do with it.

Ha. He needed to make sure he thought with his head, not with his groin. Which was ironic, in its own way. He'd never had a problem getting women, and most of them, like the models he occasionally dated, were happy with his no-commitment philosophy as long as he occasionally bought them a bauble or two.

Maybe that would be the solution. But though he knew if he picked up the phone and called, any one of them would come running, the knowledge did nothing for him. He simply wasn't interested.

No, he was better off keeping his focus where it belonged—on his plan to draw in Diego Rodriguez. He was too close now to screw it up.

Meanwhile, his most valuable horse had completely vanished.

"I don't see him." Once again, José shone the flashlight beam out into the pasture. The high-intensity light illuminated a good area, but there were no signs of the stallion.

"Keep looking," he ordered tersely, turning in the opposite direction with his own light. "The sun should be up soon."

"Do you wanna check out the—"

"No." Matt cut José off before he could finish the sentence. He gave a second, meaning-filled glance behind them. "You never know who might be following or listening."

José grimaced. "Got it."

They branched out, Matt calling Saint's name in a low voice, the way he might have called for a dog. The horse knew his voice and had even come to it once or twice, though no time had been spent actually training for this. In the predawn light, he doubted it would work this time, either.

Add to that the fact that the stallion was no doubt terrified and possibly wounded... No, they'd have to find him and corner him before he got a chance to run again.

Matt could only hope he wasn't hurt too badly.

Twenty minutes passed, then thirty. José had begun to slow down, his defeat evident in the rounding of his broad shoulders.

"You can go in if you want," Matt offered. "I'm going to keep looking."

"I still think it'd be better to wait until full light. Go back to the house, grab a cup of coffee and something to eat, and head back out."

"Eat?" Matt asked. "I doubt anyone's getting much breakfast this morning. Not with the barn still burning and the fire department there trying to put out the fire. Also, Doc Bertram is working overtime checking out my horses, so I'd say if anyone deserves breakfast, it's him."

José acknowledged the truth of that statement with a weary grimace. "Still, right now with these flashlights, it's like looking for a needle in a damn haystack."

The old cliché made Matt shake his head. He felt a deep exhaustion as well, but refused to give up until he found his horse. "Saint's worth it," he said. "Besides, you know as well as I do how many coyotes roam these parts. I can't risk it. If he's wounded and they catch wind of the scent of his blood…"

They'd surround the horse and take him down. Maybe. Still, he couldn't take the chance. Not only was Saint a valuable purebred stud horse, but he was Matt's personal mount.

When they reached the end of that pasture, they stopped. "No sign of him." Matt tried not to sound defeated.

"The gate's closed to the next one," José pointed out. "He didn't come through here."

"He can jump." Pushing away the exhaustion, Matt rubbed the back of his neck. "Normally, he doesn't, but if he's out of his mind with terror, who knows?"

"So you want to check out the next pasture, then?"

It was dangerously close to the caves. Matt wasn't

about to take the chance of Skylar following them. Though there was nothing illegal about the amount of ammo he had stockpiled, he needed to keep the location secret if his plan was ever going to work. Everyone—including the ATF—had moles. Once the cartel learned of the location, they'd simply take what they wanted.

It was how they operated.

He walked a dangerous tightrope and he knew it. While he had no plans of doing anything illegal—other than taking down the man who'd slaughtered his family, that is—he'd do what he had to do in order to ensure success.

Ironically enough, though, the one thing the ATF suspected him of was the lone act he wouldn't commit. No way in hell would he be selling ammunition to the Mexican cartel to fuel their war.

"Hey." A feminine voice behind them had them turning. Matt shot José a wry look that meant *I told you so*.

"Having any luck?" Skylar asked, walking up to them without using her flashlight. Though he supposed since they'd just been using theirs they were easy to spot, he didn't like it. Still, the darkness did appear to be lifting, even though the sun hadn't risen.

"I thought you were searching the other way," Matt said.

She shrugged, apparently unconcerned. "I took a quick look, didn't see anything and headed this way."

Lying. He didn't know how he could tell, but he knew. He shouldn't have been so surprised.

"Maybe you should have gone back to your trailer after all," José drawled.

Ignoring him, she focused on Matt. "I take it you two haven't had any success?"

"Do you see a horse?" José sniped.

Slowly, Matt shook his head in warning. "No, we haven't been able to find him."

"That's odd." Shining her flashlight out ahead of them, she sighed. "I've searched two pastures, even though I had to climb over one fence. I know most horses won't jump a fence unless provoked, so I have to ask. Do you think there's a possibility the stallion was stolen?"

For a heartbeat Matt could only stare. "Why would you think that?"

"The barn fire could have been a diversion."

"But they would have gotten Saint out first," José said, his tone indicating he gave no credence to her idea.

To be fair, Matt took a few seconds and considered it. "Anything is possible," he finally said. "But I don't think that's why the fire was set."

"Then why?" she asked, the slight edge to her voice letting him know he'd fallen neatly into her trap.

As if he'd tell her the fire had most likely been a warning from one of the large Mexican drug cartels. Since they all were at war with each other, they didn't like their suppliers dealing with other factions.

Despite the fact that Matt was not yet officially supplying them with anything, José had made sure the word got out that he had ammo to sell.

This fire was meant to be a warning. La Familia, the largest of the cartels, didn't take kindly to any opposition. The fact that several groups, including Diego Rodriguez's, had shown an interest in the ammunition had no doubt angered them. The fire was their way of showing him exactly what he needed to do. Matt felt quite certain he'd be getting another message soon to reinforce that point, whether verbal or written.

Meanwhile, Diego Rodriguez was lying low. He

knew full well the dangers of forming his own cartel and going against his former. This much ammo would certainly help him in the inevitable war that would follow.

Diego needed this ammunition. That much Matt knew.

Which meant he was much closer to hooking his fish than he'd realized.

Meanwhile, Skylar was waiting for an answer. Resisting the effort to shut her down, instead he looked at José. "I have no idea," he said. "What about you?"

To his credit, José didn't react in any way, other than with a quick cough. "No idea neither, amigo."

Skylar made a sound under her breath, just enough to let them know she wasn't happy with their answers. "Well, then, gentlemen. Let's get busy and see if we can find your missing horse."

Despite her bossy attitude, which amused Matt and pissed off José, they let her lead the way and followed her. She shone her flashlight straight ahead. Matt took the left and José the right.

Despite this, there was still no sign of the horse. Even with dawn beginning to color the horizon and turning the black night to a milky sort of gray.

Working as a team, they began to move forward, each of them searching in their own direction, sort of like a fan.

When they reached the end of that pasture without seeing Saint, Matt's heart sank. "Where the hell could he be?" he muttered.

"Did you hear that?" Skylar touched his arm, warning him to be silent. "Listen."

He froze, straining to hear. Just as he was about to tell her he hadn't heard a thing, there was a rustle that might have been a rabbit, a coyote, anything.

"I don't think that's a horse," José muttered. "Coyotes, most likely."

"Shh." Skylar held up her hand. "They're tracking something. Wait."

Then they all heard it. The sound of hooves pounding the earth, the sound of a panicked horse running for his life.

Both he and José drew their guns.

"There." Skylar pointed, swinging her flashlight in the direction of the noise.

Saint, backed into a corner. And flanking him in a semicircle were several coyotes.

Chapter 5

Matt swore under his breath. Next to him, José swore in Spanish. "How can we help him?"

About to suggest they rush forward, shouting and waving their arms to scare the coyotes away, Matt swallowed his words as Skylar stepped forward, brandishing her Glock.

"I can take care of this," she said, her voice calm and measured as she sighted. Briefly he wondered if she knew how much she sounded like a cop.

"Madre de Dios." Staring at her, José crossed himself. "How good a shot is she?"

"It's okay," Matt heard himself say. "She's a crack shot. Skylar, just don't shoot if there's even a remote possibility of you hitting my horse."

"Of course not," she promised, glancing at him, disdain flashing in her green eyes. Crouching, already getting into her stance, again she inadvertently revealed that she'd had years of training and experience. Of course, the fact that he knew what she was might have made him watch her more critically.

She squeezed off a shot. Obviously, this was meant as a warning, since the bullet went harmlessly into the ground.

The coyotes got the message. Moving in unison, they turned and fled, appearing to bleed into the predawn grayness.

Now Saint reared up, screaming in challenge and fear.

"Your turn," Skylar said, holstering her pistol. "Good luck with that."

Giving her a nod of thanks, Matt moved forward, speaking softly to the terrified horse.

At his approach, Saint quieted, or at least stopped squealing. He still snorted, tossing his head, his large nostrils flaring, but he didn't rear again.

Crooning softly as he approached his frightened horse, Matt reached out, moving in slow motion, and slipped the halter over the stallion's head.

This accomplished—which felt like nothing short of a miracle, considering the level of Saint's agitation—Matt led the huge animal over toward them.

"Let's head back in," Matt said, finally letting his exhaustion show.

Skylar fell into step with José, both of them giving Matt and Saint a bit of space. In silence they walked through the pasture, opening the gate and repeating the process in the next pasture.

Ahead he could see the barn still burning, though this time the flash of fire-truck lights also illuminated the gray sky. Once again, what had been a lingering odor of smoke became a thick cloud.

Saint began to balk. Only by speaking softly but with authority was Matt able to urge him on.

Finally, they reached the final pasture, which was lit by tall lights that flanked the gate.

"Now what?" José asked. "You can't put him in the corral with the mares."

"What about the old barn?" Matt pointed to the smaller, stone-and-wood structure on the other side of the drive. Though they hadn't used it in a long time, the old barn was still structurally safe. There was even a reinforced stall that would be perfect for Saint.

"Good idea." José turned sharply, nearly bumping into Skylar, who managed to sidestep neatly out of his way.

"Nice reflexes," José commented, giving her a look Matt doubted she'd have any difficulty interpreting. José had made it clear he didn't like her, but she'd earned his grudging respect. Still, José wanted her gone.

About to tell his friend to back down, Matt caught a glimpse of Skylar's face and held his tongue instead.

She didn't care. Her stubborn expression plainly said she'd leave when she felt like it.

José continued to glower at her. Instead of being cowed by his menacing glare, she shot one right back at him. To Matt's surprise, one corner of José's mouth finally curled up as if he were about to smile.

Truce? Whatever it was, he'd take it.

"I'll finish up here," Matt said. "After I get Saint up, I've got to get Doc Bertram to take a look at his wounds. After that, I need to have a word with the fire department. You two go on and get some rest."

Dragging a hand across his forehead and rearranging the soot, José clearly wavered. "Are you sure?"

"I'm positive." Including Skylar in his look, Matt

waved them away. "Thanks, both of you, for your assistance. Now the two of you should go on. Get some breakfast."

"I can help with all that," José said, looking from Matt to Skylar and back. Crossing his arms, he made it plain he had no intention of going anywhere until she left.

Ah, so the truce was already over.

"José." Matt shook his head. "Enough, amigo. I'm going to need you alert tomorrow to handle everything while I'm passed out. So go. Please."

"What about her?" José indicated Skylar.

Ignoring him, Skylar tilted her head and eyed Matt, plainly considering her options.

"Do you mind if I go with you?" she asked softly.

Behind her, José made a sound of discouragement.

Completely sick of the bickering, Matt shook his head. "I do mind. You go on back to your trailer. Both of you. Tomorrow, José can help me get the rest of this straightened out."

She stiffened as if he'd slapped her. Fascinated, he watched as she visibly composed herself, finally managing a weary smile.

"Of course," she said, interjecting a note of sympathy into her voice. "You're right. I'm tired, too, so I'll leave you and Saint alone. See you tomorrow."

As she turned to leave, José stood his ground, continuing to glare at her as she walked away.

Only when she was gone did both men let out their breath in identical sighs of relief.

"I'm not going anywhere," José said. "At least until I've done everything I can to help you this morning."

Giving up, Matt led Saint over to the old barn. Once they reached it, Matt sent José out for one of the veterinarians. While he waited, he led the horse into the stallion stall and checked Saint out thoroughly. No cuts or scratches. Just a few burns.

As far as he could tell, the animal wasn't too badly wounded, though the vet would have to check out the burns.

Now that he could no longer see the fire, Saint began to grow calmer. As he petted his long neck, Matt's thoughts returned to Skylar.

He shook his head. Despite who and what she was, which gave her the potential to ruin his plans, he actually liked her. She'd helped a lot and proved she had a backbone. She also appeared to actually care about his horses. It was hard to dislike a woman like that, especially when she came in such a beautiful package.

Doctor Bertram hurried over, accompanied by José. "I brought Dr. Metcalf, too. He's finishing up with your mares."

Luckily, the vet confirmed Matt had been right about Saint. Dr. Bertram cleaned the wounds gently and applied an antibiotic salve, then bandages. "You'll need to change these out twice a day," he said.

José lingered in the doorway, trying to hide a yawn with his hand.

"Go home," Matt told him. "Seriously."

"If you're sure…"

At Matt's nod, José turned and left.

Once Doctor Bertram finished with the instructions, the two men headed back outside. The fire department continued to use their pumper truck to spray the flames and actually appeared to be making some headway. Of course, nothing would save the barn. All that would be left would be ashes.

"Any idea what caused this?" Dr. Bertram asked.

"No," Matt answered shortly. "I wish I did."

Trudging wearily up to the main corral, they joined the other vet, Dr. Metcalf. He just finished examining one of the mares.

"They all appear to be okay," the doctor said, pushing back his baseball cap and scratching his head. "A few minor burns here and there. Oh, and that small filly had some wheezing from breathing in smoke."

"But all in all, I think they're going to be okay," Dr. Bertam put in.

Matt nodded. "How much do I owe you?"

"You can settle up with us later." The two vets looked at each other. "Call us if you need anything else, okay?"

Ignoring the weariness that threatened to overwhelm him, Matt thanked both men. "I really appreciate you two coming out here so early in the morning."

After the vets climbed into their pickup truck and drove off, Matt went to speak with the fire chief. On the way there, he spotted the sheriff's cruiser, which meant most likely the fire had been arson.

Hell, he thought, scratching his head, what else could it have been? There was nothing, absolutely nothing, that could have caused such a blaze.

After talking with the fire department—who strongly agreed with Skylar's assessment of arson—and answering the sheriff's questions, he and the remaining stable hands finally got all the mares put into either stalls or small runs with three-sided enclosures. That'd have to do until he could rebuild.

Spraying more water on what had now become smoldering embers, the fire department continued to work. They weren't going anywhere until they were sure no hot spots remained.

Stumbling up to the house, banking a simmering fury

that threatened to blaze up inside him, Matt focused on ordinary details. He made a mental note to call the insurance company later. Next up, he wanted a shower. He couldn't wait to wash away the soot and grim and acrid odor of smoke. And then he figured he'd better eat something before he began what promised to be a very long day.

He made it up three of his patio steps when a figure detached itself from the shadows and stepped in front of him.

Instinctively he dropped into a battle stance.

"It's only me." Skylar's husky voice didn't sound the least bit apologetic.

Relaxing slightly, he exhaled and dipped his chin in acknowledgment. Eyeing her, he couldn't help wondering how on earth she still managed to look so gorgeous and sexy after a few hours straight from hell. "What are you doing here? I'd have thought you'd be on your second or third cup of coffee by now."

"I had enough." Dropping one slender shoulder in a graceful shrug, she studied him. "I took another shower and saw you staggering across the yard. I came to see if I could help you with anything else. You look awful."

"Thanks. I feel pretty crappy." Dragging a hand through his hair, he wasn't surprised to find soot on his fingers. "Though I appreciate your offer, I've done all I can for now. I'm running on fumes. I need to go take a shower and get some breakfast. I suggest you do the same."

Opening her mouth as though she were about to speak, she apparently thought better of it. "All righty, then. See you later," she said, giving him a small, jaunty wave as she strolled away.

Despite his exhaustion, part of him stood at attention as he watched her go. Where she got her energy, he didn't know. As for him, he was done in.

Turning, he went inside, heading straight to a hot shower, dropping his filthy clothes in a heap on the floor. After a hot shower, he made a quick trip to the kitchen, where he grabbed a steaming mug of coffee and a bowl of oatmeal.

He'd barely finished eating before sound from outside had him pushing away his plate. Standing, he took a deep breath. As he did, the enormity of what had happened hit him.

Moving toward the window, his entire body sore and aching, he grimaced. Another kink in his plan, he thought, realizing there would have to be an investigation. His ranch would be crawling with law-enforcement and fire department personnel, as well as insurance adjusters and investigators. There'd be no deals with Diego Rodriguez or anyone else for a few weeks at least.

"Damn," he cursed. All his carefully laid plans were now in freakin' ashes, just like his barn.

Whoever had done this had to have known what would happen. This would not only put a damper on his ability to con Diego Rodriguez into believing he wanted to sell him ammo, but the delay would play exactly into ATF's hands, giving them a better chance to catch him red-handed, selling ammunition to the Mexicans.

After she left Matt, Skylar wandered back to her trailer. She greeted an agitated and confused Talia, put her on a leash and then went outside. She sat on the steps, watching the sunrise and waiting to see the full extent of the damage. The air, which should have smelled of grass and horses, was still tainted by smoke.

She felt restless, lonely and aching. Normally, thinking of the happy life she'd once had brought on this kind of melancholy. But this time, she hadn't been thinking of her husband and son. She'd been thinking about Matt and the beautiful, terrified horses.

She'd experienced all kinds of evil in her career, first as a police officer and then as a federal agent. She thought she'd grown a thick shell, able to unflinchingly experience the various malevolent wickedness of humanity.

Except for children and animals. Innocents who couldn't protect themselves had no place in the immoral battles of evil men.

She'd reviewed the case files and gone over every possible scenario, from the cartel guys swarming the ranch with guns blazing to Matt trying to run a truck full of ammo secretly into Mexico.

What she hadn't foreseen was the possibility that they'd attack the horses. Again the scene replayed in her mind—the terrified animals, the panicked screams of the stallion, and the fire, brutal and uncaring and swift.

Skylar took her oath to protect and uphold the law seriously. She would have died trying to get the horses out. In fact, she could have died. Only by the capricious grace of fate had she been able to escape unscathed.

Matt had been the only person there who'd shared her exact same determination. And while she intellectually knew that most men were complex and had many sides, for the first time she couldn't reconcile the two. How could a man who cared so much for his horses be involved with the brutal Mexican drug cartels?

While she was an old hand at working undercover, never before had the lines been so blurred. Usually, it was pretty easy to tell the bad guy from the good. And while even villains had their reasons and never seemed to view themselves as evil, she'd always been able to spot them a mile away.

Not this time. José, maybe. But Matt? The more she was around him, the more difficult it was to imagine him doing something like selling munitions to the Mexican cartel with full knowledge of what they'd do with the bullets.

As an ATF agent and, more specifically, as a grieving wife and mother, she knew exactly what kind of harm bullets could do. This was one of the reasons she'd left the police force to work for the Bureau of Alcohol, Tobacco and Firearms.

Sighing, she shifted her weight on the bottom step. Talia whined, her brown gaze fixed on her mistress. Absently, Skylar scratched the dog's neck, letting her pet know not to worry. With a sigh, the border collie sank to the ground and, resting her head on her paws, dozed.

Once again, Skylar experienced the gut-wrenching pain of losing her son. She blinked, trying not to remember the sight of his still, small body covered in blood. At that moment—hell, at *any* moment—if she'd been able to change places and die in his place, she would have.

As her eyes filled with tears, she clenched her teeth. *Focus. Focus.* She had a job to do and she'd damn well do it right. If Matt Landeta truly was guilty of selling ammunition illegally to the Mexicans, she'd make the bust. No matter how much she liked him.

As the sun rose higher in the cloudless sky, Skylar tried to puzzle out the problem. She couldn't afford a mistake with potentially the biggest bust of her career.

So what was wrong? Ever since the bank holdup that had robbed her of everything, she'd made a habit of being brutally honest with herself. She wouldn't change that now.

She zeroed in on the one aberration. Her attraction to Matt. This had taken her by surprise. Clearly, she hadn't planned to find him so…desirable. Unlike with his friend José, she couldn't make herself see him in the role of villain.

What she could make herself see him as was her lover.

Shocked, blindsided by the heretical thought, she gasped out loud. She hadn't taken a lover since Robbie had died, and the idea that she could even think of having sex again with a man who wasn't her husband felt like the worst kind of betrayal.

Once again, despite the fact that she'd eventually stopped the therapy, she could hear her therapist reminding her that she was only human. Her body had needs and she could only suppress them for so long. Eventually, she'd have to live again.

While she knew this objectively, for so long she'd taken to regarding herself as only a police officer, then an ATF agent. Not as a woman.

Dropping her head into her hands, she inhaled the air, still laden with smoke and water and soot, and quietly wept.

Then, calling herself several kinds of fool, she got up. Calling Talia, she climbed the steps and went inside the trailer, undressed and climbed into bed. As if a nap would fix what was wrong with her.

She lay there unmoving, wide-awake, as sunshine claimed the sky. Finally, sometime after noon, she dropped into a restless slumber, her beloved dog on the bed next to her.

The sound of knocking woke her. Talia barked, jumping to the floor and standing guard at the door. Blearily sitting up in bed, Skylar rubbed at her heavy eyes and glanced at the clock.

"Two-thirty?" That couldn't be right. She hadn't slept that late in years.

Again someone banged on her door, this time with a bit more urgency. Now she understood why—she'd overslept.

"Hang on," she said loudly, readjusting the giant Dallas Cowboys T-shirt she slept in.

Figuring she looked presentable for someone who had, only seconds before, been dead asleep, she opened the door, blinking at the bright sunshine.

Matt. Of course. He frowned up at her, his beautiful blue eyes full of worry.

Damn. How did the man manage to look so fantastic after the ordeal they'd just been through? She swallowed hard. "You look good," she blurted, mentally wincing. "I mean, considering…"

His mouth twitched, but to his credit, he didn't laugh. "Thanks," he said gravely. "Did I, er, wake you?"

Briefly she thought about lying and saying no, but since it was so painfully obvious that he had, she nodded. "I got up so early this morning that I took a nap for a few hours."

"Sorry." His gaze roamed over her, making her conscious that she wore nothing underneath the T-shirt.

Her body reacted. She crossed her arms in defense. Beside her, tail wagging, Talia tried her best to get outside to greet Matt.

"I think your dog needs to go outside," he pointed out.

"I'll take care of that."

He smiled, and her body clenched up tight in response. "Let her out. I'll watch her."

She stepped aside without a word. Talia barreled past her, but instead of running to the grass, she leaped on Matt, sending him staggering backward. "Talia," she said sharply. "Go to the bathroom."

The border collie, ever obedient, trotted off to do exactly that.

Matt moved back to the edge of the trailer steps, still staring. Was that *heat* she saw in his gaze? Surely not. She knew for a fact she didn't look at all good first thing after waking up.

"Um, what did you need?"

He blinked, as though she'd brought him back to the present. "The police are here. They've got me rounding up anyone who might have seen anything. They want to ask you a few questions."

"Of course." She wished she'd taken the time to drag a comb through her hair. "I'll need a few minutes to brush my teeth and get dressed."

"Take your time." Glancing at his watch, he took a step back just as Talia returned to the trailer. "José is on his way back here from his place in town, and the police are still interviewing the stable hands. Just come on up to the house when you're ready."

Nodding, she shut the door in his face. Her legs felt weak, so she sank back onto the bed. Beside her, Talia whined.

"It's okay, baby girl," she said, pulling the dog close and burying her face in Talia's soft fur. "Let's get you some breakfast."

While Talia ate, Skylar jumped in the shower and took care of her normal morning tasks. She put on a light dusting of mineral powder, mascara and lip gloss. Dressing in jeans and a muted yellow T-shirt, she studied herself with a critical eye and decided she looked okay. Before she spoke to the local police, she needed to make a report.

Using her secure cell phone, she phoned in. A special voice-mail box had been set up for her to leave simple updates. She did, relaying the fire and the fact that she'd be speaking with local authorities.

Once she'd concluded the call, she took Talia out once more. After she'd made sure her dog would have plenty of water, she closed her up in the camper and headed to Matt's house.

The men wearing uniforms were laid-back but businesslike, impressing her with their efficient questions. No, she hadn't seen anything suspicious. Yes, she'd smelled something that might have been used to start the fire, though she had no idea what that might have been. They finished with asking her to supply her address and phone number in case they had any further questions.

Through it all, she was super conscious of Matt leaning in the door frame, listening to her answers.

José arrived a few minutes after she'd finished, and when the police began questioning him, Skylar moved off to stand next to Matt.

"I heard from the arson investigator," he said.

"Already?" She was surprised. In her experience such findings usually took a few days.

"He's not busy," he explained. "He used to work for Dallas Fire and Rescue, but retired and moved down here. Now he volunteers whenever he's needed. This is the first time they've had to call him."

"What did he find out?"

"Arson." Matt's eyes narrowed. "Someone really wanted to hurt my horses."

"And hurt you, too," she said, instinctively touching his arm. When she saw the way his gaze darkened as he followed her movement, she hurriedly removed her hand.

"Do you have any idea why?" she asked softly, wondering what, if anything, he'd choose to reveal.

"No." Of course, he gave away nothing.

Before she could comment, José called his name, waving him over.

"Excuse me," he said and left her without another word.

Watching him go, she kept her expression pleasant. What had she expected? Him to open up about his enemies?

Slipping from the room, she headed back to her trailer to spend some quality time with her dog. After that, she'd best get busy concocting some sort of plan.

A quick game of ball helped relieve some of the tension. Up at the main house, she saw Matt and José emerge. She watched, game forgotten, as the two men climbed into the pickup and drove away. Her heart began to race. This would be her opportunity to search the house. Since the police and fire department were still questioning people and milling around, all of the household help would be distracted and preoccupied.

There couldn't be a more perfect opportunity.

Locking Talia back in the trailer, she made herself walk normally, as though she had forgotten something and needed to talk to the authorities again. As far as she knew, Matt never locked the back door, so she went through the patio, unable to keep from smiling at the lush scenery.

Once inside, she noted Matt had left the curtains open, allowing lots of light to flood in. Grateful, she did a quick search in the kitchen, still experiencing that gut-wrenching reaction of coming home. This time, better prepared, she didn't bother to try to analyze the feeling, but continued her methodical search.

What exactly she hoped to find, she didn't know. Something—anything—that might give her a clue as to where he kept the ammo stored or his reason for purchasing such large quantities.

Part of her—a tiny, really idiotic part—hoped to find something that would exonerate him.

She made quick work out of checking the kitchen and moved on to the den. This room also had few hiding places and she didn't really expect to find anything there.

Matt's study or office or bedroom—now, that was another matter. She guessed he probably had a safe and would keep any important papers there. If she found a safe, she'd be out of luck; she lacked the necessary skills to crack it. Plus, she hated to do anything without a warrant, as any evidence she found would be inadmissible in court.

In reality, she knew this search was probably a pointless waste of time, but she had to make the attempt. If she found something, she'd get the necessary warrant then.

After all, she had to have something proactive to put in her report.

Finished with the downstairs part of the house, she moved quietly to the stairs. Outside, the sun was still strong and she knew she'd need to stay away from windows, as she'd present a clear figure to anyone outside.

Upstairs there were several bedrooms. She did a cursory search of all three before moving on to what had to be Matt's personal office.

A desk, empty of clutter, revealed nothing. As she

suspected, she located a small wall safe behind a Western landscape painting, but the lock wasn't engaged and the door sat open a half inch. The inside of the safe was empty.

The rest of the office turned up nothing. Glancing at her watch, she realized she'd burned through an hour. She still had Matt's bedroom to search, so she'd better get a move on.

Crossing the hall, she hesitated in front of the only room she hadn't visited. Strangely reluctant—this felt like a violation of the worst kind—she took a deep breath and stepped inside.

Immediately, his scent assaulted her. She found it odd that she could smell him so intensely—the scent wasn't cologne or aftershave, but rather a personal mixture of spearmint and the grassy fields.

Shaking off her nervousness, she crossed to his nightstand and pulled open the door.

"Looking for something?" Matt drawled from less than a foot away.

Chapter 6

Skylar nearly jumped out of her skin. She even, to her complete and utter embarrassment, let a little scream escape, totally involuntary and completely unbefitting a seasoned law-enforcement officer.

Crap. Busted. This was not good. Not good at all.

"What are you doing here?" she asked lamely, her heart pounding. She felt flushed due to all the blood rushing to her head.

"Actually, I think that's my line," he said, unsmiling. Arms crossed, a grim expression turned his features to stone. "This is my bedroom, after all."

Mouth dry, she stared at him, searching for a plausible explanation, and came up empty. Instead, she finally nodded. "I…er…was curious?"

A muscle worked in his jaw. He didn't respond. She hadn't really expected him to.

Any moment now, in fact, she anticipated an explosion. And she really didn't want to be around when it came. In fact, she wouldn't blame him if he evicted her from the ranch.

With that thought in mind, she began backing away from him and the nightstand, hoping for a clear shot to the door. Maybe she could get out of here, hide out in her camper until he calmed down. If she had some time, she thought she could come up with a somewhat plausible explanation.

Instead, he moved with her. His hand shot out and gripped her wrist tightly.

"You're not going anywhere," he growled.

Alarmed, at first, she froze again. He was breathing harshly, his eyes glittering in the dim light. A slow heat began low in her belly, and she realized—holy hell— she was actually incredibly, unbelievably, turned on.

What the hell?

Swallowing hard, she let her gaze drift over his broad chest, flat stomach, to the apparent bulge developing in the front of his formfitting jeans. Apparently she wasn't the only one turned on.

The thought just barely crossed her mind when he made a sound low in his throat, a mixture of a curse and a groan. Then, while she was trying to process what this meant, he yanked her to him and slanted his mouth over hers. His kiss was hard and punishing and more arous- ing than any kiss she'd experienced. Ever.

Even with Robbie. Pushing away the stab of guilt she felt at the disloyal thought, she gave herself over to sen- sation. It had been so long, so damn long. His hands— oh, his hands—holding her close, stroking her, caressing her, making her want more. Right. Here. Right. Now.

She heard a moan, then realized the sound had come from her. He, too, appeared similarly affected, his heart pounding in his chest so rapidly and strongly she could feel it against her skin.

This felt amazing. And wrong. So, so wrong.

Breathing hard, she summoned up every ounce of rationality she could and pushed herself back, ending the kiss. As she stared at him, she was shocked that she could even stand since her legs felt absurdly weak and wobbly.

All at once, it dawned on her. Now the way to the door was clear. Stunned and panicked, shocked and shaking, and still way too aroused, she rushed toward it, both relieved and disgruntled when he made no move to stop her.

For the rest of the day, she hid out in her trailer. Anytime she saw movement anywhere close, she tensed, certain it would be Matt asking her to leave. She couldn't blame him. She'd react the same way if the situation had been reversed. A journalist had no reason to be snooping through his personal belongings. And no matter what, she couldn't blow her cover.

The day dragged on and there was no sign of Matt. The tightness in her chest began to ease somewhat. Maybe he wouldn't ask her to go. Which made no sense. A big fan of logic, anything illogical made her temporarily crazy. Crazy enough, in fact, that she half-assed considered marching up to the house, finding Matt and demanding an explanation.

She did not, of course. She fed Talia and took her out. At loose ends, feeling uncomfortable in her own skin, she fixed herself a sandwich from the supplies Matt had thoughtfully put in the refrigerator and ate at the camper table by herself. She watched the news on the small television, grimacing as she peered out the window every time there was the slightest sound outside.

Finally as the day turned into dusk, and dusk became night, she realized, for whatever reason, she'd been given a reprieve.

Problem was, she didn't know for how long. So she needed to step up her efforts to find the ammo. Starting immediately.

Climbing into bed early, she set her cell-phone alarm to wake her up at two o'clock in the morning. Surely by then everyone on the ranch would be asleep.

The plan she'd hatched wasn't perfect, but it was the best she could do. Matt's ranch was several thousand acres and there was no way she could explore it on foot.

Since she couldn't use an ATV even if she had access to one—the noise would wake everyone up—she planned to use one of Matt's horses.

Earlier when she'd questioned one of the trainers, she'd learned the mare they'd put in the first stall on the left in the old barn was the most gentle and the one they used for visitors who were unskilled at horseback riding. Though she wasn't a novice, she was rusty. So she'd use his mare to ride out to the far side of the ranch.

She'd lucked out with the full moon—since there were no streetlights out here, or even streets, riding in the pitch-black of a moonless night would have been a dangerous proposition.

Either way, she felt quite certain her permanent eviction from the ranch was imminent. So she had no time to waste.

Leaving the trailer, she made it to the tack room and retrieved a well-worn English-style saddle, halter, bit and reins. Crossing the well-lit parking lot might be tricky, but she had no choice. She figured everyone would be asleep anyway.

Once she reached the old barn, she realized the huge

door was closed. Praying that when she opened it it wouldn't make a lot of noise, she placed the saddle and tack on the ground, and began to pull on the door.

The squeal of metal was loud, but not deafening. Still, she froze, afraid someone might have a dog that would begin barking an alert.

But after a few seconds, when nothing happened, she pushed the door the rest of the way open.

The mare nickered softly as Skylar opened the stall door. Though moving a bit clumsily from lack of practice, she managed to get the horse saddled and place the bit in the mare's mouth.

She led the horse out into the stable yard before placing her foot in the stirrup and swinging her leg over.

Settling on the mare's back, she touched her calves to the horse's sides and urged her forward. Keeping to a walk, she rode out of the courtyard and into the first of the eastern pastures.

From the dossier she'd studied over and over, she knew Matt had divided the ranch into several pastures. The ones closest to the house were twenty acres, the next row consisted of forty-acre sections, and then after that lay open range land, fenced only at the extreme borders.

The far eastern edge of Matt's property bordered a farm-to-market road and was remote and unusable, due to cliffs and rocks. This was the area where the ATF suspected him of storing the ammo. Her task would be to locate the shed or warehouse and make notes on precise coordinates as well as surroundings. That way they could have a team in place so they'd have eyes when the actual deal went down. What Matt didn't realize—what most civilians didn't understand—was that the ATF needed just one tiny shred of evidence that he might be involved in illegal activities in order to legally swoop in and take everything.

One shred. Whether it was selling weapons and ammo without a permit or some other charge, they didn't need absolute proof, just enough evidence to convince a judge they should investigate. And since investigating could also mean confiscating everything, Matt would be out of business before he even got started.

Her job was to find that evidence.

Confidently, she consulted her compass and continued in the correct direction. When she reached the first gate, she was able to open and close it without dismounting.

It took a little longer to cross the second, larger pasture. When she finally reached the next gate, she was unable to unlatch it without getting off her horse.

Once she had, she led the mare through and closed the gate securely behind her.

Here, the land became hillier. She rode up the first rolling hill, glad the land flattened out once she reached the top. The full moon cast an eerie glow on the landscape, and she shivered as an owl hooted mournfully.

Yet despite it all, she found it breathtakingly beautiful. If she'd been there for any other reason, she would have added *peaceful* and *serene* to that description.

Ahead she could see the large boulders dotting the landscape. But no cattle, she couldn't help but notice. Maybe Matt kept them on a different part of the ranch.

By her best calculations, it would take her a good hour to reach the first area she wanted to explore. If her estimate was correct, and she took her time checking out the area, she'd have the mare back at the barn with time to brush her down well before sunrise.

Settling into the easy rhythm of the horse's steps without relaxing her guard entirely, she felt a sense of peace steal over her. She'd missed horseback riding, though she'd been unable to bear the idea of doing something alone that she and her husband had loved to share.

This time, though, for this ride she felt no sense of guilt or even loss. Possibly because she was simply doing her job rather than going for a pleasure ride.

As she crested another minor rise, the land stretched ahead as far as she could see. Matt's land, tied to him in an intimate and physical way as far as she was concerned. The moonlight gave everything a silver cast, but with the immense black night sky above and the clear view of a thousand stars, she felt a sense of how small, how insignificant she was in relation to the universe.

Humbling. Continuing to ride, she didn't dare urge her mare to pick up the pace. The uneven ground was rocky and could be treacherous to a horse, so she let the reins lie slack on the mare's neck, trusting her mount to choose the right path.

Ahead, a worn dirt trail led up a rocky bluff. Whether by instinct or habit, the horse headed for that path.

Once they reached the top of the bluff, Skylar could at last see the road that marked the eastern border of Matt's ranch. The bluff, pitted with boulders and rocks and sagebrush, ran parallel to the road.

It all appeared to be deserted.

A sound—out of place and almost mechanical—had her freezing. Reining her horse in, she slid from the mare's back and led her mount behind a huge boulder, next to some sort of short, twisted tree.

Draping the reins around a branch and tying them loosely, she crept forward alone, her heart pounding. Was she finally about to discover what until now the ATF had only suspected—illegal ammunition sales taking place? Would this night, so soon after her earlier debacle, be the one where she found the necessary evidence?

Sidling from rock to rock, keeping low to the ground, she finally made it to the other side of the bluff. Peering around cautiously, she saw nothing.

Then what had made the sound? It had sounded like a chisel hitting a rock or a hammer taking a good crack at a nail.

Or a gun cocking.

Holding herself absolutely still, she waited to see if she'd hear it again. A moment later, she did. The sharp report seemed to echo off the rocks, a moment of discordance marring the otherwise perfect night. And then again, and again. Muted, yet loud in the perfect silence.

Moving forward carefully, she peered around a boulder. There in a clearing in front of her were two huge deer, horned bucks clashing their antlers at each other ferociously. As she moved closer, she heard one whistle and another snort.

A deer fight at night.

Pushing to her feet, she made enough sound to attract their attention. Waving her arms madly, she started toward them. Instantly spooked, they took off in opposite directions.

She stood and watched them go, awed despite herself. While she'd grown up in these parts and seen plenty of deer, she'd never been witness to bucks fighting over mating rights. She'd seen the damage done to trees by them scraping the velvet from their antlers, but not the actual sparring.

Smiling to herself, she circled around and retrieved her horse. She'd done enough exploring for one night. Time to head back to the ranch.

After she'd returned to the old barn, she tied the

mare outside the stall and removed the saddle and replaced the bit with a halter. She carried the saddle and bit back to the tack room. In there, she located a curry brush and brushed the horse down before putting her back into her stall.

With a buoyant step, she hurried across the parking lot, keeping close to the shadows and hoping Talia wouldn't make a loud fuss when she returned.

She made it back to her trailer before dawn. Her watch showed a few minutes after five o'clock, which meant her little exploratory trip had taken about three hours. Though she'd found nothing and should have been frustrated, she'd honestly enjoyed her moonlit ride and unexpected wildlife encounter. The fact that she hadn't been discovered made it even better.

Talia greeted her sleepily with a muffled woof before she turned a circle or two and settled back down in her bed.

After washing her face and brushing her teeth, she changed into her large, comfy T-shirt and climbed into bed. Sometimes she had trouble going back to sleep. She'd bet she wouldn't this morning. She'd probably drop off an instant after her head hit the pillow.

In fact, lying down was the last thing she remembered before something woke her. *Knock, knock.* Jumping down from the bed, Talia woofed softly, letting Skylar know whoever was at her door wasn't a threat. Squinting at the clock, Skylar saw it was six-thirty. Still early. What the heck? Had she managed to forget some appointment?

"Skylar, are you in there?"

Matt. Again.

Belatedly, she remembered his discovering her in his

bedroom and the blazingly hot kiss they'd shared. Had he decided to wait until the morning to toss her out?

He knocked again. "Are you in there?"

"Yes," she managed. "I was asleep. What's wrong?" While she couldn't afford to be too ungracious, she'd only gotten a little more than an hour of sleep. She imagined she looked as if she'd been run over by a truck. She certainly felt that way.

"Nothing's wrong," he said, sounding close, despite the metal separating them. "We've got a big breakfast waiting up at the house, if you're interested."

Groggy, she stared at the door. Instead of kicking her out, he was inviting her to breakfast? Her stomach growled, but she was more interested in sleep.

"I know you have an article to write and a deadline, so I thought we could get started on that. I don't want you photographing the horses that have burns, but I've got several others you can take pictures of."

Her cover. Right. "When?" she asked, rubbing her eyes and hoping he'd give her enough time to down at least half a pot of coffee, liberally spiked with her favorite energy drink.

"Right after breakfast," he said. Then, to her horror, the trailer door opened and Matt stepped inside.

Gaping at him while her traitorous dog bounced around greeting him with effusive joy, she dragged a hand through her hair and winced.

Now he smiled. He looked so damn handsome her body came instantly awake. Of course, her mouth went dry as she thought of the kiss they'd shared.

Damn.

"You don't look like you've slept too well," he pointed out. She had to bite her tongue to keep from making a sarcastic reply.

"I didn't," she said instead, eyeing him and hating the way she felt as if she were waiting for the other shoe to drop.

He waited, his silent gaze challenging her to say something. Defiantly, she tossed her undoubtedly horrible hair and crossed her arms. Damned if she'd say it first.

"What were you doing in my room yesterday?" he finally asked, as nonchalantly as if discussing the weather.

Swallowing hard, she mentally cursed her lack of a believable answer. "I'm a journalist," she finally said. "I was looking for hints to the true you."

Lame, but the best she had at the moment. And closer to the truth than he'd ever know.

One dark brow arched. "You're not writing an exposé," he pointed out. "You are doing a story on my Arabians, right?"

"Yes, of course." Indignant—and that not entirely faked—she sat up straight. "But the article is also about you as a breeder and rancher." Swallowing, she managed what she hoped was a contrite expression. "I was wrong to search your room without your permission. I promise it won't happen again."

He eyed her for a moment, as though considering. When he finally gave a slight nod, she breathed a sigh of relief. "Just see that it doesn't. Now, about the photo shoot…"

Round one to him. "When did you want to do that?" she asked.

"I was going to suggest we start after breakfast." He smiled at the horrified look she gave him. "But since you're so obviously not awake, how about you meet me in the big outdoor riding arena in an hour? Will that work?"

She struggled to focus on what he was saying, trying not to stare at his mouth and wonder if she could kiss him again.

"I'm sorry, what?" she asked, knowing he'd blame it on the sleep fog that still must have been clouding her brain.

"I asked if you could meet me in an hour at the big riding arena." He dropped his gaze from her face to her chest, almost as if her thoughts had telegraphed themselves to him.

She nodded as a rush of heat suffused her. Like before, she suddenly became super conscious of the thin cotton of her shirt and her braless state, made even more evident by the fact that her nipples had decided to stand at attention, practically waving at him to notice them.

"That I can do," she said with a touch more enthusiasm than necessary. "I'll have to pass on your kind invitation to eat, but I'll be there."

Still he stood there, as if torn between leaving and climbing into bed with her. She felt an instant burning desire to lift the sheet in invitation. Horrified, mortified and more turned on that she should be, instead she pointedly glanced toward the door.

Finally he got the hint. Turning, he grasped the handle and pushed the door open. "Don't be late," he said, delivering his parting shot before shutting the door in her face.

Damn. Next time, she vowed, next time she wouldn't let him come in. He could talk to her through the metal or not at all.

Breathing hard, she staggered into her tiny bathroom and splashed water on her face. Then she started the pot of coffee, and while it was brewing, she jumped in the shower.

Later, clean and dressed, with her hair still damp, she checked her watch. Chugging her second cup of coffee, she grabbed her secure cell phone from her backpack. She had time to make another report before meeting Matt.

Punching in a number, she waited until her boss answered.

Tersely, she relayed an abbreviated account of the events of the previous night, sticking strictly to the facts. Which were, basically, that she'd found nothing.

After she finished making her report and received the standard "Good job, keep looking," she concluded the call and went into the small bathroom to dry her hair and put on a touch of makeup. She didn't wear much, just mascara and lip gloss, so she was ready well before an hour had passed.

Stepping out into the bright sunshine, she inhaled, hating that the smoke and soot smell still lingered in the air, even overriding the normal earthy scents of a working horse-and-cattle ranch.

She hurried down toward the big outdoor arena, which meant she had to pass by the ruins of the barn. When she reached it, she stared at the charred beams— all that remained of the once beautiful structure.

The yellow crime-scene tape waved in the breeze and one or two investigators or fire department staff still picked through the rubble.

Skylar lifted one hand in a wave but didn't stop to talk. Since she had her camera, she snapped a few quick photos before going on her way.

The big outdoor riding arena was just past the barn, though she had to cross a small paved parking lot and the ranch office. Inside the arena, Matt lunged one of his mares, so intent on his activity that he didn't notice her approach.

Leaning on the railing, she watched. He wore jeans and a Western shirt, along with a Texas Rangers baseball cap. She'd be the first to admit he looked good, like every woman's dream cowboy. Focused on the horse, he moved in unison with it, turning and waving the long whip just enough to keep the animal moving forward.

A wave of longing swamped her. Oh, how she'd missed this. There was a beauty to a horse's gait, poetry in the flowing movements, legs and body and neck and head, pure grace.

With an aching that surprised her, she wondered if Matt would let her ride. She needed more than a stolen trail ride in darkness. She wanted to circle the arena and put the horse through all of its paces. Just once or twice, long enough to remind her of happier times.

For the first time, she realized she'd been able to think of the past without the sharp stab of pain.

She wanted to ride. She'd ask him later.

"Hey." Noticing her, he flashed a smile and dipped his chin. "This is my newest mare. She's a roan, which is rare among Arabian horses."

Dutifully, Skylar raised her camera and began snapping pictures. She thought she got some good shots—she'd check them later when she reviewed the camera's display.

Finishing with the lunging, Matt had the horse stop and then led her over to Skylar. "Glad to see you made it," he said, smiling. Though the corners of his eyes crinkled and, for a heartbeat, her mouth went dry, she sensed something edgy inside him, as though he were trying to be in two places at once.

Shrugging this off—when would she ever stop this

ridiculous romanticizing of him?—she gestured toward the old barn across the parking lot. "I thought you'd have a bunch of employees out here, leading out the horses for me to photograph. Sort of like putting on a show."

"Nope." Still cheerful, he turned and began leading the mare toward the old barn. "This morning it's just you and me. Come with me. You can pick the next mare."

Following him, she was struck by the contrast between this barn and the newer one that had just burned down. The new one had been huge and modern and efficient. But this one had…character. Stone walls made up half of the exterior, and lumber made up the rest. The openings to the horses' stalls were large, and she could see there'd once been runs on this side. They were still attached on the other side, and it looked as if a few hasty repairs had been made.

Still, this barn was half the size of the other.

"What'd you do with the remaining horses?" she asked.

"I had some runs with three-sided lean-tos. I put the rest of them there." His smile turned into a frown. "I'm trying to get the insurance guy moving, but since it appears to have been arson and they're going to do a formal investigation, it looks like I'm just going to have to start construction on a new barn in another spot on my own."

"Seriously? Then what, get reimbursed later?"

"Maybe." He put the mare in her stall and turned to face her. "Or just have two barns. I'm lucky I can afford to build another without waiting for the insurance."

Just like that, the warm, fuzzy feeling she'd been having about him vanished. Of course he had the money. He was a criminal, after all.

"Must be nice," she quipped, careful to keep her voice warm and hide the coldness that had iced through her.

Moving past him, she stopped at a stall and began stroking the head of a beautiful gray horse. "I'd like to see this one next, I think."

"Good taste!" Offering her a quick smile, he took down the halter hanging outside the stall and put it on the horse. Clipping the lunge line to it, he led the horse out.

"Why do you say that?" she asked, curious.

"Because this is another of the horses I plan to make the cornerstone of my breeding program, along with Saint. She came all the way from Egypt. She's won numerous awards in the show ring, and now we've bred her to Saint. I have high hopes for her foal."

Outside in the bright sunlight, Skylar realized the mare was even more beautiful than she'd looked in the stall. Once they'd reached the lunge arena, a circular, fenced-in place, and she began to move, she appeared to float through the air.

Heart in her throat, Skylar raised her camera and began snapping. She didn't know if her rudimentary photography skills could even begin to do the majestic beast justice, but she'd certainly try.

Especially since *Today's Arabian Horse* magazine had agreed to consider publishing any article she wrote, as long as she was amenable to heavy editing.

This precaution had been taken in case she'd needed to prolong her cover story.

For the next several hours, she stayed with Matt as he lunged horse after horse. He kept up a running commentary, and she took notes as he gave her the bloodlines of each horse, the awards and standings in the

Arabian Horse Breeders Association, and little tidbits about their individual personalities.

She liked this part best. And when she realized she'd relaxed and was back to actually liking Matt again, this time she decided to simply postpone judgment and go with the flow.

Finally, he'd finished up with the last mare in the barn.

"Are we moving on to the others?" she asked eagerly, surprised at how quickly the time had flown.

Slowly he turned to stare down at her. All traces of friendliness had vanished from his face. "No, I thought this would be enough. These are my best horses, the ones I want featured in your magazine."

Though she wasn't clear on what had happened, she managed to nod. "Okay. I'll just write up what I've got, put the photos with it and let you read it for approval."

"Email it to me," he said.

That sounded… "I'm not sure what you mean," she said slowly. "You don't want to stop by my trailer to-morrow or the day after and take a look?"

"No." His gaze shuttered, he looked away. "Because you won't be in your trailer. I'm afraid with all that I've got going on here, I can't spare any more time for you. I'm going to have to ask you to leave."

Chapter 7

Stunned, Skylar eyed his back as he turned to walk away. While wanting to send her away was reasonable, perfectly understandable considering everything that had happened, why had he messed with her earlier and let her believe she could stay?

It didn't matter. She couldn't let him kick her off the ranch. This would blow her assignment. All because of one extremely foolish move along with an even more stupid kiss.

She couldn't fail. Not now. Her job was all that she had, and the potential for promotion would vanish if she blew this job. On top of that, her departure would only make things worse for him. The ATF would send somebody else.

She had to get him to change his mind. There was too much at stake.

"Wait!" Calling after him, she hurried to catch up.

When she reached him, she was slightly winded and sounded breathy, which she hated. "The agreement was for ten days."

His unfriendly look would have made a lesser woman cringe. Instead, Skylar simply straightened her spine and continued to look him in the eye as though daring him to renege on his promise.

"True," he finally allowed. "But now I'm thinking that might have been a little excessive. Come on. Do you really need ten days? You've taken enough pictures and an entire notebook full of notes. I think I've already given you everything you could possibly need for your article. All you need to do is write it."

With the ball back in her court, she desperately tried to think of an excuse. Hell, she realized with a sinking feeling it looked as if she was going to have to ramp up her game. Because he was absolutely correct. If she *had* been writing an article, she would have at least written the first draft by now.

Thinking fast, she swallowed. She needed to give him some other reason to keep her around. But what? Her stomach dropped at the only thing that occurred to her. Hell. Her boss might have been right. She was going to have to try harder to seduce him.

She thought of the women he usually dated, with their lithe model's bodies and beautiful skin, and wondered if he'd even take her seriously.

Still, she had to try.

"Wait," she called. Hurrying after him again, she snagged hold of his arm. Though he stopped, the look he gave her was still far from friendly.

With an effort, she smoothed out her expression, hoping she could manage to sound professional. "Okay, you're right. I am almost done with the article. But something is missing."

Still silent, he waited.

"I tried to write a first draft last night," she rushed on, trying to think like a real writer. "But something's missing. Some spark. While it's true I have all the information about your horses and your breeding program, I need a bit more."

Now she had his interest. He cocked his head, studying her. "Like what, exactly?"

Hoping she didn't sound entirely ridiculous, she continued, "Personal flavor."

His gaze narrowed. "Personal what?"

"You. You're the owner, the mastermind behind the breeding program. That's what I was looking for yesterday. Something's missing. I'm not sure what yet. But I've found interviewing the owner adds depth to the piece."

He crossed his arms. Not a good sign. "So interview me, then."

Crap. "Not right now," she said smoothly. "I'm still working up the questions. How about tonight? Maybe we could have a drink together before I go?"

"Tonight?" He frowned. "I was hoping you'd be out of here by this afternoon."

Was that squeezing emotion she was feeling *hurt?* Surely not.

"Well, what harm could one more night be?" Laughing lightly, she pressed closer. "That's all I need. I promise. One more night, to let me finish the interview. I'd like to have a drink with you, maybe dinner. Just the two of us."

Tilting her head, she hoped she hadn't overdone the huskiness she'd put in her voice.

He considered her, his expression still unreadable. But his eyes had darkened, going cobalt, pupils enlarged. His chest rose and fell and she could hear the harshness of his breathing.

A shiver ran down her spine.

Taking heart, she moved a tiny bit closer. However he might try to hide it, he *was* attracted.

As for herself, that tingle of heat, the way her body felt heavy and hot, well, it had to be nerves. Still, she forcibly didn't try to throttle the wave of desire that made her nipples pebble beneath her bra.

"Please?" she asked, swallowing hard as she gazed up at him through her lashes, privately wishing she was a bit more experienced at this seduction stuff. "Just one more night?"

When he didn't immediately respond, other than a slight hitch in his breathing, she continued pressing her advantage. "One final evening." She practically purred the words. "Then no more of your time. I already have some of the questions written up. I can finish the rest in an hour."

Truthfully, she didn't have anything, but how long would it take to whip up some interviewer-type questions?

Eyes narrowing, he stared at her. "Fine," he said, his voice harsh and not sounding happy about it at all. "I'll grill us a couple of steaks or something."

"Oh, thank you." She stood up on tiptoe and gave him a quick kiss on the cheek. "You don't know how much this means to me."

For a moment he froze, as though her kiss had stunned him. Then his mouth twisted into what could only be described as a cross between a grimace and a smile.

"Be there at six," he ground out.

She nodded, thinking furiously as she tried for a tremulous smile. "Just the two of us, okay? Some of these questions are kind of personal."

"I don't do personal," he growled. "But yes, I'll send José home. And I can manage a simple dinner without my household staff tonight."

Before she could form a reply, he turned and strode off, leaving her standing there feeling inexplicably foolish and aching for something she knew she could never have.

Blood pounding in his groin, more aroused than he had a right to be, Matt called himself all kinds of an idiot as he walked away from Skylar. When she'd told the blatant lie, he'd felt a surge of anger so potent he felt as if he were drowning. As a knee-jerk reaction, he'd asked her to leave. This was done out of a sense of panic more than anything else.

Nothing was going the way he'd thought it would. He never expected them to come here and threaten him—this still made absolutely no sense to him. As far as they knew, he was just some Texan who wanted to get richer by selling them ammunition.

Yet for some reason, someone in the cartel wanted to send him a message. He still didn't understand what they were trying to say. That things weren't moving swiftly enough? Or had the powers that be learned of Diego Rodriguez's plans to forge his own cartel?

Either way, something had gone wrong. If he wasn't more careful, his meticulously laid plans would come crumbling down around him.

Despite both his and José's assumptions that one of the cartels had set the fire as a warning not to sell the ammo to the upstarts, they hadn't received any sort of message like they'd expected. So what was the point?

José's contact was still off the grid, and the tension was about to drive Matt insane. Skylar in her thin Dallas Cowboys T-shirt with her perky breasts and come-hither gaze hadn't helped. Her lush mouth begged to be kissed. Hell, he found himself growing hard every time he even so much as looked at her.

Unexpected and unwelcome. But lust he could deal with. The uncertainty of not knowing if Diego would walk into the trap Matt had so carefully set he definitely could not.

If things weren't so close to the edge, he'd have welcomed the distraction Skylar brought. The several hours he'd spent with her, showing off his horses and watching her as she snapped photo after photo, had only made him want her more. Her tight little behind in her faded Levi's, the cute way she bit her lip when she angled her head trying to get that perfect shot.

She got to him, but that was to be expected. He'd always had a thing for gorgeous women.

Too bad everything about her was false.

Even this. He grimaced, unable to believe she was willing to go this far.

A private dinner? Drinks? What then? Seduction? Ignoring the part of him that would be ready, willing and eager to take her up on that, instead he tried to make himself despise her. The only problem was that he knew better than most how far someone could be willing to go to gain the means to an end.

But for her, it was just a job. For him, it was his entire existence.

Still, he found himself actually curious to see how far she would go.

Slamming into the kitchen, he began rummaging in the freezer to see what he had that he could grill.

"What's up, amigo?" José wandered over, biting into an apple.

"I just asked Skylar to leave."

José's dark brows rose. He took another bite, chewed and swallowed before commenting, "Are you sure that's wise?"

"She invited herself to dinner tonight to try to talk me out of it."

A slow grin spread over his friend's face. "I see."

Though one corner of his mouth twitched, Matt ordered himself not to smile back. "Alone," he elaborated.

"Her idea or yours?"

"Hers." Matt shook his head. "She was insistent about that."

José laughed. "So are you going to let her *persuade* you?"

Growing serious, Matt shrugged. "I don't know. Probably not. I don't need the complication right now."

"Yes, but you sure could use a distraction."

Since his friend had no way of knowing exactly how distracting Matt found the ATF agent, Matt went back to perusing the freezer. "I could have sworn I had a couple of T-bones," he muttered.

"You do." Reaching around him, José pulled out two thick steaks. "Here you go. Sounds like a really nice dinner for someone you don't even like."

Matt shook his head. "I didn't say I don't like her. I do. Sort of. But I'm worried she's going to get in the way if and when Diego Rodriguez decides to make a move."

"Skylar?" José smiled. "She seems clueless. If I didn't know her background, I'd think she was new to this type of thing. I'm actually starting to like her."

"I promise you, she's a crack shot. And she did a hell of a job helping me get the horses out of the barn. She must be good at what she does to be sent undercover. So who knows? Her bright-eyed, innocent thing could be an act."

"Maybe." José shrugged. "I wouldn't be surprised if she was playing you."

"Me, either," Matt agreed darkly. "And that's partly why I asked her to leave. I don't have time for these stupid games women play."

"But now you're reconsidering?" José watched him closely.

Again Matt lifted his shoulder in a halfhearted shrug. "The enemy we know is better than the one we don't. If I send her away, the ATF will send someone else. They could be more interfering."

"Or worse, they could trump up some fake charges and raid us. Claim you were operating as a gun dealer without a license, like they did to that guy in Dallas."

"Damn. I'd forgotten about that. I think I will allow Skylar to persuade me to let her stay."

José sighed. "Just be careful. I know she's *muy bonita* and all that, but you need to think with your head instead of your dick."

Matt couldn't help but laugh. "You're just jealous because you haven't gotten any tail lately."

Flipping Matt the bird, José reluctantly grinned back. "How can I, bro? These days everything's about our little operation."

"You want a day off? Take one." Matt gestured at the door. "But before you do, I still want you to try to get word to Diego. Again. Tell him we're ready. The sooner we can try to get the ball rolling, the better."

"Agreed." José pulled his cell phone out of his pocket.

"Let me make a few calls. I haven't heard from my contact in a while. I need to try to reach him. We'll talk later about me taking a day off."

While José tended to business, Matt wandered outside. One of his trainers was working one of the show mares in the large outdoor arena. Perched on the fence, Skylar had her camera up and appeared to be taking more photos.

He wondered if, as part of her undercover persona, she really was writing a story about his Arabian horse-breeding operation. If so, he imagined her efforts would all go to waste, which was kind of sad.

Matt's horses were one of the things he actually cared about. They ran a close third, after his quest for Diego and his friendship with José. He would love to actually see them, and his breeding program, featured in a reputable Arabian horse magazine.

Skylar swung her camera around as he approached, apparently taking a few snapshots of him. The uncomfortable feeling of her using them for a future police lineup made him wince, but he kept his expression pleasant.

"Hey, there." Greeting her quietly, he climbed up beside her on the fence. "Sorry about earlier. It's been a rough morning."

She cocked her head, her expression quizzical. "No worries. Do you want me to bring anything to dinner tonight? I can run to the store and get some cheese or bread or wine. Whatever you'd like."

Damn. She talked as if they were friends simply having a potluck or something. Or maybe neighbors—he didn't know. One thing for was for sure—she confused the hell out of him.

"Nothing," he said. "You don't have to bring anything."

Her smile faltered slightly at the harsh tone of his voice. Then, apparently still determined to appear light-hearted, she dialed up the wattage until she was practically beaming. "Okay, then."

Jumping down from the fence, she lifted her camera and pointed it at him. After taking a couple of shots of him refusing to smile or pose, she lifted her hand in a carefree wave and took off.

Though he hated himself for doing so, he watched her until she disappeared from view.

"Well, that went well," Skylar told herself, trying not to feel foolish as she strolled—her pace deliberately casual—toward her trailer. She'd tried to kill him with kindness, but instead of reacting the way she'd figured a typical male would, Matt had seemed to see right through her and refused to act the same way.

Was that an omen of how their dinner later would go? Heck, she hoped not.

Once she reached the camper, she opened the door and Talia nearly knocked her backward off the steps. Her enthusiastic greeting never wavered. Skylar buried her hands in her dog's fur, cuddling her and enjoying the doggy kisses that were Talia's way of showing affection.

"Did you miss me, girl?" Snapping on the expandable lead, Skylar took Talia out for a brief walk before taking her back inside and feeding her. While her dog ate, Skylar sat down at the small dinette table and reviewed her digital photos.

When she got to the last two—the ones she'd taken of Matt—she paused. Though he'd apparently been trying to appear stern and disinterested, she'd managed to capture a look of…longing, naked in his blue eyes.

Or maybe that was her imagination.

Dragging her hand through her hair, she groaned. This particular case had completely succeeded in messing with her mind. What she didn't understand was why.

Even as she pondered the question, she looked again at Matt Landeta's photo and knew.

Something about him drew her as no other man had been able to since Robbie.

As she waited for the familiar surge of guilt/anguish/anger that came as soon as she thought of her husband, she let her gaze wander back to the picture of Matt.

It took her a moment to realize she'd let her thoughts about her beloved departed husband slide back into her subconscious.

Dumbfounded, she hurriedly punched the off button on her camera. Leaving it on the table, she glanced at her watch. She had about ninety minutes to get ready. Which meant she also had ninety minutes to come up with a workable plan. Because, even though she really wanted him to permit her to stay, she knew she wouldn't be able to bring herself to beg.

Swallowing hard, she eyed herself in the distorted trailer mirror and grimaced. She shouldn't have to try this hard to look sexy. Other women never seemed to have to work so much at it.

Maybe it was because they were, um, having sex?

Even the quick mental rebuke managed to bring her a rush of heat. Damn, she had it bad. Worse, she didn't know how to deal with it. She'd never mixed business with pleasure. She wasn't about to start now.

Closing her eyes, she took several deep breaths and

concentrated on centering her core. This trick, taught to her by her therapist years ago, had surprisingly worked.

When she opened her eyes again, she felt better. She hadn't brought many clothes and had two dresses to pick from.

For this, ostensibly her last night at Matt's ranch, she chose a short halter sundress. The kaleidoscope of colors ranged from emerald-green to turquoise, and she'd been told by several of her coworkers that it set off both her hair and her eyes.

She straightened her long red hair with a flat iron and left it loose, then added blush and eye shadow to her face. Though she knew men didn't care about jewelry, she added a slender angel pendant on a gossamer silver chain and matching earrings.

Finally, she put on her favorite pair of impossibly high heels. Luckily, they were platforms, so much easier to walk in than they looked.

Dressed and ready, she gave herself one last doubtful look in the mirror and wished she could banish the fluttering butterflies in her stomach.

Maybe she needed to look at this another way—as a job. Which was exactly what it was. She had a task to complete. After all, what was the worst that could happen? Matt could turn her down flat and send her away anyway.

Literally, she had nothing to lose.

Except maybe, she thought, swallowing hard, her self-respect.

On the way up to the main house, she tried not to think. Just put one leg in front of the other and walk, all the while attempting to appear graceful.

As she approached the back of the house, she saw Matt was already outside. Though her mouth went dry at the sight of him, she kept moving. As she got closer, she saw he'd fired up the grill.

"I'm letting it preheat," he said, offering her an easy smile. Oddly enough, that smile did what her own stern talking-to hadn't been able to do. Put her at ease.

Relaxing slightly, she smiled back.

"Let me pour you a glass of wine." He had a bottle open and aerating behind him. "Is Shiraz okay?"

"Great." Now, when she needed a silver tongue the most, she could barely articulate a thought. Of course. Even though she told herself she wasn't planning to go through with...all of it?

Panic had her heart fluttering. It was one thing to make an objective sort of plan. It was another thing entirely to actually implement it. Especially concerning sex.

Once again, she resolved not to do anything that made her uncomfortable.

Hands trembling slightly, she accepted the glass, hoping he wouldn't notice. "Thank you."

"No problem." He turned back toward his grill, fiddling with one of the knobs.

Even now, completely undecided and wondering what the hell she was doing here, she had to fight an overwhelming urge to move closer to him. Would it really be so bad making love with him? Should she?

Part of her answered *Yes*. The other, more rational part was still mired in the past and screamed *Absolutely not*. After all, how could she even think of such a thing when her husband and son were dead because she had asked them to go to the bank for her?

Noticing Matt eyeing her curiously, she gave herself a mental shake and took a sip of wine. Five years had passed since the murder. Five long years that she'd spent completely alone, except for her coworkers. Married to her job—first the police force and then the ATF—she'd kept herself closed off from human physical contact, especially the masculine kind. Her body ached to experience it again.

Shocked, she let out a small gasp.

"What's wrong?" Matt asked, frowning in concern.

Tongue-tied, she blinked. "I was just thinking what a beautiful place you have here," she said. "The house, the animals, the entire atmosphere. I know the barn fire was a bit of bad luck, but you are more fortunate than you realize. I mean, what more could you want?"

Something in his expression made her stop. She couldn't blame him. She'd been babbling, after all.

"What more could I want?" he asked, his voice tight. "All of this—" he waved his hand "—the horses, the house, the land—are just possessions. I appreciate them, but people—family—matter a hell of a lot more."

The vehemence with which he spoke the words touched her in a place she usually kept shielded—her heart.

Damn him. Again she reminded herself he was an alleged criminal, but as she stared up at him, aware she needed to respond but struck speechless, she realized one truth was not going to change.

She wanted him.

Hell.

She knew she could go around and around like this all night. Arguing the pros and the cons, like two opposing political candidates locked in a meaningless debate.

As though an invisible thread pulled her, she took a step closer. Clearly still waiting for her to speak, he arched a brow.

"Are you all right?" he asked.

She nodded and then said the first thing that came to mind—the truth. "You're right. Family is important. More important than anything else—possessions, a job, whatever."

Cocking his head, his expression turned speculative. "You speak with the voice of experience."

Dangerous ground. Aware she had to keep her real life separate from her undercover one and therefore couldn't speak of her experience, she managed to lift one shoulder in a casual shrug. "Not personally," she lied. "But I'm a good observer of other people's lives."

He turned away, but not before she noticed the way his mouth tightened. Almost as if he knew she wasn't telling the truth.

Since that wasn't possible—after all, he knew nothing about her—she spoke again, focusing on banalities. "Do you grill a lot?" Slowly swiveling to face her again, he smiled. "Of course. I'm better with a grill than I am with an oven."

"Not me." Relieved to be back on solid ground, she smiled.

"How do you like your steak?" he asked. "I've got T-bones. They're kind of big, but you can refrigerate your leftovers for later."

"Medium rare," she managed. "Can I help you with anything?"

"Nope." He took a long pull of his wine. "I made a couple of salads and they're in the fridge. I baked some potatoes in the microwave and wrapped them in foil. I'm keeping them warm on the grill while I cook the steaks. Just make yourself comfortable and try to relax."

As he disappeared inside to get the steaks, she thought of how homey this was. In another life, she'd had cookouts in the backyard, only Robbie had stood at the grill, grinning as he made the perfect burger. There'd also been a young boy running, playing and laughing. Bryan. Her son.

Once again, she saw his amazingly long-lashed blue eyes, the freckles on his upturned nose. Throat aching, she remembered his butterfly kisses, the joyful way he'd yelled *I love you, Mommy!* She'd had it all back then. Everything any woman could ever want. Taken away, just like that. And she missed her family once more with a knife-sharp sense of loss.

From Matt's words, it almost sounded as if he'd suffered a similar loss. Bringing herself up sharply, she shook her head. There she went again, trying to make him empathetic. The only thing they actually shared was this amazing chemistry. Nothing more, nothing less.

Chapter 8

Inhaling, Skylar decided to cut herself a break. In the past, she hadn't found it so easy to hide her sorrow. Now, though, with the familiarity of long practice, she'd managed to shove the memories aside, to be taken out and examined another day.

Whistling under his breath, Matt returned with the steaks. He placed them on the grill and seasoned them, more relaxed while performing this mindless task than she'd seen him all day. At least, since earlier when he'd been showing her his horses.

Behind him, she realized he'd set the little metal table with silverware and bright-colored plates. A container of pale blue hydrangeas served as a centerpiece.

"It's beautiful," she said softly. He'd certainly gone through a lot of trouble for a woman he wanted gone.

"So are you," he replied.

Inhaling sharply, she searched his face. He gazed

right back, his expression serious. She expected him to rake his eyes boldly over her, but instead he held her gaze, as though searching. She couldn't make herself look away. Her body felt heavy and warm. Not so, her pulse.

That skipped and raced as though anticipating things she had barely even dared to dream about.

What was this? It shouldn't be happening, couldn't be happening, yet…here she was. With him.

The grill flared, making the steaks sizzle. The moment broken, he turned his attention back to the meat.

Damn and double damn.

Watching him, she tried to dissect what it was about him. The vitality he radiated drew her like a magnet. And she, of all people, knew better.

Restless, feeling uncomfortable in her own body, she finished the last of her wine.

"Would you like more?" he asked, smiling slightly. She felt the power of that smile like a knife in her gut.

"I can get it," she told him and crossed behind him to reach the bottle. After she'd refilled her glass, she moved slightly, standing beside him so she could see the grill. The steaks sizzled, thick and trimmed with very little fat.

"Those look amazing."

His grin widened. "They're nearly ready. Why don't you go ahead and take a seat and let me dish everything up?"

"How about I go get the salad?"

He gave her a sharp look and then nodded. "That'd be great. There are a couple of bottles of salad dressing in the fridge door. Please bring those, too."

Smiling back, she went inside.

As it had every time she'd been inside, his beautiful

house evoked so many emotions. This time, focusing on her task, she pushed them away.

Opening the refrigerator, she located the salads and the dressing and turned to carry them outside. Suddenly, the utter domestication of what she was doing hit her. It felt more than wrong. Not only was she here under false pretenses, but she was enjoying this a bit too much.

Sadly, she had to continually remind herself why she was here. What had happened to her objective professionalism?

Taking a deep breath, she pasted a smile on her face and marched outside. "Here we are." She placed the salads on the table. He'd already put the foil-encased potatoes on their plates and was now removing the steaks from the grill.

Her steak was perfectly cooked, exactly as she liked it. They ate in a companionable silence. Again she reflected on how long it had been since she felt so comfortable around a man.

Full, she finally pushed her plate away, groaning. "Sorry, I can't finish this. It was wonderful, but I'm done."

"No worries." He gestured at his empty plate. "As you can see, I didn't have the same problem."

"Wow," she said, impressed. "That looks like vultures cleaned it over. You can sure put away food."

"True. Now—" he reached across the table and covered her hand with his "—I believe you had some questions you wanted to ask me."

Though she had to force herself not to flinch at his touch, conversely he struck a chord of longing in her. But, because of this action, she knew in that moment she would be leaving. There would be no reprieve.

Regret filled her. Not only would this mean failure

at her assignment, but he appealed to her and made her senses sing. The fact that he was the first man to do so in the five long years since she had lost her husband said something. If only it had been another time, another place, a different situation.

Shuddering, she swallowed hard. Though her body ached for him, craved the fulfillment of lovemaking she knew he alone could give her, she realized she couldn't do this. Since Robbie's and Bryan's deaths, she'd thrown herself into her work. She'd been willing to do anything for her job, to be the best, solve the cases and get ahead.

Except this. She'd apparently drawn the line. She wasn't willing to do this. Not with any man, but especially not this one.

Slowly, she slid her hand out from underneath his. "You know what? I think you're right. I have enough for the article. I'm not going to ruin this perfect night by asking a bunch of intrusive questions."

He looked startled, then wary, as if he thought there would be a catch. This made her chuckle, the earthy sound more seductive than anything she'd managed to fake earlier.

Heaven help her, she tried to summon up her normal personality—the hard-nosed ATF agent—but she'd lived that sterile existence for far too long.

So be it.

Drumming his fingers on the table, he eyed her while she took another sip of wine. "What made you change your mind?" he asked.

Somehow she knew his casual tone was deliberate. She could sense the intense speculation lurking behind his smile.

"This." She waved her hand around his perfect patio,

at the perfect garden beyond. Perfect meal, perfect man. Perfect, perfect, perfect.

Too good to be true. Or real. But that didn't stop any of it from sabotaging her still-fragile heart.

"This was a lovely meal. Thank you." Abruptly pushing back her chair, she stood. "I need to get everything packed so I can get on the road. I hope it's all right if I leave first thing in the morning?"

He searched her face. "Yes." The smallest hesitation. Then "Please. Stay a little while longer tonight."

She froze, realizing she still wasn't immune to him. Something in that plea, in the harshness of his tone, the vulnerability lurking behind the lopsided smile…

With a small smile, she let herself drop back into her seat. For the first time she wondered if she would regret this, running away like a scared little girl rather than staying like the brave woman she knew she was.

"You wanted to have a drink with me."

She indicated her empty wineglass. "And so we did."

"We still have half a bottle to empty." Without waiting for her to reply, he refilled both their glasses. "Please. Sit with me and enjoy the night."

Pleased, she raised her glass and took a tiny sip. "Maybe I'll ask you a few of those questions after all."

His stare was frankly appraising. "Go right ahead. I can't promise I'll answer them, but why not give it a shot?"

So she did. The next hour flew by. They killed the bottle of wine, and when he went to get a second, she shook her head. "I'm not much of a drinker," she said, feeling pleasantly warm. Despite his earlier warning, he'd answered all of her questions, which meant they'd probably been too simple and banal.

Oh, well, they'd served their purpose.

What really bothered her, if she admitted the truth to herself, was that Matt hadn't made a single move toward her, other than the brief touch of her hand. Had all that angst been for nothing?

"Did you enjoy your visit?" he asked, his voice mellow.

"I did," she answered honestly. And then, because she had to give it one more try, she continued, "Except for one thing. There's one regret I have about my time here," she told him, leaning back in her chair, letting him know she was replete and satisfied with good food and the excellent company. Even though inside, she still felt edgy and on guard. Always on guard.

"A regret? What's that?" He sounded so wary she smiled. He was beautiful and sexy and sensual and she wanted him, though she shouldn't. None of that could matter. Too late, she'd come to her senses and could focus on what she'd come here to do. Only, her time was up.

"I wanted to go riding. Those horses of yours are so beautiful and their gait…it looks like they're floating. I'd love to experience that myself."

Again, she gave him the truth. Mentally crossing her fingers, she hoped this would be enough. Even if this bought her only one more day, she'd be one day closer to learning his secrets. She'd already decided she needed to ramp up her search. She hadn't even found a single hint of his alleged ammunition stockpile.

Of course, she could do nothing if she wasn't allowed to stay.

The smoldering look he gave her started a fire deep inside. Or, she thought dizzily, the wine might have had something to do with her imagining it.

Either way, he stared at her for a long moment before nodding as if he'd finally made up his mind.

"I tell you what. Why don't you hang around here one more day? Your article won't be complete unless you can write about the experience of riding one of my horses."

Yay! Victory. Keeping all hints of triumph out of her smile, she pushed to her feet and thanked him. "I'm going to call it a night," she said, holding out her hand.

He took it, but instead of shaking it, he pulled her to him, so close that her breath caught in her chest.

"Earlier, when…"

She groaned, "I'm sorry. I shouldn't have—"

"Don't be sorry."

Heaven help her, but she couldn't force herself to move away. "Matt, I—"

Before she could give voice to her doubts and find more excuses, he kissed her. Slanted his mouth over hers and gave her a toe-curling, insides-melting, *let's make love right here, right now* kiss. Again.

Stunned, shocked and more aroused than she'd been the last time they'd locked lips, she stood as still as a statue. At first.

Then, as he brought his other arm up and snuggled her up against him, breasts to rock-hard, manly chest, she felt the resistance go out of her like a big sigh.

"It's only a kiss," he murmured against her mouth before taking her lips again. Or at least she thought he said that—it might have only been her inner voice talking.

The kiss went on and on, deepening until her entire body felt electric with want and need and foolish, dangerous desire. He shifted, letting her feel his arousal large against her, and her traitorous body responded with a squeeze.

She wanted him—right now. Part of her wanted to give in, to go with the moment. But…

And there was always that *but*…held back, held in reserve.

Regretfully, she broke away. "Whew," she managed, praying she sounded breathlessly lighthearted rather than hopelessly stunned. "That was quite a kiss, Matt."

Now would have been when he would say something falsely charming and trite like "There's more where that came from," she supposed.

Instead he said nothing, only stood staring at her, his chest rising and falling with his own breath, those damnably beautiful eyes of his hidden in shadows.

For that, she was thankful. Mumbling something that she hoped sounded like an apology, she turned and hurried away into the darkness. Retreating, yes. Something she rarely did but knew she'd have to do now, or she'd have major regrets.

Her mouth felt swollen from his kiss. She stumbled, moving too fast in the dark, and slowed her pace. Though she didn't know how she knew, Matt wouldn't come after her. He wasn't the type to force himself on anyone.

Wasn't the type? Reaching her trailer, she pulled on the door handle and swung herself up the steps and inside. Turning the lock, she crossed the few feet to the sofa and dropped like a rock. Talia immediately came and jumped up next to her.

Snuggling with her dog, she tried to think. What the hell had just happened? Once again she touched her mouth, remembering the kiss and the heat.…

As Matt watched Skylar stumble away, he didn't know what to think. She'd given hint after hint that she'd be open to exploring other possibilities. And, even though he knew this was because she'd needed a reason for him to let her keep hanging around, he hadn't been able to banish the notion from his head.

Skylar naked, her spectacular body gleaming in the moonlight.... Despite the wine, he'd become aroused just thinking about it.

The weird thing was, he truly enjoyed her company. The time they'd spent earlier with the horses and the meal they'd just shared had made him feel they really connected. More than he'd been able to relate to any woman in a long, long time.

Which proved again that in matters of the heart he was a fool. Better to go with women like he usually did, party girls who were always ready to play.

Still, turning to gather up the remnants of their meal, he didn't understand why Skylar had run away. The kiss they'd shared had been molten, liquid fire hinting at pleasure to come.

He shrugged, forcing his thoughts to other matters. Though he'd issued an invitation to go riding tomorrow, he seriously doubted she'd stay now. For whatever reason, the passion that had flared between them frightened her. Was it because it was unprofessional, or was the rationale more intimate and personal?

In better times, he'd have gone on a quest to learn why. Now he had other things to do.

Rising before dawn, Matt took a hot shower and made his way down to the kitchen to have his breakfast. He ate his cereal standing up, rinsed his bowl and left it in the sink with the dishes from last night.

The sky had barely begun to lighten when he saddled Saint and rode out. He loved it like this, when the entire ranch still slept and he and his horse were the only ones stirring.

He rode through the various pastures, dismounting to open and close the gate. Finally, he reached the vast back part of his ranch, where small hills dotted the landscape. He'd even found a small waterfall, picturesque enough for a picnic, though he'd never taken anyone there.

Way back, near the place where his property intersected with an obscure farm-to-market road, there were caves. Since he'd taken to storing ammunition there, he'd also taken a cue from Skylar and began carrying his own firearm. He'd also set up remote surveillance cameras with sensors that would alert him if anyone got too close.

Riding out, he searched his land, absorbing the peace and sense of pride, though usually this was bittersweet as he wished his family could somehow have shared this joy with him.

With those thoughts came the harsh ones, and though he lived with them daily, he didn't want to think about vengeance now. Instead, he found his thoughts kept returning to Skylar, the woman rather than the federal agent.

He wanted her with a fierceness that startled him. But try as he might, he couldn't see a way to have her without jeopardizing everything he had planned.

Damn it.

As he rode, the sky lightened even more, signaling the imminent arrival of dawn. The peace of the wild land soothed him, and he relaxed into the saddle. As visibility improved, he thought he saw something moving up ahead. Not a horse or stray cattle, but what appeared to be a human, though at this distance he couldn't see if it was one of his employees or a stranger.

"Come on, boy." Urging Saint into a lope, then a gallop, he rode toward it. Whoever it was realized—too late—that they'd been spotted and took off at a run.

Matt rode hard, well aware there was no way a human could outrun a horse.

Too restless to sleep, Skylar rose at dawn and took to pacing the trailer. Fifteen steps to the bed and the same number back. Should she stay or should she go? This changed things. Or did it? He'd offered to let her stay another day and ride—the riding part had nothing to do with her job and everything to do with her.

But did she want to? She knew she did. And staying meant she'd have a bit more time to search and try to learn where Matt kept his ammunition. One day wasn't much, but it was better than nothing.

Decision made, she rushed through her normal morning preparations. Though the sun hadn't yet fully risen, it was light enough to see. She'd take an early-morning ride, if she could get to the mare she'd borrowed before. Hopefully, she could do this and get the horse back without Matt realizing. She'd search parts of the ranch she hadn't checked. She didn't have long. She might as well use every minute to her advantage.

The spread was huge—3,320 acres. Much of it was accessible only on horseback or four-wheeler. Previously, she'd discounted the more remote parts as a storage place because the logistics of getting the ammo out there were close to impossible. She'd made the possibly erroneous assumption that Matt would subscribe to a similar train of thought—why make things any more difficult than they had to be?

Still, she had to give it a shot. After feeding Talia and letting her out, she hurried to the barn as the sky continued to lighten.

Losing sight of his quarry, Matt slowed Saint back to a brisk walk. He'd best be careful. On this part of the ranch, there were several large boulders behind which an interloper could hide.

There were also the caves.

Matt drew his weapon, aware that out in the open he was a sitting target.

The sharp crack of gunfire was his only warning. The first shot grazed Matt's arm, which hurt like hell but wasn't serious. Reining Saint in, he dismounted in a flash, looping the reins loosely around the saddle horn before slapping his horse on the butt.

"Go," he shouted, ducking behind some boulders. The horse reared and took off at a full-out run. To Matt's relief, no one shot at Saint, and the stallion vanished into the distance.

Now to find the shooter. Drawing his weapon, he moved forward, using rocks and trees for cover. He could only hope there was not more than one.

There. Up ahead. Darting forward, he dived from one boulder to another. At the movement, a volley of gunshots erupted.

A man appeared, dark head above the boulders, gun raised. Matt squeezed off a shot.

His shot went wide, ricocheting off the rocks. More shots, this time to his left. He fired and fired again. How many men were there? He'd seen only one.

Footsteps behind him. He spun, weapon raised, and nearly hit her. Skylar.

She dived from behind her boulder to join him.

"I've got your back," she said, unsmiling.

"Damn it," he growled. "What the hell are you doing here?"

"I went for a ride." Her voice was low. Controlled. "Borrowed one of your mares—I'll explain that later. Anyway, I saw a group of strange men and went to investigate."

He didn't bother to comment on the intelligence of that act. "How many are there?"

"Four, maybe five. I'm not sure how they got here. I didn't see any horses or hear any four-wheelers."

"There's an old road not too far from here. They probably parked on it and came here on foot."

"Where's your horse?" he asked.

"I let her go." She frowned. "She should be okay, right?"

He nodded. "I sent Saint away, too. We'll round them up later."

More shots, pinging harmlessly off the rocks and trees. "You've got some good cover, but you're boxed in," she told him.

"I know, but I didn't have a choice." Narrowing his eyes, he weighed their options. "We've got to find a way to flush them out."

Another round of shots. As if they were a team, they both returned fire.

"One of them is hit," she said. "I got him right in the shoulder."

He found he was glad she was a crack shot. "Good. I think I got one, too."

"You're wounded." Eyes wide, she grabbed him. "Let me see."

He jerked away. He'd managed to forget about being

wounded until she pointed it out. Now his damn arm had begun aching. "I'm fine. The bullet only grazed me."

"You're lucky," she told him, her voice harsh. "What happened?"

"Long story short, I was out riding and saw a guy. I rode after him and into some sort of ambush."

"Deliberate?"

"Possibly." He shrugged and then winced at the unexpected pain. "I tend to think I surprised them."

She gave him a hard look. "Maybe. Or if they were expecting to catch you alone, I'm guessing they weren't expecting me. Do you normally ride out here in the morning?"

Her harsh, law-enforcement style of questioning made him grimace. Again he wondered if she realized how much that revealed. "No. I come here occasionally. I'm guessing they were on a clandestine hunting operation."

"For what?" she asked, even though he knew she knew.

"Never mind."

An ominous silence had fallen. Either their opponents were taking stock and making a plan, or they were retreating. Stuck behind this boulder, he couldn't see much.

Moving cautiously, he raised his head and tried to take a look. Though no shots came, he saw nothing, either.

"What now?" she asked.

"No idea," he told her.

"Do you want to rush them?"

"Rush them? We're completely outnumbered."

"True, but we'd have the element of surprise on our side."

He hadn't known she had a death wish. "No. Out of the question."

"Then what's your plan? We can't stay here forever. We're sitting ducks."

Though he liked her fierceness, he couldn't let her risk her life. "Hold on. Sit still and listen."

She went silent long enough to do as he asked. "I don't hear anything."

"Exactly. I think they've retreated."

Before he could stop her, she pushed away and went charging for the next large group of boulders. "Cover me."

Because he had no choice, he did. But no one shot at them. Dashing forward, he joined her.

"Come on," she told him, apparently intending to climb to the top of the rock hill. He grabbed her arm before she could.

"Wait."

Though she made a sound of impatience, she did as he asked.

Popping up, he squeezed off another shot. There was no response.

"They're gone," she said, practically vibrating with impatience. "If we can get to the top, we can get a bead on where they are."

"As long as we have cover," he cautioned. "Safety first."

She made a sound that either could have been agreement or derision. "Lead the way," she said.

Cautiously, he moved forward and up. A rock here, then a twisted scrub tree, then a large, open expanse that was the only way to the top of the hill.

"Well?" She eyed him, one perfectly shaped brow

arched. "Do you want to go for it? Every second wasted gives them more time to get away."

Since he suspected she was right, he nodded. "I'm going alone. Wait here."

Without waiting for her to comply, he dashed up the remaining distance. Somehow he wasn't surprised when she came along right behind him.

"I told you I've got your back," she said, waving away any protests he might be about to make. "Look." She pointed. "Over there, near the road."

In the distance, he could see the group of men running. A beat-up black Suburban parked nearby was apparently their destination.

"They're nearly there."

"Too far for us to catch them." He cursed. "And we're not close enough to make out the plates."

Side by side, they watched as the men climbed into the vehicle and sped away.

Chapter 9

Only when the intruders' vehicle had completely vanished did Matt turn to look at her. He wasn't surprised to find her glaring at him, her arms crossed.

"What the hell was that?" she demanded.

He grimaced. "Nothing you need to worry about."

Her mouth fell open and then she made a rude sound. "Don't give me that crap. Are you going to tell me what's going on? First a fire is deliberately set in your barn, then a bunch of guys shoots at us."

Us. The simple word sent an absurd stab of longing through him. Made even more dangerous by the fact that she could have died, and once again, it would have been all his fault.

"There is no *us*," he told her. "And the rest is none of your business. I've changed my mind about letting you stay another day. Actually, it'd be best if you go gather your things and take off."

Still glaring at him, she stood her ground. "I helped you, damn it. I'm not going anywhere until you tell me what's going on."

"You are my responsibility and you were nearly killed," he ground out, suddenly, blazingly furious. "And you still want to ask questions?"

He saw his own fury reflected back at him in her eyes. In three strides she reached him, grabbed ahold of him by the front of his shirt.

Standing on tiptoe, she tried to go nose to nose with him. She didn't quite make it, as he was still a good six or more inches taller.

Still, the fact that she even made the attempt turned him on incredibly. That and the adrenaline rushing through his body like lightning had him wanting to haul her up against him and freaking ravish her.

"I could just shake you," she cried, her frustration apparent in her voice. This had nearly the same effect as a dousing of cold water. Obviously, he didn't have the same effect on her.

"Shake me?" he asked, incredulous. "You're the one who insists on putting herself in danger. You could have been killed. Do you understand?"

"So could you," she shot back, pushing at him. "I've had years of practice. What about you? How good are you with a gun?"

Now wasn't the time to tell her he'd been a sharp-shooter in the military.

Nose to nose, chest to chest, adrenaline and anger and fear coalesced into a flash of…something else. Something white-hot and life-affirming and as dangerous as hell.

"Damn it," he growled. Then, before he could even think, she hauled him up against her and kissed him.

After half a second of stunned shock, he kissed her back.

This time, the kiss raged like a wildfire, out of control. Neither was willing to give an inch, and for the first time he relished the hotness of a woman who knew what she wanted and wouldn't back down.

She pressed against him, grinding her body into his. Already hard beyond belief, he thought he might burst through his jeans.

She grabbed his butt, pulling him closer, pulling at his shirt with fumbling hands. Impatient, he yanked hers over her head, then helped her rip his from his chest. More kisses, touches, groans. On fire, they shed the rest of their clothing, just as the sun rose over the horizon in a blaze of gold.

Finally, naked, he dimly registered the truth of her body—every bit as splendid as he'd dreamed—before she was on him, taking as much as she gave.

He tried to hold off, to bank the fires so they'd burn longer, but she would have none of that.

Pushing him back, she straddled him. "Are you ready?" she growled.

He thought he'd never seen anything as erotic as her, crouched over him in the early-morning light, wild and sexy and…

Before he could even finish the thought, she took him inside her in one swift move. Sheathing him, so tight, so wet, so damn perfect.

A moan escaped him. "Skylar," he managed, unable to articulate anything but her name.

She began to move. He moved with her, bucking, trying to keep to the slow rhythm she set, but his body had other plans.

They took each other—not making love so much as

taking possession—and it was fierce and fiery and re-affirmed to both of them that they were alive.

After, sweaty and spent, they held each other briefly before she pushed away and sat up. Gazing at him, she swallowed hard. "I hadn't intended for that to happen."

Finally, honesty. Slowly, he shook his head. "Me, either."

"It's time for some truths," she said.

Weary of it all, he shook his head. "Fine. You want the truth? Then I'll tell you. I already know what you are."

At that, she went very, very still. "What do you mean?" she asked, but her voice sounded off.

He eyed her. She watched him, her wariness evident in the way she held her body. Stiff, remote, as though they hadn't just shared the most intimate of acts.

"You're ATF or DEA," he continued. "Undercover. Don't bother denying it."

Finally, her shoulders sagged, just the tiniest bit, but it was enough. "How long have you known?" she asked.

He saw the way she tried not to glance toward her weapon. Did she really think he was that big a threat? That after all that had happened between them he'd really hurt her?

"Go ahead." He gestured toward the gun. "Hand me mine while you're at it."

She goggled at him. "What?"

"Do you really think I'm going to hurt you?"

"I don't know," she cried. "My cover is blown, you're not what I expected, so who the hell knows what's going to happen next?"

"You don't have to worry about me," he told her. Then, because he wanted no lies between them, he added, "Unless you get in my way."

"Your way." Dragging her hand through her hair, she looked vulnerable and beautiful and the exact opposite of the tigress who'd attacked his body only moments before. When he didn't respond, she sighed. "Are you going to tell me the truth about what's going on? Who were those men? Why were they shooting at us? Did they set the fire at the barn? And are you going to call the local police?"

Once again, she hammered questions at him the same way she'd attacked him. Full-out, holding nothing back.

"Those men were most likely members of the Mexican drug cartel."

She stared. He wasn't sure if it was because she hadn't expected the truth or because even the truth was a bit difficult to swallow.

"The Mexican drug cartel never comes this far north," she finally said. "They have people on this side who take care of distribution for them."

"True." He smiled, though it felt more like a grimace. "And since you know I'm not dealing drugs…"

"Then what are you doing?" she interrupted. "We know about your stockpile of ammunition."

"Which is not illegal."

"I know the law, thank you," she snapped. "Are you selling or do you intend to sell that ammunition to the Mexicans?"

He widened his eyes. "Now, *that* would be illegal," he mocked.

"Matt, please. I'm trying to work with you here."

"Then arrest me, if I've done something wrong. Otherwise, I want you off my ranch."

Slowly, she shook her head. "You've done nothing wrong."

"I know I haven't. So what's your next step? I've

heard stories. How when you people can't find a legitimate reason to move in, you manufacture one."

Her expression went mulish. "That's bull."

"Oh, yeah? I saw on the news how you raided some guy in Dallas who had an ammo stash. The charge was that he was *suspected* of being a weapons dealer without a license. You had no proof of anything. But you went in anyway."

To give her credit, she looked down. "That was an isolated case. I'm sure they found something after it was all over."

"Are you? I'm not."

She sighed. "Look, you've already told me my cover's blown. I really do want to help you. Not as a federal agent, but as a…person."

As a woman? He let it go, still not entirely sure he could trust her. But he wanted to, oh, how he wanted to. The depth of his longing shocked the hell out of him.

More proof he was truly a fool.

Frustrated, he turned away. "No."

"Off the record," she urged. "I promise. I'm willing to assist you any way I can."

"Why?" Studying her, he searched her face for any hint of a lie.

His question seemed to stop her cold. For the first time, she appeared uncertain. "Honestly, I don't know. Maybe because I actually like you."

Strange as it seemed, he believed her. Still, they were on opposing sides of the fence. "I refuse to ask you to compromise your job."

"I would never do that," she shot back. "But I can help you. If you're in a bind, let me lend a hand."

As tempting as her offer was, he knew she couldn't help him with what he wanted to do. It would be against everything she stood for. After all, she'd come here under false pretenses, and for all he knew, she was still lying.

He could do nothing about the powerful attraction they shared, but he couldn't allow it to factor into his decision. He had too much at risk. "The best thing you can do is pack, get in your little VW and get the hell out of here."

She crossed her arms, still spectacular in her nakedness. To his disbelief, his body stirred. Immediately, he snatched up his discarded clothing and began getting dressed. She simply stood there and watched him.

"Please," he urged. "Put on your clothes."

To his immense relief, moving slowly, stiffly, she dragged on her jeans and her T-shirt, running her fingers through her hair. Once she'd finished and was fully clothed, she faced him again. This time, at least he could look at her without becoming too aroused.

"I'm dressed. Now, don't ask me to leave, because I'm not going anywhere until you tell me the truth."

Frustrated, tired of the lies, exhausted from the pretense, he swallowed.

"Please," she added, touching his shoulder lightly.

It was the contact, the feel of her hand on his body that did it. For one brief, shining instant, he no longer felt so alone.

So he told her some things, things that José was the only other person to know. Careful not to reveal everything—like his real name or how he'd come by his millions—he stuck with the facts, trying to remain unemotional. He told her about his family, about his brother, Ricardo, and his dealings with La Familia.

"The largest of all the Mexican drug cartels?" she asked.

"And the most dangerous. Yes." And finally, he told her about coming home to find his family all dead, shot execution-style and left in the blazing sun to rot in the field behind their house.

There were things he left out. Most important, what he had planned. His *revenge.*

As his words trailed off into silence, he looked up, saw the silver sheen of tears on her cheeks and felt a curious swooping pull inside his chest.

"No." He shook his head. "Don't cry for me. It's too late for that," he told her.

"What are you planning?" she finally asked, her voice flat, as if she'd tried to suppress all emotions. "Using the ammo to draw them here and then...what?"

"Planning?" He lifted his chin. She was too astute for her own good. "I'm not planning anything."

"Now who's not telling the truth?" Expression calculating, she stared at him. "You've accumulated a large amount of ammunition. There has to be a reason—that was one of the things our intel never got figured out. You probably made sure the cartel knows about it, too. Why?"

Instead of answering, he dodged the question. "They don't know where the ammo is. I've made sure of that."

"But they're looking for it. That's what those men who shot at us where doing here—searching for your ammo."

"Maybe. But they'll never find it."

"Then what are you doing? I know you have some sort of plan."

He'd already gone this far. What the hell? She'd never be able to prove any of it. "The two men who killed my family are trying to break away from La Familia and form their own cartel. La Familia doesn't take well to that kind of thing."

"So they both want your ammo. Why?"

He shrugged, deliberately casual. "Maybe they both have heard it's available."

"You really intend to sell it to the highest bidder?" She looked so disappointed and furious that he had to smile.

"No. I don't intend to sell it at all." He waited while she processed that.

"Then what?" Her frustration was evident in her voice. "What do you plan to do with it?"

Instead of answering, he glanced back toward the ranch. "You know, sooner or later someone is going to discover Saint without a rider and come looking for me."

"Let them look." She shrugged. "We're dressed. Now tell me what you're planning to do with the ammo. I'm guessing it involves revenge."

"End of discussion," he said.

"All right." She crossed her arms. "The ATF never could learn where you came by your money. That's one of the reasons why they suspect you of illegal activity."

"And you want to know where I got it?"

"Yes."

He sighed. "I won the lottery. Right after I got out of the military, before I went home to find my family killed, I bought a ticket and won two hundred and fifty-one million dollars."

Of all the things she might have expected, it hadn't been this. "But Texas law won't let you remain anonymous."

"I know." Scratching his head, he grimaced. "I hired a lawyer and a financial adviser. They helped me set up various corporations—all legal—in which to claim the money."

Her skeptical expression told him what she thought of that. "Still, I'd think there'd be some sort of trail to your name."

"I worried about that, too. After my family was killed, I changed it." He paused, studying her as if debating whether to continue. "I used to have a different name."

Now her expression softened. "Do you regret that now?"

"Sometimes. I'm used to being called Matt Landeta now, but when I think of having a son, I regret he won't be able to carry on the family name."

"Then why don't you change it back?"

Before he could answer, someone shouted his name. José. And close. Not bothering to hide his relief, he turned and waved.

"Tell me," she pressed. "Before he gets here."

"I've already revealed enough, Skylar. When we get back to the ranch, I want you packed and gone before breakfast. Is that clear?"

"Clear as mud." Rather than compliant, she sounded mad as hell. "I have nothing to lose. My cover is blown. If you're not illegally selling ammunition to the Mexican drug cartel, then tell me what you're doing. If you're convincing enough, I might be able to persuade the ATF to leave you alone."

Now, that would be nice. But could he trust her? He wanted to, damn he wanted to. But the stakes were too high and he couldn't risk it.

So he did what he did best, deflected. Or tried to. "Look, I'm just a regular guy who happens to have a lot of ammo. Just because—"

"Spare me the crap." She sounded disgusted. "I get it, Matt. The cartel murdered your family and you're out for revenge. But this isn't the way to go about it. Those people don't play. They're ruthless and they have no qualms about killing."

"You don't have to tell me that." He spat the words, the old ache mingling with fury in his chest. "I'm well aware of what they do. I'm the one who found my mother's body, right next to my father, a few feet from my brother. So don't talk to me about what the cartel is willing to do."

His voice had been rising as he spoke, and by the time he got to the end of it, he was shouting. She looked at him as though he'd sprouted horns.

Glancing back down at his friend, he saw José had nearly reached the bottom of the hill. Once he started climbing, he'd be there in a matter of seconds. Matt wondered how much he'd overheard.

"Go," he told Skylar, refusing to look at her now that he'd laid bare his grief. "Pretend like we never talked."

"Shall I also pretend like we never made love?" she asked, deliberately scathing, before moving away and beginning the hike back down the trail.

She lifted her hand as she passed José, but didn't stop. Instead, she kept going, back toward the ranch house, moving away. Away from him and out of his life.

Though he knew this was all for the best, that didn't stop it from hurting.

Pigheaded man. Skylar strode past a startled José, steaming back toward the ranch. She was a trained federal agent. She could help him. Why couldn't he accept her words at face value? If he wanted justice, she was willing to help him capture the man or men responsible and make sure they stood trial.

She would not, however, be a party to murder or illegal ammo sales. Not even for him.

The distance was farther than she'd remembered and the sun beamed down hotly. She began wishing for water after ten minutes, and the unfamiliar soreness of her body turned into an actual ache by the time the ranch house came into sight.

Also, for no good reason, she felt perilously close to tears.

Stupid man. And foolish Skylar. Because for the first time in a long time, she hadn't made her job her number one priority. She'd let her cover be blown, and rather than try to bluff her way out of the discovery, she'd actually *admitted* the truth about who she was. That was her first mistake.

Her second was even worse. Despite everything, she'd actually begun to care for someone who cared only about revenge.

Hurrying to her trailer, she let Talia out and then began packing to leave.

"Are you all right?" José asked when he reached the area where Matt stood. "I knew something was wrong when one of the field hands reported Saint running around saddled but without a rider."

"I'm fine. Did you make sure Saint was unsaddled and brushed out?"

"Of course." José looked disgusted that Matt had even asked. Though he wasn't a horse person per se, he took pride in making sure Matt's animals were well taken care of.

"He's back in the barn, safe."

"Good. What about the mare Skylar took? Did you find her, too?" Matt asked, starting out for home.

"Yep. What the hell happened to you?" José eyed him up and down. Matt knew he looked like crap, covered in mud and grass with a bit of blood thrown in for good measure.

"Someone took a few potshots at me," he said. "I squeezed off a few of my own, and I'm thinking I scored a hit, judging from the amount of blood."

"Are you all right?"

Matt nodded, indicating his arm where he'd used a strip torn from his shirt as a makeshift bandage. "Surface wound. He barely hit me."

"Do we need to get you looked at?"

Matt suspected José already knew the answer to that, so he didn't bother answering. Instead, he focused on what they needed to do next.

"I want word sent that I need to meet with Diego immediately," Matt said. "This is a bunch of bull."

José raised a brow. "I doubt it's Diego's men who are shooting at you."

"You don't think so? It's either them or someone from La Familia. Either way, Diego knows who did this."

"You might be right." Now José looked pissed. "I'm thinking whoever it is might be trying to locate where you've got it stored. Getting a good price on it is one thing. Getting it for free is something else entirely."

They'd talked at length about this possibility. No one except the two of them had any idea where the ammunition was stored. Matt wanted to keep it that way.

"What about the Fed?" José asked, gesturing in the direction Skylar had gone. "How was she involved?"

"She wasn't at first. I was out riding alone at dawn like I sometimes do. When I caught sight of one of them and tried to chase him down, the others opened fire."

"Were you…"

"Nope, nowhere near the caves." At least this was a bit of good news. He grimaced. "I never saw the rest of the shooters until they jumped into their vehicle. But I still think I got one of them."

"They're probably aware you're a sharpshooter," José put in.

"You think? I don't know about that. Either way, Skylar showed up and covered my back. She hit one, too."

José stared. "Seriously?"

Matt described what had happened.

"Damn." José hurried to keep pace. "So now she knows Mexican cartel members are involved. Great, just great."

"Of course she does. Who else would be searching my land? ATF agents wouldn't look without a search warrant, despite sending Skylar here undercover."

José's expression turned even grimmer. "Do you think they found the caves?"

"No. That I'm sure of. The sensors didn't go off, which means no one got within ten feet of the caves."

"Yeah, but still. It's bad they had the balls to show up here."

"And shoot at me. I'm not sure what the outcome would have been if Skylar hadn't shown up."

"I don't like the way you say her name." The look José shot him was both disgruntled and worried.

Matt shrugged again. They walked in silence for a bit, each man lost in his own thoughts.

"I told her almost everything," Matt said as he and José reached the bottom of the first hill and strode across the pasture. Skylar was no longer anywhere in sight.

"You did what?" José stared at him, shock and disbelief written all over his face.

"I told her the truth."

"All of it?"

Picking his steps carefully, Matt nodded. "Almost."

José winced. "Why'd you go and do that, man?"

Silence. They were almost at the house.

Since Matt hadn't responded, José asked the question again.

"We, uh, made love." He didn't use the far more crude term he might have because this was Skylar he was talking about. The slight narrowing of his friend's eyes told him José had noticed.

"So she got to you. I hate to say I told you so, but, dude, I've seen that coming for a while."

Matt shrugged. He supposed he should have felt angry or betrayed or worried. Instead, he felt a weird sense of relief, strangely glad the subterfuge was over.

"Do you think she believed you?"

"I don't know. It doesn't matter. I also told her she has to leave."

"Oh, no." José shook his head. "That's the worst thing you could have done. Revealing the truth to her was bad enough. If she goes, you know she'll make a report on everything. That could seriously mess things up."

Considering his friend's words, Matt stepped up onto his rear porch, entering his house through the back door.

Once inside, he got them both bottled water, taking a deep pull of the cold liquid before speaking. "What are you suggesting?"

"You need to keep her here." Water bottle in hand, José began to pace, a sure sign of his agitation. Matt watched him, wishing the tightness in his chest would ease up and wondering if he'd really made a mistake in talking honestly to Skylar. It didn't feel like it. But that could also be because they'd made love.

Made love. He nearly snorted out loud. Who was he

really kidding—José? It had been sex. A purely physical thing, nothing more. And he knew once José thought about it, he would try to figure out a way to use that tidbit of information to manipulate Skylar somehow.

Which would actually be perfect, except…Matt didn't want to do that.

So he closed his mouth and watched as José struggled to come up with a plan.

Finally, José stopped, right in front of the window that overlooked the guest trailer. "She's loading up her car. You've got to stop her."

Matt didn't move. "Why? If she knows we're not trying to sell ammo, she'll tell her superiors at the ATF and they'll leave us alone."

Without taking his gaze from the window, José shook his head. "First off, they'll never believe her. If—and this is a big *if*—she actually thinks you told her the truth and puts this in her report to her supervisors, they'll think it's a story fabricated to throw them off the scent."

"So? Either way, it'll keep the ATF out of our hair. I send her away and refuse to let anyone else onto the ranch."

Now José faced him, his expression grim. "And then what? The ATF sends someone else. What if this leaks to the cartel? You know they have moles everywhere. That's the last thing you need."

Matt cursed.

"So once again, I ask you, what the hell were you thinking?"

"I wasn't, obviously." Dragging his hand through his hair, Matt exhaled. "She had my back in the shoot-out. That's got to count for something."

"She was just doing her job," José said, turning his attention once again to the window. "I still think you should go down there," he said. "Of course, it's your de-cision, but the enemy we know is better than the enemy we don't. If keeping her here will keep the ATF out of our hair..."

Finally, Matt pushed himself away from the wall. "Fine. I'll go talk to her. Though what I could possibly say to convince her this time to hang around, I have no idea."

"You'll think of something."

Matt only hoped his friend was right. Jaw clenched, he headed outside and down to the trailer.

Chapter 10

The VW's doors were open and Skylar had begun stacking her belongings on the backseat. As Matt approached, she emerged from the trailer with a large duffel bag. At the sight of him, her entire body stiffened.

"Yes?" she asked, her voice chilly. Talia, staying close to Skylar's side, wagged her tail and cocked her head uncertainly.

"I came to apologize," he said, winging it and hoping like hell he managed to make sense by the time he was through. "I shouldn't have treated you that way."

When she didn't respond, instead continuing to regard him suspiciously, he knew he'd have to say more. But what?

Since honeyed words and such were foreign to him, he took a deep breath and went with the truth. "Don't go."

This stopped her in her tracks. Staring at him, her

frown deepening, she narrowed her eyes. "Again? Make up your mind. You just told me, not even an hour ago, that I had to leave."

"I know." Eating crow was never pleasant, but he swallowed his pride and continued, "I was wrong. Please stay."

"You're like a yo-yo, you know that? This is the second time you've done this and then changed your mind." She continued to regard him suspiciously. "Why?"

"Because I need your help." Simply put, the instant he spoke he realized it was the truth. "Now that you know what I'm trying to do..."

Though she still stared at him, to his relief she slowly lowered the duffel bag to the ground. "Are you serious?"

"Definitely."

Her gaze searched his face. "You want me to help you catch the men who killed your family?"

Since no more words were necessary, he simply nodded.

"It won't bring them back, you know."

Anger flashed through him. What did someone like her know of loss, especially the kind of loss he'd suffered? Squashing that fury, he spoke carefully. "I'm aware of that. But my family's honor requires this."

She cocked her head, considering his words. "I'll help you, but I have several conditions."

"Go on."

"One, if we catch these guys, we'll arrest them and make sure they stand trial."

Crossing his arms, he didn't bother to tell her how unrealistic that idea was. The government of Mexico was so corrupt, so afraid of the cartels, that if Diego and his men here in the U.S. were arrested, once they were extradited they'd be given a free pass to freedom.

And then their vengeance would be a bloodbath.

When he didn't respond, Skylar narrowed her catlike eyes. "Do you agree?"

He sighed. Though he hated to lie, he suspected if he told her the truth she'd refuse to stay. And despite the fact that he figured she wouldn't be satisfied with a half-truth, he still gave it a shot. "I'll consider that possibility."

"Not good enough," she responded, crossing her own arms. "I'm sworn to uphold the law. I will not help you murder a man in cold blood."

Suddenly, despite José's warning, Matt realized he'd had enough. "The fact that you could say such a thing makes me wonder how much you actually know about the Mexican drug cartels," he said, his voice harsh. "Are you truly familiar with the way they operate?"

"Of course I am," she responded. "I've read up on them. Their crimes are notorious."

"Reading up is not going to cut it. You need to experience it in person. Go hang out in some of the border towns, even on the U.S. side. I promise you that you'll see and hear things that will help you realize these men are no more than animals. Cold-blooded killers."

"Maybe so, but they're still entitled to a fair trial," she said stubbornly.

"Fair?" His voice dripped with scorn. "The cartels don't know the meaning of that word."

She took a step closer. "Take it or leave it," she said softly. "I'm not staying any other way."

Damn. Matt considered himself an honorable man, but she left him no choice. After all, she wouldn't be able to stop what he meant to do when the time came.

Unfortunately, this meant that once again he was back to lying.

"Fine," he said, glad she didn't know him well enough to be able to know when he wasn't telling the truth. "We'll try it your way."

Regarding him in silence, she stood a moment longer. Finally, dipping her chin in a nod, she turned and carried her duffel bag back to the camper.

She made two more trips, waving off his offer to help. When she'd finished, she dusted off her hands. "Let's go talk to José," she said. "I'm guessing he's watching us right now from your house."

He felt a quick flash of discomfort. With anyone else, he'd have wondered how much she knew of José's involvement. But since she was ATF, she'd no doubt been briefed. José was wise to want to keep her around.

"I have to ask one favor first," he said. "I need you to keep all of this out of any reports you make. Just in case there's a leak, you understand."

To his surprise, she chuckled. "You know, if I tried to report something like this, they'd want to work with you to set up a sting."

"If they believed me, that is."

Looking thoughtful, she nodded. "You do have a point. I'll keep quiet, for now. But I won't do anything illegal, understood?"

"Perfectly." He dredged up a smile. "I appreciate the favor. Come on, let's go find José."

José waited exactly where Matt had left him. Arms crossed, he watched them approach, unsmiling.

Apparently undeterred, Skylar walked up to him and stuck out her hand. "José Nivas? I'm Skylar McLain."

At first Matt thought José wouldn't respond, but finally he shook, quick and fast. "Matt told me you're helping us now."

She smiled modestly. "As much as I can. What do you need me to do?"

Matt waited to hear what his friend would say.

"Whatever Matt wants," José finally said, lobbing the ball back into Matt's court.

Fine. He'd always been good at winging it.

"Do you make reports?" Matt asked, realizing what he needed her to do.

Skylar nodded. "Of course."

"How often?

She shrugged. "When I can. If nothing is going on, every couple of days."

"I want you to make a report now. Tell them you've discovered the location of the ammo."

"But I haven't…" She bit her lip. When she spoke again, her voice had gone flat. "You want me to lie to my boss."

"You said you'd do whatever it took to help me," Matt pointed out. "I can't take the chance of them trying to interfere."

"Then I make the bust, the arrest. Right?"

Hating that he had to lie, but well aware that he'd long ago vowed to do whatever it took, he nodded. "Right."

He watched while she considered, her internal struggle plain on her face. When she finally nodded, he resisted the urge to share a high five with José.

"Where do you want me to say it is?" she asked.

For this, he looked at José. "What do you think?"

José shrugged. "You've only got a couple of choices. You could say you rented a warehouse in town."

"No. That's too easy to check out."

"Okay. We can't say any of the barns—we don't want to endanger the horses."

"True." Matt thought. "The tack room and office

aren't big enough. We've got the hay storage building. What about there?"

"Who in their right mind would put explosive ammunition with highly flammable hay?" Skylar pointed out. "I'm not sure anyone would believe that."

"Good point."

"What about the ruins?" José finally spoke up, referring to a pile of rocks that had once been the ranch homestead a hundred or so years ago.

"All that's left of that is the chimney," Matt said. "Where could we hide anything?"

"The cellar." Now José grinned. "It's fully intact. Remember you were talking about using it for a tornado shelter, if you could move it closer to this house?"

"Perfect." So perfect, in fact, that Matt had to wonder why they hadn't actually stored the ammunition there. It would have been a hell of a lot easier to secure than the caves. He'd had to install steel doors like a bank vault with a keypad to which only he knew the combination. And as a further security measure, he'd set up remote security cameras.

"We could actually move it there," José said, as if he'd read Matt's mind, "and then leak the real location instead. Maybe even leave a few boxes there as a decoy."

"Damn, that's brilliant." Clapping his friend on the shoulder, Matt grinned back. "But since I've got the true hiding place all secured, I don't want to move anything, not with the cartel snooping around."

Glancing at Skylar, he noted her frown as she followed the conversation. "What's wrong?" he asked.

"You're both acting like this is a game."

Behind her, José rolled his eyes. "*Chica,* it *is* a game."

With a stubborn tilt to her chin, she ignored him,

keeping her gaze trained on Matt. "Is it a game to you, too?"

Abruptly, he sobered. "No, Skylar. It's not. It's intensely serious. But sometimes, it helps to joke to break up the tension."

"I see." She tried to summon up a smile, falling short. "Well, I'm sorry, but I can't find the humor in what I'm about to do. I've never made a false report in my life. I could lose my job over this."

Now she'd succeeded in crushing his earlier optimism. "Once again, I don't want you to do anything you're not comfortable with. If you can't make the report, we'll figure out something else."

Once again, the choice was hers.

Crossing to her, Matt put his arm around her shoulders and pulled her close. "Go back to your trailer, play with your dog and think about what you want to do. We don't need a decision immediately."

From the rigid way she held herself, he could well imagine what she'd choose. When she moved away from him, she wouldn't meet his gaze, reinforcing his hunch.

"All right. I'll be down at my camper. I'll let you know later what I'm going to do."

At the doorway, she turned. "When I get back, I'd like to go for a ride. I find it helps me clear my head. I'll take out the same mare I rode earlier, if that's all right with you."

"No, I'd prefer you didn't." Matt smiled to take the edge of his words. "I have another horse I want you to try. We'll go together."

Instead of accepting his offer, she narrowed her gaze. "Safely in numbers and all that?"

He nodded.

"I'll be back in under an hour," she said. "We'll ride then."

Both Matt and José watched in silence as she walked away.

Once she was out of sight—and hearing—José cursed. "I don't think she's going to be of any help at all."

"I agree." Refusing to let the knowledge get him down, Matt set his jaw. "So we'd better come up with an alternate plan."

"Yeah, especially since I have news. I didn't want to tell you in front of her, but I heard from Diego's man," José said, his voiced laced with calm resolve. "He's agreeable to a meeting with you, the sooner the better."

Matt pushed away the fierce rush of joy. "Where? I refuse to go down to Matamoros."

"You're in luck, then. I don't think they want to take a chance with border patrol. As you suspected, they must have people on this side of the border. He's sending someone to talk to you."

Instantly, Matt shook his head. "No good. I meet with Diego himself or no one."

"Hear me out." José held up his hand. "This is the first meeting. There's no way he's going to handle this himself. It takes time to instill a sense of trust. They're going to want proof that you can deliver."

José made sense. Still, he didn't like it. "Proof? As in what, show them the ammunition?"

"Pretty much," José said. "We can do that. Blindfold whoever they send, drive him around the ranch and then let him see the ammo."

"Fine," Matt agreed, blowing his breath out. "As long as we don't give them any clue where it's really hidden."

"About that," José said. "I think it's time to move it

off the ranch. Have you given any thought to my idea of renting a warehouse in town?"

Scratching his head, Matt nodded. "I have, though I like the abandoned-cellar idea better. I'll be honest, though. It sounds too risky. We'd have to move it in secret, in small increments, and there's a huge chance someone would see it."

"I take it that's a no, then?"

"I'll think about it." Matt wouldn't, and they both knew it. "Right now, I think it's safest where it is."

With a grimace, José dipped his chin to show he understood. "I'm curious. What are you going to do with all that ammunition once you accomplish what you want?"

Matt smiled. "Donate it, if I can. I'd like to give it to underbudgeted police departments or something."

Apparently surprised, José gave a grudging nod. "Sounds like a plan."

"Will you look into that for me?"

"Sure." José's expression turned troubled. "What about me?" he asked quietly. "What am I supposed to do once you're gone?"

"Gone?" Attempting to lighten the mood, Matt gave the man he considered a brother a light punch in the arm. "I have no plans to go anywhere."

"Humph." José made a rude noise. "Messing around with La Familia? If you don't get killed trying to get Diego, you'll probably end up doing some jail time."

"Not if I do it right." Infusing his voice with more optimism than he felt, Matt shook his head. "No worries, old friend. Whatever happens, I'll make sure you have a job here."

José looked away, but not before Matt caught a glimpse of something strange crossing his friend's face.

"What's wrong, man?" Matt asked.

Jaw rigid, José sighed. "I don't like this. I think we should have gone with the original plan. It'd be way better if you could get into Mexico and take him down there. Drug-cartel killings are so common there that the *policia* barely notice them anymore."

"We already discussed that. Too much risk. Once I shot him, I'd never get away. The cartels have too many eyes. Someone would take me down long before I could make it back across the border."

"Maybe." A hint of stubborn defiance sparked in José's eyes. "But with you being a sharpshooter and all—"

"I'd need a specialized type of weapon, impossible to get through customs and difficult to obtain in Mexico without someone noticing."

"I could have made arrangements—"

"No." Matt held up his hand, impatient. "Come on, bro. We've talked this to death already. It's too damn dangerous. Plus, I want him to know why he's being killed. If I took him out at a distance, he'd never know."

"Face-to-face is stupid and more dangerous than going down into Mexico," José shot back. "You are so obsessed with your vengeance that you can't think clearly."

"Enough!" Matt growled. Inhaling deeply, he gathered his shredded calm around him like a cloak. "José, I know I've offered this before and you've refused, but if you want out, you can go with my blessings."

José looked away, a muscle working in his jaw. "It's just that I'm worried about you," he finally ground out. "Neither of these plans is ideal, but I want to minimize your risk."

"Me, too," Matt lied. The one thing he always made

sure of was that his best friend didn't know the truth. All Matt lived for was the vengeance. Once Diego Rodriguez was dead, Matt didn't really care what happened to himself.

"You know," José pointed out, his voice studiously casual, "if she decides to go along with our plan, Skylar will blame herself if anything happens to you."

"That's possible," Matt said. "But nothing will."

"Still…"

"She'll get over it." Again Matt had to clamp down on his irritation. "We've only known each other a week. She's a strong woman."

"For a reason."

Matt stared. "What do you mean?"

"Wait a second." Turning, José began rummaging in a small stack of folders. "Here we go." He extracted a copy of what looked like a newspaper article and handed it to Matt. "I did some research. I found this on the internet."

Dated five years earlier, the story talked about the vicious gunning down of several people in a Dallas bank robbery.

Reading it, at first Matt didn't see what this had to do with anything. Then he saw the last line.

Among the victims were Robbie and Bryan McLain, the husband and seven-year-old son of Dallas police officer Skylar McLain.

He looked up. José watched him expectantly.

"Her family?" he asked, although he already knew the answer.

"Yeah. I kind of imagine she blames herself." *Like you.* José didn't say the last two words. He didn't have to.

"Why would she do that?" With a sinking heart, Matt

hoped his friend wasn't right. "It was a random, sense-less shooting in a bank robbery gone wrong. There's no way she could have prevented that."

"Maybe. Maybe not. Just like there's no—"

"Stop." Matt held up his hand. "Don't even go there. I'll always believe I could have prevented my family's murder if I'd been there. Nothing you can say will change my mind. You should know that by now."

Slowly, José shook his head. "What if she's like you, amigo? This Skylar McLain also lost her entire family. You don't know whether or not she blames herself."

"Why does it matter?"

José turned away. "Listen to you. Since when do you not give a damn about hurting innocents? You already think you have to carry the world on your conscience. How are you gonna feel if she thinks she's responsible?"

Clinging to the last tatters of his patience, Matt glared at his friend. "Responsible for what?"

"If all of this implodes on you. People could get hurt or worse, killed. Have you considered that?"

That did it. "The only one getting killed is Diego Rodriguez," Matt said, his tone pitched to let José know he was finished with the discussion.

But as usual, his friend had to have the last word. "I guess you figure anyone else is collateral damage, huh?" he asked before walking out of the room.

Back in the camper, Skylar picked up her cell phone and stared at it as if its blank screen held the secrets to the universe. She placed it back on the kitchen table and grabbed Talia's ball. She needed to do something else so she could clear her head.

As usual, her border collie was up for the game. Skylar threw, and Talia leaped and twirled and caught, returning to drop the ball at Skylar's feet.

Finally, when she thought her pet had gotten a good workout, Skylar whistled and they went back inside the trailer. While Talia slurped water from her bowl, Skylar took a deep breath and picked up her phone.

Could she do this? More important, did she want to?

Stomach churning, she scrolled through her contacts and pulled up the number. Punching Call before she talked herself out of it, she spoke in a low voice to the—thank goodness—recording. She said she'd learned the location of the ammo but, protecting herself, she hadn't been able to investigate personally to make sure her information was correct.

Then, taking a deep breath, she said she believed the ammunition had been stored in the cellar of the ruined original ranch house. She would investigate as soon as she could and report back.

When she'd finished, she punched the off button and sat staring at her phone, her heart pounding.

She'd done it. Given the first—and hopefully last—false report of her career. She was now in with Matt and José, 100 percent. For bad or for good.

The only bright spot was the one thing she was achingly certain of. If the Mexican drug cartel showed up trying to break into the cellar, she'd know Matt was right and there truly was a mole inside the ATF. That issue would have to be dealt with, as well.

Otherwise, she'd learn she'd been played for a fool.

Dusting her suddenly sweaty hands off on her jeans, she shoved her phone into her pocket and stood. "Be good, Talia," she said, scratching her pet behind the ears.

Grimacing as another feeling of misgiving swamped

her, she left her camper. She'd go find Matt and tell him what she'd done. And then she'd claim that ride.

Matt was waiting where she'd left him, though José was conspicuously absent. He watched her approach, his face completely devoid of expression.

"Hey," she said softly, holding his gaze and wondering at the unfamiliar softness she felt inside her. "I did like you wanted. I called it in and said I'd learned the ammunition was stored in the cellar of the abandoned house."

"Thank you." He reached out as if to touch her, but at the last minute withdrew, leaving her inexplicably aching.

She spoke quickly, needing to fill the awkward void. "Now, how about that ride?"

Her words seemed to bring him back from whatever dark place he'd gone.

"The ride. Yes. But are you sure you want to do this?" he asked, flashing that lopsided smile that made her chest ache anew. "Remember, the last time we tried to go riding, even though it was separately, we got shot at."

Wishing she could manage to smile back, she nodded. "We also made love."

He cocked his head, the heat in his gaze making her entire body flush. "That, too. Once again, are you certain you want to go riding?"

The undercurrents swirling between them had her dizzy. The thought of making love with him again... Her breath caught.

Somehow, despite everything, she'd crossed an invisible line. She couldn't go back. Hell, she wasn't even sure she wanted to. Resolutely she raised her chin. "Yes, I'm positive. You said you took necessary precautions, right?"

His grin faded, his expression turning grim. "I've got men checking all the ranch perimeters, especially near the farm-to-market road. No one can come onto my property without me knowing about it."

"And," she put in casually, "there's nowhere to hide, right?" Even though his stockpile of ammunition remained hidden, no doubt in plain sight.

"Nope." He didn't even hesitate, though he had to know what she was talking about. Giving her a hard look that, oddly enough, made her feel as if she'd disappointed him, he beckoned her to follow and headed out the door.

Side by side, they walked to the barn. At first, each lost in their own thoughts, neither spoke. But when they reached the old barn, he threw open the door and turned to her.

"Your choice," he said quietly. "Any of the mares in this barn. I have a few geldings, as well. I'll be riding one of them."

"Not Saint?"

He shook his head. "Not for this ride. Go ahead, choose."

Feeling like a child faced with a mound of brightly wrapped packages at Christmas, she slowly moved down the barn's wide aisle.

Several of the horses looked at her, swishing their tails. A few completely ignored her. Only one crossed to the stall door and poked her head out to greet her.

"This one," Skylar said, stroking the bay mare's long, black mane.

Matt nodded with approval. "Good choice. That's Cinna." He pointed toward a small room toward the back of the barn. "That's a makeshift tack room. Grab a saddle and halter and bit."

For the next several minutes, they worked in companionable silence saddling up their mounts. Matt had chosen a big chestnut gelding. Watching him as he worked, his muscular arms stretching his shirt over his broad shoulders, she felt a little shudder of desire deep inside her.

"Are you ready?" he asked, bringing her out of her sensual daze.

Blinking, she swallowed hard before nodding. Slipping the bit into Cinna's mouth, she secured the halter before leading the mare down the barn's wide aisle. The clip-clop of hooves sounded both familiar and alien.

Once outside, she stuck her foot in the stirrup and swung her other leg over the horse's broad back.

Already astride, Matt gave her an unsmiling nod of approval before he put his heels to his horse's sides and rode out.

"Come on," he called back over his shoulder.

With a moment's hesitation—after all, this was the first time she couldn't separate her ambivalent personal feelings from the detached professionalism the job required—she rode after him.

"We're going to take the complete tour," he told her, gesturing toward his saddlebag. "I had the cook pack us a picnic lunch. This will take almost all day."

Of course, she'd keep an eye out for anything suspicious, and she knew he had to be aware of this. Ergo, he'd most likely keep her far, far away from his secret stash of ammunition.

Although, really, now that she knew what he had planned, maybe he would even show it to her. Now, that, she thought with a wry grimace, would be something.

Chapter 11

Matt eyed Skylar sitting so comfortably on one of his best mares, cursing himself for not considering how badly he'd have to battle temptation around her.

A kiss hadn't been enough. And sex, powerful, raw and intimate, had done nothing more than stoke the embers of desire to a roaring flame.

He wanted her again. With a fierceness that rivaled his desire for revenge. He'd thought nothing would ever equal the strength of that.

This craving both worried and enchanted him. Skylar didn't seem to realize how beautiful and sexy she was with her riot of red hair and emerald-green eyes. Matt, however, could hardly think of anything else.

Focus. Damn, this was the worst time for him to be infatuated with a woman, the absolute worst. No matter what, he needed to hold it all together and keep his sights trained on his goal. No way was he messing it up when he was so close.

The sun was warm and the slight breeze kept it from feeling too hot. Though he tried to relax, he couldn't. His senses had gone into a sort of hyperaware overdrive and his chest ached with the effort to appear nonchalant.

"Where are we going?" Riding up alongside him, Skylar handled her horse with the natural seat of a born horsewoman.

"I told you, the grand tour. I'm going to take you to see everything." He managed to smile at her, hoping he at least appeared more relaxed than he felt.

"Everything?" She smiled back, starting a slow burn in his groin. He'd just about decided to try to relax and enjoy the day when she cocked her head and gave him a quizzical look.

"When you say *everything,* do you mean you're you going to show me where the ammo is stored?"

As far as lust-killers went, this one was a doozy.

He supposed he should be grateful. Instead, he could barely contain his irritation. "Why would I want to do that?"

She lifted her chin in that obstinate little gesture he was coming to know. "Why not? I stuck my neck out for you. I lied to my superior. I think I at least deserve to see it."

Reining his horse to a halt, he eyed her. "Why? Why would you even want to?"

If he expected her to fumble for a response, he was wrong. "To prove to myself it's really there. All this time, with the ATF claiming to have proof that you've amassed a stockpile, I've been searching for it. Now you've leveled with me and we're on equal footing. I think I have a right to see it."

Inhaling deeply, he hoped his grimness wasn't reflected in his expression. "That doesn't even make sense. Tell me the rest. Again, why do you want to see my ammo?"

Gazes deadlocked, neither would look away. A thousand possibilities spun in his mind—from her finally being able to call in the ATF with some trumped-up charges to her actually working for Diego Rodriguez. Which was ridiculous. She'd lost her family, just like him. With something like that in common, he knew she'd never betray him.

He trusted her—up to a point. Just not enough, not yet.

"I just do," she responded stubbornly. Her answer didn't make him feel any better.

He glanced at his watch. "You know what? I suddenly remembered an appointment. The local Cattle Ranchers Association is meeting in town in half an hour. I was going to skip it, but now I think I'd better go. We'll have to head back in. I guess I can give you the ranch tour some other time."

His patently sincere tone didn't fool her. He didn't care.

"You can go with me if you'd like. Come on." Turning his horse toward home, he waited for her to catch up. But when he glanced back over his shoulder, he saw she hadn't moved.

So he rode back to her, cursing under his breath. "What are you doing?"

Her eyes blazed emerald fire. "Refusing to play stupid games. What are *you* doing?"

She had him there. Dragging his hand across his chin, he winced. "There's no need for you to see the ammo."

"Really? I'm beginning to wonder if there even *is* any ammo."

Whatever. He wasn't rising to the bait. "I've told you everything I can. And while I do appreciate you helping me out by giving a bit of incorrect information to your agency, there's no reason for you to see anything at all. Understand?"

"No. Actually, I don't."

Frustrated, he caught himself staring at her mouth. Hell, he'd much rather kiss her than waste time with this pointless arguing. But kissing her would likely lead to something hot and unstoppable in no time—and that was a risk in and of itself.

"You really don't see, do you?" Shifting in her saddle, she appeared every bit as aggravated as he was. "I've dedicated my life to my job. So far, I have never failed to make the arrest. This case—your case—was supposed to be an easy one. Assuming it went well. Which, so far, it has not."

He waited, aware there had to be more.

After taking a deep breath, she continued, "While I did what I could to help you, I have to believe that this is still going to end up being the best bust of my career. Oh, not of you—" she waved away whatever comment he was about to make "—but of key players in the Mexican drug cartel. Maybe this time we can get some charges to stick before they're extradited back to Mexico."

Now it took every ounce of willpower he possessed not to comment. It was obvious Skylar had no idea how these criminals worked. If captured, Diego Rodriguez would never make it to trial. He'd be shot and killed within the first forty-eight hours, if that long.

Rather than some cartel employee who was killing for hire, Matt wanted to be the one to kill him. Simple as that.

"Come on, Skylar." He gestured. "I wasn't joking about the meeting. Let's go."

"What about our picnic lunch?" she asked.

"We can eat it in the truck on the way."

Reluctant—and not bothering to hide it—she finally turned her horse around and rode with him back to the ranch.

Once they'd removed the saddles and brushed down the horses, Matt eyed her once again. Careful to keep his distance—he didn't want to take a chance on even brushing up against her and inflaming his already semi-aroused body—he checked his watch once more.

"I'm going to head to the house and clean up. If you want to go to town with me, I'll meet you out front in fifteen minutes."

"No thanks." Though her tone sounded serene, the smile she gave him hinted she was up to no good. "I think I'll just grab my own lunch and hang out here."

"Suit yourself." Confident she couldn't get into any trouble, he left her, feeling both relieved and disappointed all at once.

Hating that she couldn't articulate why she wanted to see the ammo, Skylar watched Matt go. It didn't help that he was right, in part. To him, it made no difference whatsoever if she viewed his stockpile. Her cover was blown and her usefulness limited.

But not to her. If she truly knew where his stash was kept, she'd have that much to hold in reserve if and when everything else went south. Which, she admitted, it so easily could. One phone call and she could bring the well-trained team of agents down here like rain.

But not if she didn't have a single shred of proof the stockpile truly existed.

Well aware her limited window of opportunity was growing ever shorter, she knew she'd have to take advantage of every chance that came her way.

Therefore, she'd begged off attending the cattleranchers meeting with Matt. It had sounded boring anyway.

After all, having a few hours to herself would give her the perfect opportunity to do a little more snooping. Though she couldn't imagine where he'd hide such a huge amount of bullets, this time she planned to search the ranch office, which was housed in a building near where the big barn used to stand. Luckily the fire hadn't spread to it.

Returning to her trailer, which had a good view of the drive, she stood vigil, watching until she saw Matt's red Ford F250 pull away. Then, feeling absurdly nervous, she took a stroll down to the old barn, ostensibly to pet the horses, in case anyone asked.

But for late in the afternoon, the stable yard was curiously deserted. She went directly to the barn to make her rounds admiring the beautiful horses before exiting and strolling toward the ranch office.

This door, too, was kept unlocked; lucky for her, because there was no way in hell she could easily explain picking the lock.

The late-afternoon sunlight had begun to wane, fading into the rosy dusk of early evening. A perfect time when overhead lights would not be necessary, though she had a handy flashlight app on her phone that she could use if the lighting inside the ranch office was too dim.

She still didn't see another soul.

Odd. Quietly she walked up the wooden steps to the

small porch. Grasping the knob, she pulled open the door and slipped inside.

Whew. The hard part over, she stood still until her breathing quieted. It was then that she realized she wasn't alone. Grunts and groans, endearments whispered in Spanish, the instantly recognizable sounds of two bodies intertwined, the distinctive and unmistakable sounds of lovemaking.

Horrified, Skylar froze. As her eyes adjusted to the dark room, she saw José and a blonde woman, naked on the office couch. Neither had noticed her arrival.

Crap. What the hell should she do now? Her best option would be to beat a graceful exit, especially since once he got past his embarrassment, José would undoubtedly demand to know what she was doing snooping around the ranch office.

Luckily, the two of them were so involved with each other that they still didn't know she was there.

As their caresses grew more intense, the woman raised her head. Skylar recognized her from photos she had in her file on Matt. The woman—Chantal something—was a model and Matt's former girlfriend. From all the news stories she'd seen on TV and in the magazines, the woman was extremely high maintenance. She needed a man with a lot of money, like Matt. How a man like José could afford her, Skylar didn't know.

Great. Just great. Skylar hastily looked away, praying she could make a quick exit. Her only option would be to go back out the way she'd come.

Heart in her throat, she began backing away. When she could reach the doorknob, she made a hasty exit. Once outside, she ducked around a corner and waited to see if there was any pursuit.

So far so good. Nothing happened.

Okay, then. Hurrying back toward her camper, Skylar tried to think. She hadn't even known about the ruins of the old house or the fact that there was a cellar. On the off chance that the ammo really was there, maybe she should check it out first. Once she found out where it was, that is.

She'd go grab her dog and check the place out. With Talia in tow, she headed on foot across the first pasture, breathing deeply of the clear country air, when her cell phone rang. Her entire body tightened when she realized it was her boss, David.

"Thanks for the information," he said, sounding pleased. "I've passed it on to my superiors."

Skylar made a noncommittal sound. She knew there had to be another reason behind the call. David wasn't in the habit of phoning just to praise her.

"We have a bit of new information about José Nivas," he said. "A deposit of twenty-five thousand dollars was posted in his savings account a few days ago. Any idea where he might have come by that amount of money?"

Though she had no idea what kind of salary Matt paid his friend, she knew it wouldn't be anywhere near that kind of money. "No," she answered. "No, I don't."

"We think he might be running a little business on the side, selling off some of Landeta's ammo. I want you to keep your eyes out for anything incriminating. We just might come away with two arrests instead of one."

Stunned, she agreed to do exactly that and pressed the button to end the call. Only then did she realize she'd forgotten to mention stumbling in on José having sex with Matt's former supermodel, high-maintenance girlfriend. If that wasn't a motive for needing money, she didn't know what was.

She had to tell Matt. Or did she? José was his closest

friend—hell, the two men were like brothers. Worst-case scenario, Matt would refuse to believe her, and her attempt to keep him informed would result in yet another wedge being driven between them.

"I wonder if he keeps an inventory on his stockpile," she mused out loud, causing Talia to wag her plumed tail.

Damn. Really, she needed to find a way to let Matt know. He'd grown so used to watching for enemies without that he hadn't once considered looking within.

She found the old house—correction, old ruins—easily enough. The site gave off an aura of sadness and neglect. Sighing, she turned in a slow circle, trying to see the place as it once had been. Hard to believe that this pile of rubble had ever been a home where children played in the yard.

Most of the house was gone. Only the chimney still stood. Walking around carefully, she found a concrete triangle still standing, into which had been set a rotted wooden door. This had to be the entrance to the cellar.

Yanking the door open as carefully as she could, considering it must have weighed close to twenty pounds, she brushed away spiderwebs and peered down into the dank darkness.

Should she go down there? Was it safe?

She only debated a few seconds. After all, she was here on assignment. She had to learn if Matt had really stored the ammunition here. She didn't have time for fear.

Descending the steps—which blessedly were concrete—was an exercise in control. She'd worked hard over the years to contain her terror of small, enclosed spaces. Unfortunately, she would have felt a lot better if someone were here with her, just in case she got stuck.

Since she hadn't even been able to tell anyone where she was going, she'd have to rely on Talia to fetch help if needed.

Hopefully, that wouldn't be necessary.

"Talia, sit." Once her pet had obeyed, she gave the palm-forward hand signal for *stay*. "Wait," she said.

Then, inhaling deeply, she turned to go down into the dark and empty cellar.

While she hadn't brought one of the huge flash-lights—too conspicuous—she had a penlight she'd clipped to her purse. Its steady pinprick of light was welcome as she went down into the darkness.

After each step, she paused, carefully counting, and shone her little light around her. When she'd finally reached the bottom, stepping cautiously, she illuminated the entire small concrete room.

Except for stacks of rotted lumber and piles of old rocks, it was completely empty.

She nearly laughed out loud. Of course it was. Had she really thought Matt and José would direct everyone to the ammo's true hiding place?

Breathing deeply, she turned to begin her ascent.

And heard the thud of the door closing above her.

Heart pounding, she told herself not to panic. It might have been the wind. After all, no one else was out here and Talia hadn't barked.

Nevertheless, she hustled up the steps in the pitch-black darkness, her small beam of light leading the way.

When she reached the heavy wooden door, she pushed, using her shoulders and every bit of strength she could muster.

The door didn't budge.

Don't panic, don't panic, she chanted over and over to herself. "Talia," she called, knowing her dog wouldn't have broken the stay. She gave the only command she could. "Come. Talia, come."

A happy bark from the other side of the thick wood told her Talia had obeyed.

Now came the tricky part.

"Go find help," Skylar said in desperation. Then, realizing her pet would have no idea what that mean, she reconsidered. "Talia, bring ball. Go bring ball."

The border collie barked once, then, hopefully, took off. Her ball was inside the camper, so Skylar assumed she would sit outside the trailer and bark until someone came along.

Then Skylar had to pray whoever saw Talia would realize something was wrong and come looking for her.

Meanwhile, she was trapped in this dark and exceedingly confined space. With spiders and who knew what else.

She shuddered, then sternly ordered herself not to think about that.

Sitting down on the bottom step, she turned off her penlight to save the batteries, closed her eyes and began doing the deep-breathing exercises she'd learned in a yoga class. Hopefully, someone would come to let her out. The sooner, the better.

Each time terror threatened to overwhelm her, she somehow managed to talk herself out of it. When she began feeling as though she were suffocating, she tried to find calm.

But the dark! The idea that no one might ever find her, that there were spiders and rats and other things that came out at night…

She felt herself losing it. Launching her body at the door, she tried to claw her way out, cursing and screaming and crying.

Of course, she couldn't.

Heart pounding so hard it felt as if it would leap from her chest, she gasped for air. Would that run out, too?

Hyperventilating, she tried again to attack the door, but as she pushed to her feet, everything went blurry. She fell, barely conscious as her head slammed into the concrete step.

The Cattle Ranchers Association meeting took longer than expected. Driving back to the ranch, Matt found himself consumed with thoughts of Skylar. As he entertained himself with carnal fantasies, his stomach rumbled. Reaching into the picnic hamper, he discovered chicken along with carefully packed containers full of potato salad, deviled eggs and biscuits.

Too bad he and Skylar hadn't taken the time to have their picnic. They could have feasted on each other for dessert. His entire body went warm at the thought.

When he pulled back into the driveway, Skylar's dog came barreling out to greet him.

"Hey, Talia." He reached down to pet her, but the border collie seemed agitated. Matt felt the first prickling of alarm.

Pushing it aside, he grabbed the meal and headed toward her camper. Talia ran circles around him, barking, barking, barking.

"Where's Skylar?" he asked, his unease growing. When a quick inspection revealed she wasn't in the trailer, Talia barked again, running off toward the field and then returning, giving him a bark to make it clear she wanted him to follow her.

Placing the remains of his lunch on the camper table, he climbed back outside. "Show me, girl," he urged.

This time, when the dog took off running, Matt was right on her heels.

They crossed two pastures. Talia had to circle and come back for him several times, as he couldn't keep up with her. When the ruins of the old homestead came into view, he realized where Skylar had gone.

The border collie barked once more, dashing into the rubble and standing before the cement that led to the cellar.

The heavy wooden door was closed.

Talia barked again.

"Skylar?" Matt called, gripping the weathered metal handle and pulling. The damn thing wouldn't budge.

He called her name again. She still didn't answer.

"Maybe she's not in here, girl," he told Talia. He gave the door another try, but couldn't get it to move.

Cursing, he began looking around for something he could use as a makeshift crowbar.

Unfortunately, the half-burned two-by-four wouldn't cut it. That didn't stop him from trying it anyway. The rotted piece of lumber came apart in his hands.

Talia barked. "Sorry, girl," he told her. He'd have to head to back to the ranch to find an actual crowbar.

He took off running, wishing he had a horse. The dog chased after him, barking and trying to herd him back toward the ruins. She nipped at his ankles, nearly tripping him. As he stumbled, he saw the piece of metal pipe on the ground, glinting in the sunlight.

"What the…" Hefting it, he shoved aside any questions about what it was doing in his field and tore back toward the stubborn door.

The pipe worked perfectly, and after only three attempts, he was able to wedge the door open.

Talia watched him, appropriately solemn. The instant

he had the door open, the dog dashed past him down the steps, barking.

Pushing the heavy thing back so far it splintered, Matt rushed after Talia, hoping against hope that Skylar was all right.

He had no flashlight, and despite the tiny bit of light that leaked from above, the darkness felt absolute. When he nearly tripped on something, he thought at first it was the dog. But when he reached down, he realized Skylar was lying on the concrete floor.

Somehow, he got his arms under her and managed to lift her. Staggering, he made his way slowly up the steps, blinking as he emerged into the afternoon light.

Skylar. Once they'd cleared the cellar, he carried her outside and placed her gently on the grass. A small trickle of blood showed she must have hit her head—close to the temple, but hopefully not near enough to do any serious damage.

But then why was she still unconscious?

"Skylar..." Brushing the hair away from her face, he checked for a pulse. Her heart beat steady and strong.

Talia barked, urgently this time. Skylar's eyes fluttered open. "Tali?" she whispered. Then, as her memory apparently came flooding back to her, she gasped and tried to climb to her feet.

"Easy, easy," Matt said. "It's okay. I've got you."

She gasped, inhaling as though she feared she'd run out of air. "I thought I was going to be trapped in there forever. I didn't want to die like that."

He gave her a gentle smile. "You can thank your dog for coming to find me. I'd just pulled into the driveway and she came running."

"Oh, Tali!" Wrapping her arms around her pet, Skylar

laughed as Talia licked her face, tail wagging furiously. "Such a good girl you are. What a good girl."

When Skylar had finished cuddling her dog, she struggled to get up. Matt put his arm around her and helped her.

"Maybe we should run you into town and get your head looked at," he said.

"No." She started to shake her head and then winced instead. "I'm fine. I think."

"You might have a concussion. I really think..."

"No." She cut him off emphatically. When she went to move forward, it quickly became apparent she was still a bit shaky on her feet.

"Let me help you. It's a good walk back to the ranch."

Facing straight ahead, she didn't look at him. "Thanks."

Noting the twin spots of color high on her cheekbones, he wondered if he ought to override her protests and force her to get checked out at the medical clinic.

Envisioning the struggle that would be, he decided to simply keep an eye on her for now. Talia also, he noted, appeared to be watching her carefully. Even though the dog ran circles around them, she kept coming back and trotting at Skylar's side, her canine gaze intent on her mistress.

As they slowly and painstakingly made their way home, Skylar's strength seemed to gradually increase. Eventually he was able to remove his arm from around her waist, allowing her to walk on her own.

"Do you mind telling me what happened in there?" he asked.

She swallowed hard. When she spoke again, her voice had gone flat. "I panicked," she said. "I've always been claustrophobic, but I really thought I'd over-come that fear. I found out otherwise."

Stopping, she lifted her hands, letting him see her raw, bloody fingers and broken nails. "I tried to claw my way out of there," she admitted, her voice still shaky. "It was a pretty bad panic attack." Swallowing, she continued, "In the middle of all of that, I slipped and hit my head."

He didn't know what to say, so he didn't speak. He didn't have too many fears himself, not these days anyway. For a while after he'd returned from Iraq, he'd had PTSD and jumped at every sound. He'd taught himself to overcome it, but in the process he'd closed himself off from people, focusing on his animals instead.

Silently commiserating, he took her hand in his and held it all the way back to her trailer.

Chapter 12

Skylar's throat closed up at the kind gesture, and to her horror she realized she had tears in her eyes. Matt had no idea how much it meant to her, the simple act of holding her hand. Offering comfort rather than wanting to discuss—and cure or mock—her irrational, all-consuming fear.

The most horrible part of it wasn't that she couldn't seem to stop shaking. No, the worst part was how much she despised herself for her weakness.

After losing her family, she'd vowed always to be strong, no matter what she faced. Thus far, she believed she'd succeeded. Until today. All alone in the cramped, dark space, she'd given way to her fears and nearly lost her mind.

This was the very first time she'd failed so horribly. And even worse, she'd done so in front of someone else. Someone who was a potential criminal and whom she'd been sent undercover to investigate.

Once they reached the camper, Matt opened the door for her and kept his hand at the small of her back as she climbed the steps.

Spying the picnic hamper on the table, she turned to Matt. "Did you…"

His smile seemed tentative. "Yes. I ate a few bites of chicken on the way back from town. There's plenty left. I thought you might still want to go on a picnic. Of course, I had no way of knowing…"

As his words trailed off, again her eyes filled with tears. What the hell was wrong with her? She was never a weepy sort of person.

Angling slightly away from him, she swiped at her eyes.

Then, hoping he hadn't noticed, she lifted her head. "Let me get cleaned up, okay?"

Without waiting to hear his response, she stepped into the tiny bathroom. Scrubbing the dirt from under her nails—even this reminded her of her missing son—she cleaned her face, grimacing as she rinsed away the blood. She'd have a bruise there later.

When she emerged, still avoiding his gaze, she rummaged in one of the cabinets and found paper plates. Putting two down by the hamper, she slid onto the bench seat on one side of the table, indicating he should take the other.

"Any other time, I'd have loved a picnic." She smiled, albeit a bit wobbly. "But for today, let's eat here."

He didn't move. "You want me to stay?"

Surprised, she cocked her head. "Of course. Why wouldn't I? Look at all this chicken! Plus, there's potato salad and deviled eggs that you haven't even touched."

He shrugged, then took the seat across from her.

"It's just, after the time you had, I didn't know if you wanted to be alone."

His words gave her pause—after all, any other time, in such a situation, she *would* have wanted to be alone. But he… "You're different," she admitted, refusing to feel embarrassed. "Plus—" this time her smile was genuine "—you saved me."

He looked at her. She looked back. As their gazes locked, everything else—the food, her fears, her self-loathing—faded away.

"Eat," he said, breaking the spell.

Talia whined, making Skylar laugh. "She knows that word and it's past her dinnertime. Let me feed her real quick."

Busying herself pouring kibble into a bowl, Skylar felt anticipation buzzing through her, tingling in her blood, under her skin. Something had changed between her and Matt, though she would readily admit the transformation might be a bit one-sided.

She trusted him. While she'd been attracted to him from the moment she'd met him, she'd held a part of herself in reserve, afraid to allow herself to believe he wasn't a criminal.

Now…that doubt had vanished as if it had never existed.

Returning to the table, she wouldn't look at him, as if he could somehow see the truth in her eyes. Instead, she set out the chicken, potato salad, deviled eggs, beans and biscuits. He'd gotten them each a bottled iced tea, and she put straws in each drink.

"Quite a feast," she said brightly. "I'm starving. How about you?"

"Hey." The quiet rumbling of his voice again brought the stupid pricking of tears to her eyes.

Slowly, she raised her face to look at him, blinking furiously to push them away.

As soon as he saw her face, he pushed to his feet. "Come here." He held out his arms. "You need a hug."

Moving as if she were in a trance, chicken all but forgotten, she stood. On wobbly legs, she went to him and let him envelope her in his embrace.

"Shh," he murmured, one hand smoothing her hair. "You seem like you're about to shatter. Maybe you really should be alone."

"No." Alarmed, she clutched him. "Don't go. Please. I don't want to be by myself right now."

Hearing her own words, she closed her eyes. "You have no idea how much it cost me to say that," she said. But still she did not release her hold on him.

"You'd be surprised," he told her. "Because I don't want to leave you, either."

She opened her mouth, but she had no response.

He kissed her then, covering her mouth with his softly, gentle when she craved rough. Making a sound of frustration, she kissed him with a hunger that was more than physical, though she demanded a physical response.

When he lifted his lips from hers and shook his head, she was stunned—and secretly, since she was all about admitting the truth to herself lately, hurt.

"Not now," he told her, putting his hands on her shoulders and gently turning her back toward the table. "Sit down and eat something. You've had a big shock. You need to get some nourishment in you."

Resisting the urge to pout—who *was* this person she seemed to be turning into?—she did as he asked, sullenly taking the largest, crispiest chicken breast and a leg, her favorite. She grabbed a heaping spoonful of potato salad and two deviled eggs.

The instant she bit into the now-cold chicken and flavor exploded in her mouth, she knew he was right. Chewing and swallowing, she resisted the urge to take another huge bite before giving him a muffled thank-you.

He nodded and they both dug in.

After they'd eaten until they were full, Skylar wiped her greasy fingers on a napkin and took a long drink of her iced tea.

"I needed that," she said, sighing. "It was really good."

"I did, too," he admitted, one corner of his mouth lifting in the beginning of a smile. "Do you feel better now?"

Suddenly shy, she nodded. When he didn't respond, she let her gaze roam over his features. She felt breathless, like a young girl again, dizzy just from being in the same room as him.

Still he made no move toward her. She wondered how to prove to him she wasn't so delicate.

"Any news?" he asked.

For a moment she didn't understand what he meant. Her quick frown must have telegraphed this to him, so he elaborated.

"Has anyone contacted you since you made your report?"

Bam. Just like that, she came crashing back to earth. Should she tell him what she'd learned about José?

"I can see someone has," he said, leaning across the table and watching her intently. "What's going on?"

Though she hated to ruin his evening—*their* evening—she told him about the twenty-five thousand-dollar deposit into José Nivas's account. She couldn't yet bring herself to speak about stumbling across José and Matt's former girlfriend having sex in the barn office. If she did, she'd have to explain what she was doing there in the first place.

"Twenty-five thousand dollars?" Matt looked simply thoughtful rather than flabbergasted as she'd expected.

"Did he mention that to you?" she asked, although she knew he hadn't.

"No, but he doesn't tell me everything." Drumming his fingers on the table, he stared out the window. "Maybe he got a loan for something."

"The ATF found no evidence of that."

When he looked at her, his blue eyes seemed darker. "Why are your people investigating him anyway?"

"You know why."

He sighed. "He did his time. He's reformed. You can't hold that against him."

"We don't," she shot back. "Especially if he's innocent. But he has ties to the Mexican cartels, even now. And even I'm not entirely sure what his role is in this thing you're trying to set up."

"He has nothing to do with it." His denials seemed to come a little too quickly. Still, she let it go.

"Are you going to ask him about it?"

He grimaced. "Probably. Yes. He's gone home for the night, but he'll be here in the morning. I'll speak to him then."

Standing, she began to bag the bones up for the trash. "I'll have to take these out so Talia doesn't get into them."

"I can take them with me," he said.

Disappointed, she nodded. Was he leaving, then? She'd hoped for a bit of body-to-body comforting.

As she tied up the trash bag, he came up behind her and took it from her. Placing it on the stove, he turned her around to face him. "How are you feeling?"

Instead of answering, she reached up and pulled him down to her, pressing her lips to his and kissing him with reckless abandon.

He responded in kind, his tongue sending a jolt of desire to her lower body. Demanding more, she caressed him, thrilling at his muscular chest, loving the leashed strength she knew lay behind his gentle touches.

Curling into him like a cat in heat, she moaned as he slipped his hand inside her T-shirt, cupping her breast.

Somehow they made it to the bed and shed their clothes. She writhed beneath him, desperate to take him inside of her.

"Slowly," he told her as he let his fingers work magic over her breasts, slipping down her belly to touch her there, where she was already moist and so damn ready she thought she might scream.

As he continued his torturous exploration with his mouth, she felt as if she were part fire and part ice. And damn him, he was enjoying this, too, if his huge arousal was any indication.

When he finally slipped inside her, she gasped in sweet agony, her body clenching in a spasm of pleasure.

And then he began to move and all rational thought left her. They danced together, naked bodies slick with perspiration, coming together and apart in perfect harmony.

As she reached the pinnacle and began shattering into a million tiny stars, she cried out, calling his name over and over.

A moment later, he joined her, his head back, eyes closed, so damn beautiful she wanted to weep.

After, as their breathing slowed, he continued to hold her. Neither spoke—she knew there was no way in hell she could reveal her feelings to him. Especially since realizing how she truly felt was absolutely terrifying to her. Never mind that it would freak him out.

"Do you want to spend the night here?" she asked, wincing as she heard herself say the words.

"Not tonight." Kissing her forehead, he moved away, standing up and looking on the floor for his clothes.

From underneath the sheet, she watched him get dressed, refusing to let go of the drowsy warmth of satisfaction that had spread through her.

"Do you want me to let Talia out?" he asked once he was fully clothed.

She nodded, absurdly grateful she didn't have to leave her cozy cocoon.

Once he'd taken care of her dog, he grabbed the trash bag of chicken bones and crossed over to kiss her mouth softly.

"See you in the morning," he said.

And then he was gone.

Out of habit, she got up and locked the door behind him before climbing back into bed.

Not wanting to analyze or even think about what had just happened, she turned on her side and tried to will herself to sleep.

Vulnerable. Matt walked to his barn, breathing in the familiar scents of hay and horses, and tried to clear his head. Skylar had been vulnerable. Not usually a word that he'd use to describe her, but he'd seen a side of her that he'd never have imagined.

For the first time since he'd met her, she'd asked for something from him without an ulterior motive. She'd needed comfort, which he'd readily given. And then the heat they always seemed to generate between them had blazed to life, offering them both a welcome distraction. Recreational sex.

He swallowed hard, his chest tight. Maybe for her that had been what it was. Not for him. For him, it had become something more.

Returning home, Matt turned on the TV and watched several old movies in succession, paying very little attention to the plot or the dialogue. He drank a few beers, roamed his large, empty house and deliberately stayed up late, hoping when he finally did go to bed he'd fall into a deep and dreamless sleep.

Instead, he tossed and turned. His thoughts alternated between his newfound—and unwanted—feelings for Skylar and his worries over what José had gotten himself into.

He got up an hour before his usual rising time of 5:00 a.m., feeling tired and out of sorts. After showering, he made a pot of strong coffee and carried a mugful out to the back porch. Watching the sun rise, which was usually his way to meditate about the coming day, failed to inspire him. Soon he found himself downing his third cup of coffee, pacing and checking his watch for the twentieth time.

When seven o'clock rolled around, he gave up and went inside. José was late. Since his friend was always on time, Matt called José's cell. No answer. In fact, the call went straight to voice mail. Matt didn't leave a message. He figured whatever José was doing it must be important if he'd turned his phone off.

José would turn up eventually. He always did.

But as morning turned into afternoon, lunchtime came and went, and the sun began to hang lower in the sky, Matt's gut began to hurt. Soon it would be evening and he still had no word from his friend. Matt couldn't help but worry. He knew he should have driven to town to look for him, but he kept remembering what Skylar had told him about the large amount of money recently deposited into José's bank account. While he trusted his buddy with his life, he hated having to ask such a thing. Worse, he couldn't even imagine what kind of answer José would give.

He'd seen Skylar from a distance, and though he didn't consciously avoid her, he kept himself busy enough that they didn't cross paths all day.

Though now, with all the chores finished and still no sign of his friend, he knew eventually he'd have to seek her out.

Instead, she came to him.

He'd finished his evening meal by himself—warmed-up leftovers eaten with grim determination—and walked back outside to stare at his empty driveway, when he realized he was no longer alone.

"What's wrong?" Skylar asked, perched on the edge of one of his patio chairs as though about to take flight.

He stopped pacing, about to ask her how she knew anything was wrong, then realized he was being foolish. "I can't reach José."

She regarded him curiously. "Is today his day off?"

"No." He grimaced. "He didn't show up this morning."

"Maybe he's sick."

"He didn't call."

Frowning, she cocked her head, considering. "He could be too sick to call. That's one possibility."

"And the other?"

"He could have run off with the twenty-five thousand dollars."

"True. Or, since twenty-five grand isn't a lot in the scheme of things, maybe the cartel got to him," he countered. "He's in some kind of trouble. He'd have called me if it was anything else."

She eyed him, clearly trying to determine whether he was normally so paranoid or if he had reason to be. Finally, she nodded. "If you're that concerned, let's drive over to his place and check it out."

Taking action—any action—felt a lot better than sitting around wondering. He snatched his car keys off the ring in the kitchen and hurried back outside.

The moment he reemerged, she stood. "Let's go."

Though he wasn't sure how José would feel about him bringing Skylar to his home, Matt wanted her company. Her presence helped quiet the jangling sense that something had gone very wrong.

She waited until they'd left the ranch and reached the blacktop heading into town before speaking again. "Look, I know the cartel is messing with people on this side of the border. Look what happened to those people they burned alive in the car in Arizona. But that was on the direct drug route, and the victims were most likely involved with the cartel."

He glanced at her. "And your point?"

"I need to know if José is involved with the Mexican cartel."

"I like your directness," he said, stalling.

"Do you? That's not an answer."

Tightening his grip on the steering wheel, he sighed. "As I'm sure you're aware, José did have a relationship with one of the cartels in the past. He was arrested, convicted and served his time. Since he's been out, he's been clean."

"You're positive of that?" She sounded skeptical. He supposed he couldn't blame her.

"He works for me, Skylar."

"Even so, what about since he was released? Any contact?"

He sighed, seeing no way around it. "Yes, he's had contact with a few members of the cartel."

"Old friends?"

"Maybe," he allowed. "The truth is, anything he's done has been on my behalf."

"Because of the revenge thing."

"Exactly."

She went silent for so long he wondered if she'd nodded off. But no, a quick look revealed her staring off into the darkness, clearly thinking.

"I hate to say anything." When she finally spoke, her voice was troubled. "Before I do, what's your reasoning as to why the cartel has been targeting you—shooting at you, burning down your barn, et cetera?"

Jaw tight, he answered, even though he believed she already knew the answer. "We have ammunition. More than one warring faction wants it. Each of the two cartels who are in the know don't want me to sell it to the other."

"I disagree." She shook her head, sending her thick hair swirling around her shoulders. "If that were the case, I believe they'd have been more direct. These people are accustomed to taking what they want without asking."

"Exactly." He pounded the steering wheel for emphasis. "That's why they were shooting at us. They've been sneaking onto my ranch trying to find out where I've hidden the ammo."

Now she sighed. "I'll let you have that, even though I can't shake the feeling there's more to it than that. Are you certain you trust José?"

"Yes." He didn't even have to think about it. "He's like my brother. I'd trust him with my life."

"Then I guess you'd better hope you're wrong. If the cartel took him, he's a dead man."

They both fell silent for the rest of the drive. José lived in town, in a neat frame house a few blocks from the railroad tracks.

Pulling into the empty driveway, Matt killed his engine and shut off his headlights.

"The place looks deserted," Skylar pointed out. "No lights are on inside and there's not even a car or pickup in the carport."

José's truck was gone. Matt's stomach clenched. "Damn it."

They got out together. He wasn't surprised to see that Skylar had drawn her Glock. He did the same.

"Do you have a key?" she asked in the clipped, law-enforcement tone she sometimes used.

"No." He shook his head. "José's personal life is private. As long as he checks in with his parole officer and passes the drug tests, I don't worry about him."

She nodded. "Stay close to me." Keeping to the side of the front door, away from any windows, she rang the bell. They both could hear the chimes echoing through the small house.

But no one came to the door. With a sinking heart, Matt realized he hadn't actually expected anyone to. After all, José's truck was gone.

"Let's go around back," she whispered. He nodded in agreement.

Hugging the side walls, they made their way to the back of the house, which was not fenced.

José's back door was wide open.

Matt swore. Skylar stopped, though she kept her pistol out, apparently assessing the situation. She looked capable and yet still as sexy as hell. He'd never realized he had a thing for strong women.

But then, he hadn't known many before her.

"Are you ready?" she asked, jerking her head toward the door. "We'll go room by room."

He nodded, hoping like hell they wouldn't find José's body.

"Now!" She leaped forward. Keeping close to each other, they dashed inside the dark house. He went for the light switch and flicked on the lights.

"Clear," she said, coolly professional, barely glancing at him before she moved into the kitchen.

He headed for the bedrooms. Both of them were off a small hall off the main living area.

The first bedroom, the smallest of the two, José had made into a study. "Clear," he called out, barely registering the scattered papers before heading toward the master bedroom.

Skylar had beaten him to it. "Clear," she told him, holstering her gun. "There's no one here."

"And no signs of a struggle." Putting his weapon away, he turned back toward José's study. "It looks like someone has been searching for something in here."

But as they gathered the paperwork, he realized they were only José's credit-card statements, bank-account records and mortgage statements. Nothing to do with Matt or ammunition or drugs.

"Except that there's another deposit of twenty-five thousand dollars in his bank account." She held up a deposit slip. "He made the deposit yesterday, in cash."

Matt tried to think, but came up with nothing. "I have no idea. I pay him every Friday, but he doesn't make anywhere near that much money."

Her expression seemed carefully blank, which told him she was thinking the worst and trying not to show it.

"He's not selling drugs," he protested. "I'd know if he was using."

"Maybe not drugs," she said softly. "But how close of a tab do you keep on your ammunition stores?"

"He wouldn't do that to me." His gut twisted at the thought.

"You do keep some sort of inventory, right?" she persisted.

Defeated, he let his shoulders sag. "José takes care of that. All the records are at my house."

"Would you know if he's updated them?"

"Of course. But José wouldn't—"

"I know, I know." She put a gentle hand on his arm. "He's your best friend. I understand. If it's any consolation, it would take a lot more than fifty thousand dollars to go on the run."

Unless… Matt didn't voice the thought out loud. Unless José was setting things up for an even bigger payoff and the cartel he wasn't selling to had grabbed him in retaliation.

Even the thought of his best friend backstabbing him felt wrong. Not to mention disloyal. But it wouldn't go away. "Why would anyone have taken him?" Matt asked, frowning and hoping she could come up with some other, more acceptable scenario. "Especially if he took some sort of bribe. It doesn't make sense."

"Maybe he failed to deliver," she said. He wasn't sure he liked the way she watched him, cool and calculating, more of her ATF persona than the Skylar he'd come to know.

"I'll check the stores," he said, holding up a hand when she started to speak. "And no, you can't come with me. The fewer people who know where I keep the ammo, the better."

Still staring hard at him, finally she gave a reluctant nod. "Let's get out of here."

"I'm with you on that one." They each climbed into the truck and buckled up. He reached to put the key in the ignition, when she put her hand on his arm, stopping him.

"What about Chantal?" she asked quietly. "Do you think she knows something about this?"

"Chantal?" He didn't get how she could go from rational ATF agent to this. "What does she have to do with any of this?"

Skylar swallowed hard. "She and José are...together. I saw them in the ranch office."

He wasn't sure he understood. "I haven't seen Chantal or even talked to her since we broke up—mutually, I might add—last year. So when you say they're together, what do you mean? Together how? Working together?"

Slowly, she shook her head. "Um, no. Together like a couple. I walked in on them in the barn office. They were having sex."

Even in the dim light of the single streetlight, he could see her fair skin had turned a fiery red. "That's impossible," he said. "José would never..."

"Steal your girlfriend?"

"No, not that." Dragging a hand through his hair, he struggled to make sense of this latest revelation. "José knows Chantal's not my girlfriend. But he would have mentioned it to me, if only to make sure I wouldn't take issue."

She watched him gravely. "Would you have? Taken issue with them dating, I mean?"

He didn't even hesitate. "Of course not. Chantal means nothing to me. José knows that. What bothers me is the fact he felt he needed to keep that hidden."

"Like he kept hidden the two twenty-five-thousand-dollar deposits in his bank account?"

Clenching his jaw, he nodded. He felt angry, true, but also confused and, well, frickin' hurt. José was his best friend.

"Pretty incriminating," she said.

"There's got to be more to this than we know," he finally said, aware she'd think he was a fool, but not caring. "I refuse to give up on José until I hear the truth from him."

"Okay." She gave a decisive nod. "Then we need to find out what happened to him. I can contact the local authorities and put out an APB."

"No." Inserting the key in the ignition, he started the truck. "Let me see what I can find out before we do that. If it was the cartel, I don't want to give them a reason to kill him."

Neither one said what he knew they both were thinking. If José had been grabbed by the cartel, he was probably already dead.

Chapter 13

Once they returned to the ranch, they parted ways. Though Skylar had offered to keep vigil with Matt, he'd turned her down. He wouldn't be good company, he'd said.

She'd tried like hell not to let his rejection hurt.

Another restless night, then. Unable to face more tossing and turning, around midnight she whistled for Talia and went for a walk. Up at Matt's house, lights still blazed yellow from the windows, letting her know she wasn't the only one unable to sleep.

If she had more nerve, she'd go up there, knock on his door and seduce him. Her body came fully alive at the thought. But she couldn't go through with it. She was too afraid of how she'd feel if he turned her down.

Yet again, she had to wonder when she'd become such a coward.

Reaching the old barn, she opened the door, flicked

on the hall lights and slipped inside. A few of the horses nickered sleepily, but none of them came to the stall door.

Breathing in the unique scent of horses, manure, hay and grain, and leather, she felt a sort of peace steal over her. Though this wasn't her place, she felt a sense of *home*. This notion was so foreign, so wrong, she gasped out loud.

She'd learned the hard way that home wasn't a place, but rather where the ones you loved were. She hadn't felt this way since she'd lost her family.

Was this because of Matt? Did her feelings for him, so new and unsteady, run that deep?

Matt. And once again, she'd come full circle. He was on her mind, always on her mind, and she wanted to be with him more than she wanted anything else.

Foolish.

Still, she glanced at her watch, wishing she could shake this absurd and completely bizarre need to be with him. At first, she'd felt like a teenage girl with a crush. Now that they'd made love, now that he'd given her a glimpse into his true nature, she ached for him with a need that was almost physical and blotted out everything else.

Completely unacceptable for an ATF agent and totally wrong for a widow who should still be consumed by grief.

Closing her eyes, she tried to conjure up Robbie's face. To her horror, she could only get as far as his blue eyes and blond hair. The rest of the details were shadowy, at best.

Hell, it had been five years. Still…how could she forget?

Digging in her purse, she found her wallet. There, in

the section where other people kept credit cards, she had three pictures. One of Robbie, one of their son, Bryan, and the third of them all together.

It was this last one she pulled out to stare at. She and Robbie had looked so young, so happy. Bryan had been so fiercely independent that the moment before the photograph had been snapped, he'd been scowling at the camera. The photographer had managed to coax a smile with a toy robot, the very same one she'd had to buy Bryan the following day. It had been his favorite toy—he'd slept with it, and it accompanied him everywhere.

She'd buried his tiny little body with that robot.

Raising her head, she waited for the tears—she always, always, always, always cried when she looked at this photo. To her shock, not this time. She felt sad and the familiar aching sense of loss, but she did not weep.

One more thing she wished she could share with Matt.

"Is that your family?" Matt's voice, as though he'd felt her need pulling at him.

She narrowed her eyes. He'd come up behind her without her noticing. More proof she wasn't 100 percent on her A game.

Plus, she hadn't told him anything about her past.

Maybe it was time.

"Yes," she told him, resisting the urge to put the picture away. "They're both gone now."

"Let me see," he asked, holding out his hand.

Heart skipping a beat, she gave it to him, noting the solemn, reverent way he examined it. This warmed her heart and—she was almost ashamed to admit it—gave her hope.

"They're beautiful," he said, handing it back. "You must have loved them very much."

"I did," she said. Again to her surprise, her voice sounded steady, sad but unbroken. "I miss them every day. Even though it's been five years, I've never stopped longing for them."

He nodded as if he understood. Remembering what had happened to his own family, she realized he probably did.

"I'm sorry for your loss." He swallowed, his gaze far away. "Believe me when I say I know how that feels."

Again, almost as if he'd known what she'd been thinking.

Under any other circumstances, with any other person, she might have concurred and changed the subject. But this was Matt and he wasn't just mouthing platitudes. He truly understood the gnawing ache of loss.

"Thank you," she said.

"Tell me what happened."

So she told him. "I was running late for a meeting. My husband, Robbie, had taken the day off and was going to take our son, Bryan, to the park. I needed to cash a check, so I asked him if he'd mind stopping at the bank for me on his way home."

Now fat tears rolled down her cheeks. Ignoring them, she continued, "At least they had their day at the park. They even stopped for lunch at Bryan's favorite hot-dog place. The last stop they made was at the bank."

He covered her hand with his, offering comfort. She swallowed hard, willing herself to continue. She hadn't managed to make her way through this story in its entirety even once without breaking down, even with her psychiatrist.

But continue she did. "They were waiting in line for the teller when the robber came through the door. Just one, and he was high on crack or crystal meth.

He shouted for everyone to hit the floor. I'm guessing they did, but the bank guard made a move the robber didn't like and he sprayed the bank with bullets. Seven people lost their lives that day. Robbie and Bryan were among them."

When she'd finished speaking, letting her words trail off, she waited for him to talk, to offer condolences or to comment that he remembered hearing about that horrific bank robbery on the news, or some other banal attempt at making her feeling better.

Instead, he took her picture from her and gently placed it on the table. "Do you still cry over them?" he asked gently.

"Not as much as I used to," she admitted. "It's probably the same with you, isn't it?

He gave a casual shrug that didn't fool her one bit. "I never cry."

Guy talk, and she wasn't buying it. "Surely you did right after you lost them."

Slowly, he shook his head. "Not even then. I focused on the rage instead of the grief."

This so saddened her that she felt her eyes fill. Seeing this, he took her into his arms and held her. Tight, as if he never wanted to let her go. Offering her comfort, when she should have been the one to offer it to him.

Shocked, she stood frozen, at first feeling like a bird trapped in a snare, unable to fly. Then, as the warmth of his embrace took hold of her, as he simply gave her the strength of his muscular body by way of comfort, she let herself relax, burrowing her face into the hollow at the side of his neck and breathing in the wonderful, masculine scent of him.

He rubbed her back, the gesture obviously not meant to be anything but comforting, certainly not sexual. But the longer she stood there, molded to him, she felt as if her body was being set ablaze, one minuscule section at a time.

His breathing hitched and changed, letting her know he felt it, too. Current surged between them, soothing becoming something more, something with potential. Raw and sexual.

She wasn't sure who moved first, him or her or maybe they both did at the same time. But before she could blink, they began kissing, the slow, drugging kisses born of pent-up frustration and mutual need.

Kissing him, their bodies pressed so close, out of habit she found herself waiting for the flash of familiar guilt, so soon after talking about her family.

To her uneasy surprise, it never came. In its place blazed desire.

Waking up in the morning with Skylar curved into him, her delectable derriere pressed up against him, felt like Thanksgiving and Christmas all rolled into one. Matt set about waking her by placing kisses on her satiny skin, starting just below her ear and traveling down her neck, toward her collarbone.

He'd just begun to reach interesting territory as Skylar stretched and yawned, arching her back and perfectly placing her beautiful, full breasts in the exact position for him to kiss, when his cell phone rang.

Damn. Briefly closing his eyes, he froze. After all, it was six-thirty in the morning and who called at that hour unless it was an emergency?

José.

Rolling over, he grabbed the phone, coming fully awake as he saw an unfamiliar number on the caller ID.

Hurriedly, he answered, "Hello?"

"Matt, it's me."

Thank God. Relief flooded him. "José? Where are you? Are you all right?"

José's laugh sounded forced. "I think so, man. They've been keeping me in the dark. This is the first time they've let me make a call. And this is a burn phone, to be used this one time before it's destroyed, so don't bother trying to use GPS to locate me."

"Keeping you?" he repeated. "What's going on? Who's got you?"

Beside him, Skylar sat up, wide-awake. She grabbed the notepad and pen from the nightstand and scribbled a note. *Maybe we can trace the call using GPS.*

He shook his head, taking the pen from her and writing, *No. Burn phone.*

"Matt? Are you there?" José asked, sounding a bit worried.

"Yes. What's going on, amigo?"

"The cartel has me." José spoke with the kind of fear usually reserved for a demon from the depths of hell.

This, Matt could understand.

"La Familia? Or Diego Rodriguez?" Just saying the name made Matt clench his jaw. Diego had already taken his family from him. Was it possible he might take his best friend, as well?

"I don't know," José muttered. "I haven't seen Diego. All I know is these guys are Mexican nationals and they work for the cartel."

"What the hell do they want with you?"

"Maybe insurance." José sounded oddly hesitant, a personality trait Matt recognized. He'd known José all his life, and José was one of the worst liars Matt had ever met.

"Truth," Matt reminded him, not sure if someone was listening or not. "Come on, man. Tell me the truth."

"I'm trying." José sighed heavily. "Here's the deal. They want me to take them to where the ammunition is stored, tomorrow night. They're going to load it up and haul it off. You will not interfere because I will be their hostage. If you have Feds there, or anyone even within a half mile, they will shoot me. They mean business, Matt."

Something inside Matt, some bit of intuition perhaps, told him José's story was a mixture of truth and lies. Was it possible that Skylar was right and José was working with one of the cartels for his own ends? That would fit, as they'd be making the payment directly to José.

They'd been children together, always had each other's backs. He hated to think their trust might have come to an end.

He had a right to know. "José, tell me. Does this have anything to do with the two payments of twenty-five thousand dollars you deposited into your bank account?"

Silence. Then José cursed virulently in Spanish. Without answering, he ended the call.

Damn. The actions of a guilty man, whether Matt wanted to believe it or not. He resisted the urge to fling his phone into the wall.

"Are you okay?" Skylar asked, the expression on her face telling him she knew he was not.

Gut twisting, he relayed everything José had said. And not said.

"So you don't think he's telling the truth?" she asked. "You believe he's lying because he's working with your enemy?"

"That's what it seems like."

She touched his shoulder. "You know as well as I do that everything is not always what it appears."

"True, but this…" He shook his head. "I don't know. I wish I did."

Dejected, he got up and crossed the room, heading for the bathroom. "I'd really like to believe my friend. But he's making it more and more difficult to do so."

When he got back, she flashed him a half smile and stood, heading off to take her turn in the bathroom. "When I return," she said, glancing at him over her shoulder, "we'll talk about what we're going to do."

A few minutes later, Skylar stuck her head out the door and asked Matt if it would be okay for her to take a quick shower as she was tired of the camper kind. Since he knew that in the trailer she'd had to use the shower nozzle to wet herself down, then shut it off while she soaped off, then turn it back on to rinse, he readily agreed.

A moment later he heard the shower start. Though he entertained a brief fantasy about joining her, he knew that wasn't going to happen, not after the news he'd received from his friend.

The phone call—and what he'd learned about José— was tearing him up inside. He truly didn't know whose side José was on. Matt's, as he'd always so steadily professed, or a Mexican drug cartel's?

When his cell rang again, this time showing Private Caller, Matt jumped. His heart began to pound as he pressed the answer button. "José?" he answered, hoping against hope that his friend had somehow been able to escape.

Instead, he heard a low, guttural laugh that sent a chill up his spine.

"No. This is Diego Rodriguez," the husky, heavily accented voice said.

Matt's jaw clenched. "A personal call? To what do I owe the honor?" He knew the other man could hear the mockery in his tone.

If Diego did, he chose to ignore it. "We have your friend José. We have also learned you have an ATF agent on your ranch. The woman Skylar McLain. Since the ATF has been a thorn in our side for a long time, we will do a trade. José for the federal agent. As part of the deal for the ammo."

"A federal agent?" Matt pretended to be surprised, especially since this was completely different from what José had said before. Diego was still talking about making a deal, while José had said they wanted him to reveal the location so they could forcibly take it. And why the hell was Diego bringing Skylar into it?

Did that mean La Familia had José? The only other alternative was that José was acting on his own. Matt refused to accept this until he knew for certain. For now, he could only play along. "What are you talking about? What do you mean, a federal agent?"

"Cut the bull," Diego snarled. "José has told us that you know all about this."

Matt froze. José. Again. None of this made sense. "Let me talk to him," he demanded. "I need to make sure he's safe."

Again the chilling laugh. "Do not worry, Señor Landeta. José is still alive. We have given him something to help with the pain. Perhaps you're familiar with his addiction to heroin?"

Damn it. Matt closed his eyes. José had been doing so well. He'd dried out while in prison and had stayed clean the two years since getting out. He regularly attended his Narcotics Anonymous meetings. If they had given him heroin…

Tamping down a burst of pure fury, Matt bit back any response. It wouldn't be good for this scum to know what a bull's-eye his words had been. One thing he had learned over the years was to never let your enemy know your weakness. Never.

Especially since he couldn't be certain Diego was telling the truth.

"I'm still waiting for your answer," Diego said, his voice impatient.

Answer? How could he decide anything until he knew the truth?

In the bathroom, the shower cut off.

Matt needed to talk to Skylar. He could use her clear head to help him come up with some sort of a plan. "I need some time to think." Hopefully, he could stall Diego.

"You have one hour, no more. I will call you then." And Diego ended the call.

When Matt looked up, he saw Skylar watching, her hair still wet from her shower, her hands jammed into her pockets. "I take it that wasn't José," she said drily.

"No." For the space of a heartbeat their gazes locked. "Everything has gotten way too far out of hand," he said. "This time it was Diego Rodriguez."

She frowned. "What'd he say?"

So he told her. When he'd finished, she dragged her hand through her hair, her expression mirroring his shock and disbelief. "I don't understand," she finally said. "There's still a chance that Diego's lying about having José, but why?"

"Or—" he hated to say it, but had no choice "—José

is working on his own with La Familia and is somehow double-crossing Diego Rodriguez."

"That would be playing an extremely dangerous game.

"He knows I'm an ATF agent." She stared off into the distance, considering. "And the heroin thing. How would he know something like that?"

"Exactly. He'd have no way of knowing unless José told him."

"You've been sort of doing the same thing, you know," she said. "Playing two powerful factions off each other. Both are inherently evil."

"No, that's where you're wrong. Diego is the one who is trying to break away from La Familia. All I've done is pretend to offer him the necessary ammunition to help him do it."

"Perhaps." She conceded the point with a slight smile. "But you still had to realize La Familia would get involved."

"Actually, I was hoping they wouldn't. I don't know how they found out, but Diego is a dead man. They don't mess around when their own people are disloyal."

"Then he must be even more desperate."

"I'm thinking he needs the ammo more than ever, especially if he's managed to amass a small army of followers. He's got nothing to lose, so if he goes out in a blaze of gunfire, that's better than torture and mutilation."

"More desperate equals more dangerous," she said. "And what's up with this whole trading-me-for-him thing? What the hell good is that going to do?"

"He says he plans to use you as a bargaining tool to get the ATF off his back."

She shook her head. "Obviously he has no clue how

this works. If he was holding me, the ATF would pull out all the stops to rescue me and get me back safe and sound. They'd call on other agencies, if necessary."

While in Special Forces, Matt had been a part of a few of these rescue attempts himself, so he knew she was right. "Well, if he doesn't know that La Familia is onto him, I'm guessing he thinks the might of the cartel would protect him."

"I guess so." Skylar gave him a grim smile. "But in this case, he'd be wrong." Taking a deep breath, she continued, "So let's outline what we've got. José says he's being held and that they're ordering him to reveal the location of your stockpile."

"Right." He nodded. "And the ATF already *does* know the location, though we have no idea where they got the info."

She played along. "And since the other person who knew that besides you is José, he's the only one who could have told them."

Though he blanched, he had no choice but to agree. "That would mean he's playing several sides at once."

"Yes, it would."

"Meanwhile," he continued, "I don't understand why Diego Rodriguez would want to trade you for José. What's the point of that?"

After a moment, she snapped her fingers. "I know. Here's what I think. Whether or not José is working with them or is a prisoner, let's assume Diego is the one who has him. He gets José to give him the location of your stockpile. He wants to set up this trade—knowing it's not going to happen, but thinking you'll try—as a distraction so he won't have a problem getting the ammo out."

Considering her words, he nodded. "In that scenario, José warning us wouldn't be part of the plan."

"True. But it would mean that José somehow found a way to call us without them knowing."

"Or that they ordered him to phone but the person listening to the call spoke only Spanish, not English."

She smiled. "It could happen. It's a little far out there, but you never know."

Exhaling, he wished he could express to her how much her determination to help him get to the truth—as opposed to trying to bulldoze him to her way of thinking—meant to him.

"Thank you" was all he could say.

Her smile widened. "You're welcome."

"We have one hour. Now we just have to figure out what we're going to do."

"I like the way you included me in that," she said lightly. "Thank you for that."

"We're a team." Though he kept his tone casual, he knew she understood how important this was to him.

A muscle worked in her jaw as she swallowed. "We are that, aren't we?"

Touching her shoulder lightly, Matt pulled back so he could see her face. Though her eyes were suspiciously bright, she hadn't started crying, for which he was grateful.

"I think we make a good team," he said softly.

"So do I," she agreed.

He took a deep breath. "Can I ask you something?"

She shrugged. "I guess. About what?"

"About you."

Though she frowned, she readily agreed. "Go ahead."

Bracing himself for her reaction, he pushed ahead.

"Did you get him? The man who killed your husband and son?"

She stared at him, her green eyes going dark with remembered pain. "You mean did I get vengeance, like you want to do with Diego Rodriguez?"

"Yes."

Straightening her spine, she inhaled deeply. "No. Not like that. I got justice instead. He was captured—the Dallas police were able to make an arrest. I attended when he stood trial. He was found guilty and is now serving life imprisonment without parole."

Her brusque tone told him she was finished, that she no longer wished to discuss this particular topic,

But he wasn't. Though he knew he shouldn't ask, he couldn't help himself. He truly needed to know. "Did that help you at all, Skylar? Were you able to sleep better at night, knowing that son of a bitch is behind bars?"

The tiny lift of her chin told him how she was going to answer. "No," she admitted. "Not at all."

"There you go." Hoping he'd made his point, he waited for comprehension to dawn in her beautiful eyes.

"I see what you're trying to say," she admitted, her expression still grave. "But I can't say it would have helped any more if he'd been killed in a police shoot-out or sentenced to death by lethal injection."

"I find that hard to believe," he said.

She shrugged. "Believe what you want, Matt. But in the end, nothing can bring your family back."

Stunned, he eyed her, wishing—hell, *yearning*—for her to be wrong.

But he knew she only told the truth.

He swallowed hard. "You know what? José said the exact same thing."

And one more truth—one final thing he wouldn't

say out loud. He'd known José was right all along and he hadn't cared. Nothing would bring his family back. That was a given.

But he owed it to them—and to *himself*—to avenge their deaths. Because he honestly believed once he did the hard knot that clenched like a vise around his heart might finally disintegrate.

Chapter 14

Leaving Matt to wrestle with his own demons, Skylar headed out to the camper, ostensibly to let Talia out. With everything that was going on, especially after learning of José's capture, she had a few calls of her own to make. It was time she told her supervisor everything, including the fact that her cover was blown. Everything except the fact that she'd told a tiny white lie about where the ammunition was being stored.

She considered herself lucky that David himself answered the phone. Keeping her voice unemotional and professional, she reported to him exactly what was going on, including the fact that her cover had been blown.

David cursed. "That's not good. Not good at all."

Inwardly wincing, she took a deep breath. "I know. And there's more. The cartel is also apparently aware that I'm ATF. They want Matt to exchange me for his friend José."

"What?" Now she'd succeeded in shocking the unflappable David. "He told you this?"

"Yes."

He cursed. "Is he crazy?"

"No. We—I—believe Rodriguez feels if he had me as a captive it would give him some sort of bargaining leverage against the ATF."

David snorted. "You and I know differently. Out of curiosity, what does Landeta want to do?"

"He isn't sure. He asked my opinion."

"I see." The phone line went silent while David considered. "You do understand that this is out of the question? I cannot allow any of my agents to be at risk."

Skylar forced a chuckle. "Of course, sir. I honestly think this is just a ploy. They're throwing a lot of scenarios out there and trying to see which ones stick."

"Even if that's the case, I'll need you to come in" was his response, as she'd expected. Standard procedure, for her own protection. After all, her boss was a play-it-by-the-book type of person.

"I think I can still do some good here," she said, still warring with herself internally whether or not to spill all of the beans.

"How so?" he asked mockingly. "Your cover is shot to hell, and people are disappearing left and right. Even the damn Mexican cartel knows who you are. You could be next."

"Maybe," she conceded. "But I don't think so."

"Explain."

Taking a deep breath, she told David what Matt had said about his family and the cartel, and how he'd stockpiled the ammunition merely as bait to bring Diego to him.

"And you believe this nonsense?" David's scathing

tone told her he did not. "Matt Landeta is all about the almighty dollar. He's gone through elaborate methods to keep his wealth hidden—we know he's a multimillionaire several times over, but haven't been able to pinpoint the source of all that money."

"So you think that means it was gained illegally?" she finished for him.

"Exactly."

"Not true. He told me he won the lottery."

David snorted. "And you believed him? He's lying, Skylar. Face facts."

"But Matt's not the kind of person who—"

"Who what?" David barked, making her realize she'd just revealed way too much.

This time, she had enough sense to remain silent.

But it was too late. She'd already given herself away.

"You're coming in," he said. "Now."

"But, sir—"

"Do I have to remind you that none of this is personal?" Relentlessly harsh, he hammered the words through the phone. "You are a federal agent and are there to uphold the law. Nothing more, nothing less. If Matt Landeta is breaking the law, you—or in this case, we—will have no choice but to arrest him. Regardless of the reason behind his actions. Where the law is concerned, reasons don't matter. Is that understood?"

Textbook. She'd learned all this at Quantico. Well aware of how much she'd managed to make herself look like a fool, Skylar swallowed hard and answered in the affirmative.

A long silence while her boss considered. "We'll debrief you fully when you get back to headquarters. In the meantime, is there anything else you would like to report?"

"No, sir. That's everything." Throat tight, Skylar knew for the first time in her career she was going to disobey a direct order. Up until this particular assignment, her job had been more important than anything.

Now she'd found something that meant more.

Saddened but resolved, she decided to give it one more try. "Sir, please let me stay. I've worked super hard on this case. I think I can still do some good here."

"No." He didn't even hesitate. "I'm pulling you now. You're in too much danger with your cover blown."

Aware that no amount of arguing would sway him, she kept quiet.

Taking her silence for assent, David continued, "Now that we've settled that, let me fill you in on what we've learned. The cartel—La Familia, to be exact—is now aware of the location of the stored ammunition. Perhaps this is due to their capture of José Nivas."

Skylar waited expectantly. Would the location be the false one she'd reported earlier? If so, Matt and José would be right. There had to be a mole inside the ATF.

But David's next words were worse.

"Your intel was wrong, incidentally," he continued. "The stockpile is not inside the basement of the original ranch house. Landeta keeps it in some large caves on a remote part of his property."

"Seriously?" she blurted. "Where are they located?"

"We're getting the exact location now. We've got somebody undercover working the border. He got word that La Familia has been looking for the site and finally was successful."

"What about the other group?" she blurted. "Diego Rodriguez and his people, the ones who've supposedly captured José Nivas. Do they know where it is, as well?"

"That, I couldn't tell you. But it's highly likely," he

said. "We've learned that there are two groups involved. La Familia, the big, bad guys. And a second, splinter group, headed by your Diego Rodriguez. La Familia plans to take the ammo. We believe Diego is the one with whom Landeta has been making arrangements for purchase. Rodriguez is apparently trying to split off from them and form his own fledgling cartel. La Familia doesn't take kindly to stuff like that."

He cleared his throat while she sat stunned.

Good intel, she thought. It was as accurate as if she'd been reporting the truth all along. Which she should have been doing. Damn.

When he continued, his brisk, businesslike tone had taken on a bit of sympathetic warning. "To sum this up—you've got two warring groups both heading for Landeta's ranch after the same ammo. Either way, it'll be a bloodbath."

Add to that the ATF special-operations teams, which she assumed he'd be sending in. Damn and double damn. "I can assume you're planning to try to arrest the Mexicans?"

David snorted. "I doubt there'll be many left alive, but yes. We'll extradite them back to Mexico to stand trial there."

Back to Mexico. Exactly like Matt had said. Where if they were connected well enough, they'd go scot-free. Otherwise, they'd be executed by their former compadres before they ever made it to trial.

Either way, the situation was even worse than Matt thought, especially if the ATF and both Mexican groups knew the real location. A powder keg waiting to explode. She shuddered. All she could think of was how badly she needed to find Matt and let him know.

"When?" she asked. "When is all this going down?"

"Word has it that La Familia is making a move soon—likely tomorrow night—and that they plan to leave no one alive."

She thought fast. "Unless, of course, we're able to intercept them and prevent it. If we can help it, we've got to stop them from getting their hands on that much ammunition. I think I can do that, sir."

"Do you?" The sarcasm in his voice wasn't lost on her. "This assignment has been a colossal failure on your part," David mused. "We'll go over that in person, but I have to say we've learned more from outside sources than we have from you."

Clenching her teeth, Skylar didn't respond. What did he expect her to say anyway? Apologize? Damned if she would. She'd done what she'd thought was right. She'd done her best.

As the silence dragged on, she debated ending the call. David had always liked to make her squirm, but until now, he'd had little to use against her.

"Maybe next time things will go better," she finally said. This was about the safest, blandest statement she could come up with. If she said what she really wanted to say, she'd be fired.

"Next time?" A hint of steel colored David's dry tone. "I'm not sure there will be a next time. We do have more capable undercover agents, you know."

Skylar winced. "So you're pulling me, and then what? You don't have anybody else in place. You've got the most powerful cartel in Mexico making a move tomorrow night, which will result in what you yourself have just described as a bloodbath. What are you going to do about it?"

"Right now we've got a request in before the judge for a search warrant. As soon as that's in place, we're moving a couple of teams in." David sounded smug and satisfied. "They won't be expecting us, so we'll have the element of surprise on our side."

Gripping the phone so hard her hand hurt, Skylar wanted to scream and curse at him. She wanted to tell him what she thought of his high-handed treatment. But she didn't, partly because if she did so it would only reinforce his already low opinion of her and partly because she knew in some aspects David was actually correct.

She had failed. But how could she make things right if he wouldn't give her a chance to redeem herself?

"Maybe you're right," David said, making her realize she'd said the words out loud. "There *is* something you can do to assist us."

It was all she could do to keep holding on to the phone. "What is it?" she asked. "I'll do anything I can to help."

"Talk to Matt," he said, surprising her. "You've got to warn him. Hell, it should be easy enough to do now that your cover's blown."

Confused, she agreed. "How is that going to help anything?"

"Simple. Tell him we can abort this whole thing if he'll just give us a confession. We won't need to wait for the warrant then, so our teams can swoop in and remove the ammunition, plus deal with the Mexican nationals once they arrive."

A confession. Briefly, she closed her eyes. Matt would never confess to something he hadn't done. And worse, Matt wanted Diego Rodriguez so badly he was blind to the disaster about to unfold.

David spoke again. "Meanwhile, we're going to keep the request for the search warrant in motion. If I don't hear from you within one hour, I'll go ahead and green-light the original plan."

"Yes, sir." She took a deep breath. "I'll do my best."

Evidently he felt it was necessary to give her yet an-other warning. "Remember, a lot of bloodshed can be avoided if Landeta will simply confess. You make sure to tell him that, will you?"

"Got it." Skylar heard the unnecessary reminder. Still, there was one more important thing that hadn't yet been mentioned. "Oh, I need to know something else. What about José Nivas?"

"What about him?" David sounded slightly impa-tient, as though he'd already moved on to other, more important tasks.

"Are we going to do anything to get him out?"

There was the briefest of hesitations, enough to give Skylar her answer. Shocked, she couldn't push the accu-sation past the lump in her throat. This was the organi-zation she'd devoted her life to for the past several years. They were, every one of them, sworn to uphold the law. And at this point, no matter how bad things looked, both José and Diego were innocent until proven guilty.

They couldn't just abandon him to his fate. She had to be wrong about this. She had to be.

"We'll see what we can do," David said. "We've got a couple of sharpshooters on the special-ops team. I'll try to designate one to protect Nivas. After all, we wouldn't want him to become collateral damage, now, would we?"

"Not at all." In this, they were in agreement.

"Oh, and, Skylar? One more thing. I don't have to stress to you how important this is. Our entire opera-tion—not to mention your career with the ATF—is riding on this. Get it handled and head in for debriefing. Got that?"

Wishing David would hurry up and end the call, she realized her hands were shaking. Her entire career. And there you had it. Though she knew Matt trusted her somewhat, she understood there was no way he would agree to confessing. No way in hell.

Truth be told, she didn't want him to.

Still, she had to at least give Matt the opportunity. As she went to find him, it dawned on her that she had the perfect bargaining tool: herself. Maybe Matt would consider doing what David wanted if they agreed to help him get José back safely. Once José was returned unharmed, they could clear up the mess that would be created by Matt's false confession. She certainly would testify on his behalf.

It was a long shot. But she had no choice.

David cleared his throat, reminding her he was waiting for a response.

"I understand," Skylar replied.

Satisfaction rang in his tone. "I'm sure you do."

After she ended the call, she sat motionless, trying to think. Without saying the actual words, her supervising officer had told her what would happen if she didn't swing this case around the way he wanted.

Collateral damage. She knew that was exactly what José would be if she and Matt didn't do something to free him.

Still…they wanted Matt to give a false confession. Simply so they could close the case and tie everything up neatly with a bright red bow.

Taking a deep breath, she went to find Matt and fill him in. Striving for calm, she'd try to present the news as objectively as possible.

He listened attentively while she described her phone conversation with David. When she'd finished, steeling her nerve, she asked him to consider confessing to a crime he hadn't committed.

She felt as foolish as if she were requesting he jump off a cliff into a pool full of ravenous sharks.

"You want me to do what?" Matt stared at her as if she'd grown two heads. She didn't blame him.

"I'm not sure I agree with this myself," she said. She spread her hands. "I know it doesn't make sense. But he says if you confess, the ATF will come in and remove the ammo, and we can avoid this entire gun battle."

"They can do that anyway once they get their search warrant. You know as well as I do that they can trump up some charge."

"We don't operate like that," she said automatically, even though she was actually beginning to wonder if that were true. "Once we get everything settled, I'll help you sort it out."

"No." Crossing his arms, he shook his head. "I won't confess to something I didn't do. You know that. Not just no, but *hell* no. Absolutely not." The icy look in his eyes told her he now regarded her as his enemy. This hurt more than she would ever have believed possible.

"I'm sorry," she said, well aware that wasn't enough.

"Why would you even ask me to do such a thing?"

"Because my boss asked me to," she replied.

"And you?" he asked, his gaze searching her face. "What do you want?"

She spread her hands. "I've been ordered to come in. They're pulling me. I wanted to make sure you knew all of the options that are available."

"This is not an option." He shook his head. "Skylar, your boss is right. I think it's best if you leave. You've made it clear what side you're on. I want you off my ranch. Today. Now. Just go back to your little camper, pack your stuff, grab your dog and go."

Damn it. Frantically she tried to find the right words, wishing she could somehow make him see. "Please listen, Matt. It's not the best solution, but it's logical. You can keep a lot of blood from being shed."

"Logical? To whom? You?" He practically spat the words. "That'd be fantastic for you, wouldn't it? Your big case all wrapped up in a tidy ribbon. You'd get your promotion and I'd go on to prison, never to be heard from again. José would be what—collateral damage? And Diego and his men would go free. I don't think so. It's not going to happen."

"I don't blame you for thinking that," she said. "But hear me out. The ATF has put in for a search warrant. Both La Familia and Diego's group are headed here. You'll be lucky to survive."

Slowly he backed away, his normally expressive face like stone. "I'd rather die with honor than confess to a crime I never committed." He pointed toward the door. "Go."

She didn't move. "You were planning to kill Diego," she cried, feeling as though she were splintering into pieces.

"I told you I'd consider letting you arrest him." The contempt in his voice was the final straw, especially since they both knew he'd do no such thing.

"Matt, please. They're descending on your ranch in a matter of hours. If you want to have a prayer of defending yourself, never mind get José back alive, you've got to let the ATF help you."

"Help me?" He shook his head. "By getting me to confess to selling ammunition to the cartel?"

"You're the one who set that up. You did a damn fine job. For all intents and purposes, that's what it appears you are doing."

He didn't respond. He didn't have to.

She cleared her throat. "They're coming regardless. What are you going to do? If you allow this shoot-out, then what? You have no intention of turning Diego Rodriguez over to the government, do you?"

"What's it to you?" He practically spat the words. "You're finished. Done. You can walk away and never look back."

"I'm not going to," she told him, praying he'd read the truth in her eyes. "Despite my orders, I refuse to leave."

"That makes no sense." He dragged his hand through his hair. "At least you'll be safe."

"Not without you." Crossing the space between them, she wrapped her arms around him and held on. He held himself stiffly, as though he found her touch repellent, but she knew better.

Or thought she did. At least until he methodically removed her hands and stepped away from her.

"I'm staying," she repeated. Then, relentless, she went in for the kill. "In a matter of hours, your ranch is going to be in the middle of a firestorm. You've got La Familia at war with Diego Rodriguez and his faction. On top of that, the ATF is swooping in with SWAT teams."

"And José is still a captive." Eyes narrowed, he watched her.

"Exactly. You've got to choose your top priority. Protecting the ammo and trying to get Diego, or bringing José back safely."

He didn't even hesitate. "José. Of course. José."

"Then if you won't take the ATF's offer, you'll have

to let me do the exchange like Diego requested. Me for José."

"What?" He inhaled sharply, almost a gasp. She'd managed to shock him. "No. I can't risk—"

"For a man who just ordered me off his ranch, you're acting awfully concerned for my welfare all of a sudden," she pointed out. "I can handle it."

Moving forward, she placed her hand on his arm. Though he tensed at her touch, this time he didn't remove it. "I'm a crack shot, a trained law-enforcement officer and a veteran ATF agent."

Dismay flickered in his eyes, the first real softening since she'd asked him to do the unthinkable and confess. He grabbed her hand, crushing it in his larger one. "You have a death wish," he said slowly. "I should have seen this coming."

"Oh, for the love of—" Silently counting to five, she took a deep breath. "I don't have a death wish. And I'm not saying we really trade me for José. All we need to do is make it look like we will. You're a sharpshooter. I read that in your file. You'll have my back. I feel quite certain you can defend me if need be."

He stared at her without speaking. The sudden speculative gleam in his gaze told her what he thought and why.

"Before you go thinking that I'm giving you permission to take down Diego Rodriguez, you should know this. I really believe this people exchange is just a distraction. Assuming they've even really captured him, there is the possibility that they really don't plan to exchange José at all."

A muscle flickered in his jaw. "I was afraid of that."

"If they even have him," she reminded him. "We still don't know what's really going on with him."

Disregarding her words, he continued, "Does your boss think he's already dead?"

"He didn't say, but we can only hope not." Briskly, she moved on, aware that to dwell on what-ifs would only make them indecisive and ineffectual. "He did promise me a sharpshooter to help in his rescue. Either way, José is a distraction."

"A distraction to camouflage what?" he asked. "Their war with Diego and his group?"

"That's part of it." Lifting her chin, she met his gaze straight on. "I don't know if Diego is aware that La Familia is onto him. I'm pretty certain he doesn't know they're moving in, as well. But Diego wants to keep everyone busy so they can swoop in and steal your ammo."

"They don't know where it really is," he began, then stopped and looked at her, correctly reading her expression. "Hell. They do know, don't they?"

She nodded. "I'm afraid so. I was told it's kept in some caves on your property. The location is near the old farm-to-market road."

"That's right. But how do they know this unless José told them?" An expression of horror crossed his face as he realized this had to be the case.

"José had to tell them," she concurred. "He's the only other person who knows. Remember, Diego mentioned that's also how they found out I'm a Fed."

He swore, looking as if he'd like to punch something.

"I'm sure he didn't tell them of his own free will," she said, leaving unspoken what they both already knew. Unless, of course, José was really working with them. Which would explain the fifty thousand dollars he'd received from someone.

Matt looked grim. "I'm going to have to believe they tortured him. They had to. That's the only way he'd reveal something like that. I'm sure of it." He cursed again.

She still didn't bring up José's questionable behavior. Now was simply not the time.

"What do you want to do?" she asked. "Your choice. But you've got to make a decision quickly. We're running out of time."

"I've already told you. We've got to save him. No one else should die due to my actions."

No one else? She went still. What more didn't she know about this man? "No one else? What do you mean?"

"My family." His mouth twisted. "My family died because of me."

"Because of you?" Concerned, she frowned. "Is there something you forgot to tell me? In what way was it your fault that your family died?"

"I wasn't there," he said instantly and fiercely. "If I'd been there, at least they would have had a fighting chance."

She reached out for him, but he easily evaded her.

"You can't blame yourself for that," she told him softly, aching.

The pain-filled gaze he turned on her damn near broke her heart. "Just like you can't blame yourself for what happened to your husband and son?"

Feeling as though he'd just clubbed her in the head, she staggered back. "Touché, Matt Landeta. Touché."

Instantly contrite, he crossed to her and wrapped his arms around her, holding on tightly. She let him, even though part of her was reeling. Not because he'd been wrong, but because he'd been right.

Capricious fate had dictated that her husband and young son be at the bank that day. Though she would have changed places with them in a heartbeat, what had happened that day wasn't her fault.

It had never been her fault.

She looked up at him, wishing she could magically bring him the same sort of healing epiphany.

Though now was most definitely not the time.

"What is it?" he asked, his gaze searching her face. "You look as though you've seen a ghost or something."

Standing up on tiptoe, she pressed a quick kiss against his mouth. "No, I've seen the light."

One brow quirked in a question, he waited for her to continue. Instead, she moved away from him and crossed her arms.

"None of that matters right now," she said. "But we've got a decision to make. So what will it be?"

He cursed but didn't answer.

This she could understand, but she needed him to choose. Again she glanced at her watch, wishing she had a more exact timetable.

"I need to know. What it comes down to, Matt, is you've got to decide what you want to do. This time, it's all up to you."

And then, though it felt like one of the most difficult things she'd ever done, she left the room, giving him time alone to make his decision.

Chapter 15

In Matt's kitchen, a room she still loved, Skylar made herself a cup of tea and sat at his kitchen table, staring out at the perfectly landscaped patio. She knew how badly it was tearing him apart—he'd lived for years focused on revenge. Now he'd not only begun to realize it would be futile, but he was having all his carefully constructed plans ripped away from him by the cleverness of a monster.

Several things could happen to Diego Rodriguez. He could get killed by the very organization he was attempting to leave, he could get lucky and get away with the ammunition, or he could be arrested by the ATF and deported back to Mexico. But he wouldn't be meeting his end at Matt's hands. Killing him wouldn't solve anything. Matt wouldn't get his shot at revenge.

José's rescue was another story. Whether or not José was truly being held captive, for now she'd go with

Matt, who believed in his friend. José didn't deserve to die this way. And she truly doubted he'd get any help from the ATF. Her own agency would be too intent on the situation with La Familia, Diego Rodriguez and the ammunition stockpile.

Only, it didn't have to be that way. They—she and Matt—could work together to rescue José. If, as an added bonus, Diego Rodriguez got caught in the cross fire, so be it. Matt was a sharpshooter, after all. She'd even gone so far as to mention that he could defend her. From there, it was a short leap to what else he could do.

And while she, as a federal agent who had a duty to uphold the law, couldn't point out the obvious to him, she could see it clear as day. Diego didn't know Matt's real identity or what he'd done to Matt's family.

She didn't know if their plan would work. But Matt had absolutely nothing else to lose.

Her cell phone rang. David. "McLain speaking," she said.

"We got the search warrant," her boss said without preamble.

"You did?" Surprised and a little disappointed, Skylar sighed. "That was quick."

"We have a damn good case," David informed her. "We've got two teams en route to the location now."

Damn. Time had truly run out.

"Did you learn where exactly it is?"

"Yes. How familiar are you with the ranch?" Without waiting for Skylar to answer, David pressed on. "Apparently on the eastern boundary, there's a hilly area, one with lots of large rocks. There are some large caves out there. Mr. Landeta has had them outfitted with steel doors, similar to those in a bank vault."

Skylar cursed. "I've been near there. That's where

that gun battle occurred, the one I wrote about in my report. It's near an old gravel farm-to-market road."

"That's where our people will be in place. You need to get out now. Fair warning—it's going to be a danger zone."

"What about the sharpshooter?"

"Sharpshooter?" David said the word as though it were foreign and he didn't comprehend its meaning.

"You said you'd try to spare resources to help us free José Nivas. Remember?" No way was Skylar letting her boss off the hook for this one. No way in hell.

"I'll see what I can do," David said, but Skylar could tell it was an empty promise. As her boss disconnected the call, Skylar knew she and Matt were completely on their own. If José was going to be rescued, they would have to be the ones to do it.

When she hung up, she raised her head and saw Matt watching her.

"I called Diego," he said. "He's agreeable to an exchange tomorrow at dusk."

Interesting timetable, she thought. "He wants to do it right when all hell is going to break loose. I told you José was just a distraction."

"Assuming Diego even knows that La Familia is on their way," he countered. "But you're right. Diego is planning something. He wants the exchange to happen here, in the parking lot in front of the ranch office. Who called you?"

"That was my boss at the ATF. They got the warrant. They have teams on their way now. They'll be in place by the time this whole thing goes down."

He nodded. "And they're going to help us get José out?"

Again, she'd give him complete honesty. She could

do nothing less. "He said he'd see what he could do. But I'm thinking it's going to be up to you and me. You're going to have to be our sharpshooter," she told Matt. "That is, if you're willing to focus on José's rescue rather than getting ahold of Diego Rodriguez."

"I think you already know the answer to that," he said, lifting a case and placing it on the table. Opening it, he gestured for her to take a look. "This is my rifle." Outfitted with a scope, the gun appeared to be military issue.

"So you'll be the sharpshooter?"

"I can handle that," he said.

"Good." She took a deep breath, knowing he wouldn't like what she had to say next. "I'm going to go out there for the exchange. I'll need you to cover me."

He froze. For a second she thought he'd contradict her. Instead, his gaze sharpened as he studied her. Finally, he nodded.

"There's no way in hell I'm going to let you come to harm." He sounded fierce, as fierce as the hard, possessive kiss he gave her. "Do you understand?"

"I know you won't." She grinned. "Just to be on the safe side, I'm going to get the bulletproof vest from my car." Even though the damn thing weighed close to ten pounds and was uncomfortable and hot, wearing it could save her life. Since most people aimed for the chest or back rather than the head, it was the best protection she could get.

"Go ahead and get it," Matt said. "While you're out there, grab your stuff and bring Talia up to the house. Both of you are staying with me from now on. There's no reason why the cartel would wait. I think this will be going down any moment now. While it's just us here at the ranch, I don't want to take the chance of either of you being in any kind of danger."

Grateful and moved beyond words, she nodded. The thought had already occurred to her, too. José knew she was staying in the little camper. Anyone wanting to target the ATF agent would go there. No way was she risking her beloved dog.

As she turned to do as he'd asked, Matt fell into step beside her. "I'll go with you," he said. "Until this is over, I'm not going to leave your side."

That night, though she tried, she couldn't sleep. Though they didn't speak about it, she knew Matt lay wide-awake at her side, going over various scenarios in his mind the same way she was.

In the morning, he rose before she did and padded off to the bathroom. She sat up, gritty-eyed, and whistled for Talia. After she'd taken her dog out, Skylar headed for the guest bathroom to shower and dress.

Today they were both warriors rather than lovers. Neither of them needed any distractions.

After breakfast, Matt showed her the remote surveillance cameras he'd installed near the caves. "They also have a sensor that alerts me if anyone gets close to them."

Studying the live feed, she nodded. "Are we waiting here until we see activity on the camera, or do you have something else in mind?"

"We're not waiting here" was all he said.

For the third time in twenty minutes, she glanced at her watch. This was the part she always hated, the waiting. Once she went into action, she didn't have so much time to think.

"Let's go over the plan at least once," Matt said. "Assuming, that is, that you actually have one."

"Of course I do," she scoffed. "It's simple. When it comes time to make the exchange, I walk out there, count to five and tell José to drop to the ground. You take out his handlers, and we get the hell out. There's no way we could mess this up."

"Right." He looked away from her. They both knew that was a lie.

She ached to soothe him. "It's going to be all right."

"I know," he grumbled. "But speaking from personal experience, rule number one is that nothing ever goes as simply as you planned it."

"True." She flashed him a quick smile. "There's a reason Diego set up the exchange at the opposite end of the ranch from your ammo. You do understand it's entirely possible we might not make it back there in time, right?"

His eyes flashed an emotion that could have been anger or frustration. "In time for what? From what you tell me, the ATF will have people positioned all over the place. Diego will either be dead or captured if he puts in an appearance there."

She studied him. He sounded way too calm. "You don't expect him to, do you?"

"No," he admitted. "He's too valuable in his brand-new organization to put himself in danger. I doubt he'll even show up for the José exchange. He'll be somewhere nearby, close enough to keep an eye on things but completely out of the line of fire."

She caught the leashed excitement in his voice and realized he was still thinking of his revenge. "Do you think you can figure out where he'll be?"

The shrug he gave her was too studied, too casual,

and she realized if he did, he had no plans of clueing her in. With a flash of insight, she realized what he meant to do once José was safe. No matter what the cost, Matt was going hunting, even if he had to follow Diego Rodriguez into Mexico.

This knowledge crushed her. But conversely, it also strengthened her resolve. She wouldn't let him self destruct like this, not if it was within her power to stop it.

She'd have to stay one step ahead of him somehow. "I disagree," she said. "Diego's taking a big—and dangerous—step, trying to form his own new cartel. La Familia isn't going to take that lying down. He won't take chances with anything. I don't think he'll trust anyone else to handle this. I think he'll be here."

"Maybe, maybe not." Matt didn't sound too concerned.

With Talia safely closed up in the house, they sat outside on the porch and watched the sun slowly make its way overhead.

Again she checked her watch. "Not too long now," she said.

"Look." Matt pointed. Two helicopters, neither one military-issue, appeared over the horizon. As they drew closer, they split apart. One went east, toward the caves, and the other headed directly toward them.

"Are those your people?" Matt asked.

"I…I don't know." She stared, momentarily shocked into silence. "I hadn't expected this," she said. "Though those aren't military helicopters, I suppose it could be the ATF."

"Or Diego's people. Or even La Familia." Standing, Matt moved his hand in a dismissive gesture. "Rule number two—expect the unexpected."

Since he didn't appear too concerned, she forced herself to try to relax.

"Are you ready?" Matt asked, shouldering his rifle and shooting her a quick look.

Heart in her throat, she checked her own weapon and nodded.

He placed a hard kiss on her lips. "Then let's go. We'll stay hidden until we find out who exactly is inside this chopper."

"Agreed."

Hurrying across the lawn, they took refuge behind a large stack of baled hay. From there, they still had a good view of the chopper, but had enough cover to be able to avoid any shots that might be fired at them.

As the helicopter drew closer, Matt's cell phone rang. Answering, he shot her a quick look while he listened. After a few seconds, he hung up without saying another word. "That was Diego. He claims to be in the helicopter heading toward us."

Shading her eyes with her hand, she nodded. "What about the other one? Who's in that?"

"I didn't ask," he said. "I'm guessing they're heading over to try to steal the ammunition. Good luck to them. My first concern is José."

Impressed, despite herself, she gave him a thumbs-up.

They both watched silently as the chopper drew closer.

"There." Matt pointed. "In the passenger seat, waving. That looks like… It's José."

"Waving?" Narrowing her gaze, she eyed Matt. "What the hell?" José waving could mean only one thing. He wasn't Diego Rodriguez's captive. This was a setup, meant to set the ATF and Diego at each other so La Familia could get away with the ammo, and José was in on the whole thing.

Matt's scowl told her he was thinking the exact same thing.

"What do you want to do?" she asked urgently. "The chopper's going to be here any second."

He didn't even hesitate. "Nothing's changed. Everything is a go—just like we planned."

Heart pounding, she stepped from their hiding place into the open, hugging the side of the hay. Though she wanted to be seen by the chopper, she made sure she had access to ready cover in case she needed to jump back out of their line of fire.

The pasture where Diego's men had chosen to land bordered the parking lot. It was flat and relatively tree-less, a good place for a large helicopter to set down.

Skylar waited, motionless, as the chopper grew closer. She'd have preferred to be right there when they opened the doors, close enough for the wind from the blades to ruffle her hair, but she and Matt had decided she'd hang back. At least until they saw what exactly Diego had planned.

When the helicopter had completely set down, the pilot kept the blades spinning; she figured he did so to enable him to make a relatively quick getaway if he had to.

Tense, she felt horribly exposed as she waited for someone to get out. If José truly were a captive, no doubt he would be flanked by two or three guards. Like Matt had speculated, none of them were likely to be Diego.

On the other hand, if José was part of this, she was a dead woman. Her fingers tightened on her pistol.

Seconds dragged into minutes. The helicopter continued to vibrate, still in place, but no one exited.

What the…

A prickling on the back of her neck warned her. Acting purely on instinct, she sprinted backward toward the stack of hay she'd chosen as cover. She'd barely taken a dive behind it when gunfire erupted from the chopper.

"Hell." Peering around a large bale, she returned fire, taking grim satisfaction as she watched one of the men—not José—fall out of the chopper's open door.

"Are you all right?" Matt had moved up beside her.

"Yes." She shot him a furious look. "How sure are you that José was the one waving earlier?"

His frown deepened. "Pretty sure.

"Not a hundred percent. We still don't know if he's a captive or part of this."

She swore again. "True. Hell we don't even know if he's even in that chopper."

"Either way, it's a setup. Just a distraction."

As if confirming his words, the helicopter slowly began to rise. As it did, someone inside sprayed the ground with bullets.

"If they get directly above us, we're sitting targets," Skylar warned. "We've got to take cover."

"The truck's too far away." Matt grabbed the side of a bale of hay. "Help me. We can make enough of a makeshift shelter to block us from them."

Quickly they swung hay into place, crawling underneath once they had enough room. Skylar braced herself, hoping Matt was right and the thickness of the hay bales would protect them. She tried to remember if she'd ever seen any studies or watched any videos of what happened when a bullet—or in this case multiple bullets—was shot into hay bales.

But instead of hovering over them, the chopper took off, flying due east, moving fast.

"They're joining the other one," Matt said, helping her out from under the hay.

"Let me have your cell phone," she ordered. As he dug it out from his pocket, she snatched it out of his hand and hit the redial button for the last call received.

She didn't recognize the voice that answered, but truly didn't care. "What the hell was that?" she spat. "I was willing to trade myself for José Nivas. Where is he? What have you done with him?"

Mocking laughter greeted her. "Ah, the federal agent. You're *muy estúpido*—much more stupid than I thought."

Keeping a leash on her temper, she snarled, "What have you done with him?"

"The better question," the man, who must have been Diego Rodriguez, said silkily, "is what we're going to do with all that free ammunition."

"Is this Diego Rodriguez or someone from La Familia?" she said, equally smooth.

Silence while he digested her words.

"What do you mean by that?" he asked carefully. She thought she could finally detect a note of fear in his voice.

"I guess you'll have to find out, now, won't you?" she said and ended the call.

"Well?" Matt demanded as she handed him back his phone.

"I still don't know anything. Other than scaring the crap out of Diego—if that was him—all he said was he was planning to nab the ammo."

"It's not that easy," Matt told her. "I've got reinforced-steel doors with a combination, just like a bank vault. They'll have to use explosives to get in there. And if La Familia shows up…"

"Not to mention the ATF. How long will it take us

to get over there?" she asked, eyeing his pickup and wondering why he seemed to feel no sense of urgency.

"Depends. If we stick to the roads and go in by the old farm-to-market road, maybe four or five minutes tops. Longer if we drive on the ranch."

"Well, come on." She grabbed his arm. "Let's go check on your ammunition."

Instead of moving, he shook off her hand. "No. I don't care about that anymore. Your ATF people can take care of Diego and the cartel."

"But…" She stared at him. "I thought… Don't you care about—"

"I care about José," he told her bluntly, his expression bleak. "I just want him back safe. I'm done with all the rest—the cartel, Diego, revenge."

"You are? Why?"

Instead of answering, he shook his head. "Now is not the time. Plus, I guess I shouldn't have said I was done with the cartel. They've changed all that by taking José. Now I've got to get my best friend back."

She said the first thing that came to mind. "You don't think there's a chance he's in the other chopper? Maybe they brought him to pinpoint the exact location of the cave?"

He cursed. "I didn't think of that. Come on. Let's go."

They ran to his truck and hopped in. Matt pulled out, tires screeching, driving fast.

"Hold on," he told her, the set of his jaw grim. "The roads are gravel and bumpy. Make sure you have your seat belt on."

She did—old habit—so she simply nodded.

They rocketed down the road, skidding on dirt and gravel, hitting ruts so hard they bounced, only their seat belts kept them from hitting the roof.

"How far now?" she asked, gritting her teeth to keep them from knocking into each other.

"Once we hit the farm-to-market road, it's about three miles."

As they crested a hill, she saw the choppers parked side by side in a field. Several government-issue vehicles were parked ahead, blocking the road.

"Looks like the ATF has arrived," she said.

"They're real fond of black, aren't they?" Matt asked wryly.

"Yes, they are," she answered, wishing like hell she could see what was going on inside the perimeter. "It doesn't look as if they've secured the helicopters yet."

"I don't know. The blades aren't moving."

"Good point." When they reached the first Suburban, which had been parked sideways across the road, two heavily armed agents rushed out to block their way.

Matt parked. Skylar flashed her ID. "This is the landowner," she said, indicating Matt. "Let us pass."

With the window open, she could clearly hear the sharp report of gunfire.

"We can't," the agent said. "A bunch of heavily armed Mexicans are shooting at each other. There's been a gun battle going on there. Our team got caught in the cross fire. We've radioed for medics. As best I can understand, we have two down."

"Out of how many?" she barked. "How many men did we send in there?"

He gave her a startled look before answering. "Twenty-four. Two teams of twelve. INS officers are en route, and the Texas Rangers are sending men, too. We've got the situation under control. Now please stand back."

Moving back to the pickup, Skylar and Matt did as he asked.

"What now?" Skylar asked.

"There's a back way in," Matt told her. "Get in the truck. We'll drive until we're out of sight and then we'll park and go in on foot."

"And then what?"

He made a sound of frustration. "I don't know. I'm guessing we'll look for José and see if we can rescue him."

"While I'm all for action," Skylar told him, "since we have no way to make the ATF teams aware of our position, between them and the Mexicans, not to mention the INS guys and the frickin' Texas Rangers, there's an overwhelming likelihood we'll get shot."

He nodded, his expression fierce. "I understand. You can stay here if you want. But if there's any way I can get José out, I'm going to take it."

Well, damn and double damn. Since hell would freeze over before she'd let Matt go in there on his own, she knew she had no choice. "Fine. I'm in."

They drove down the winding road until they could no longer see the ATF vehicles. Matt pulled over and killed the engine.

"Listen, Skylar," he began. "This isn't your battle. You don't have to do this."

Leaning over, she planted a hard and fast kiss on his mouth. "Enough of that nonsense. We're a team, remember? Come on. Let's go."

Out of the pickup, they could hear the sounds of the gunfire much more clearly. With a sinking heart, Skylar knew that if La Familia had their way, no one would be leaving there alive.

And the worst part of it was they still didn't know

what José's true role was in all of this. For his sake, she hoped he hadn't chosen the wrong side.

Rifle slung over his shoulder, Matt strode off, looking like a dangerous mercenary from an action flick.

Hurrying after him, she nearly jumped out of her skin when her cell phone rang.

"Wait," she called to Matt. "It's my boss."

Answering, she barely got out her last name.

"Where are you?" David barked. "Tell me you're not on-site, disobeying orders."

"Um." Done with skirting the edges of the truth, she grimaced. "Not yet. But we will be there soon."

"Hold back," he ordered. "We've secured the scene. We have Diego Rodriguez, José Nivas and various Mexican nationals in custody."

Listening, she realized the gunfire had stopped. She repeated David's words out loud so that Matt could hear.

"How many dead?" she asked.

"Two of our men were wounded. I don't have a body count for the others yet."

Again she repeated what she'd heard.

"Who are you talking to?" David demanded to know.

"Matt Landeta. He and I were going in the back way to try to rescue José Nivas."

"I'm not sure he needs rescuing." David's hard tone told her what he thought of men who betrayed their friends. While she could sympathize, she refused to pass judgment until she heard José's side of the story.

"What about the ammunition?" she asked dazedly, amazed at the speed with which everything had been settled.

"That's why I'm calling you." David sounded grim. "We just blasted into the caves. We need to have a word with Mr. Landeta."

"Why?"

"Because there's no ammunition in there. The damn place is empty."

Chapter 16

As soon as she and Matt showed up at the storefront the ATF was using as temporary headquarters, they were separated.

Trying not to show her impatience, she answered every question accurately, not really caring if the truth damned her and ruined her career. She'd already disobeyed a direct order. She wasn't sure she even wanted to continue in law enforcement anyway.

When she'd finished, she was put in a holding cell and left alone. Her own agency was treating her like a common criminal.

Her repeated requests to talk to Matt were completely ignored. She didn't know where they'd taken him or even if he was being charged with some sort of crime. Since they hadn't found any ammunition, she doubted they'd have a leg to stand on, but that didn't mean they wouldn't try.

Even her questions about José Nivas were deflected. She supposed she'd find out eventually when she finally got ahold of Matt.

At last, after twelve endless hours, she was released and instructed to return home, with orders not to contact anyone involved in the case—especially Matt Landeta. She had a final debriefing scheduled for the following morning at the Dallas ATF office, which was the one she worked out of.

"I've got to go to Matt Landeta's ranch first," she told them. "My dog is there, as well as my belongings." What she didn't say was that she had to find Matt, too.

The special agent in charge—who was not David— nodded. "We'll send an escort with you."

"I don't need an escort."

The cold look he gave her made her frown. "Actually, you do. We've seized the Landeta ranch until further notice. No one, including Mr. Landeta, is allowed on or off the property without strict supervision."

Stunned, she managed not to show it. "Thanks," she snapped. "Then why don't you go ahead and drum up this escort so I can be on my way?"

Her attitude wasn't earning her any brownie points, she could tell from his furious expression. Again, she found she didn't care. She had more important things to worry about.

The wrought-iron gate was wide open. Escorted by two decidedly unfriendly agents, Skylar hurried to the main house and located Talia. Her pet was overjoyed to see her, jumping and spinning in circles. Despite the border collie's friendly greeting, Skylar's escort ignored the dog. She wondered if they were made of stone.

Once she'd taken Talia outside, she went to the little camper and gathered the last of her belongings, trying to ignore both the lump in her throat and her ever-present, unsmiling escort.

Since disobeying the order to report back for a debriefing, she'd expected this. Whatever other repercussions would come from her actions, she guessed she'd find out when she returned to the office on Monday morning, after taking a few days off, plus the weekend. No doubt David would give her an earful.

The little rented Volkswagen had vanished. Upon questioning, her escort told her it had been seized and would be returned to the rental agency. She had a brief moment of disquiet, wondering how the heck she was going to get back home, then realized her escort had most likely been told to drive her.

Though she kept hoping, she saw no sign of Matt.

Telling herself everything would get straightened out soon enough, she squared her shoulders, lifted her chin and marched out to the government-issue vehicle, carrying her bag, with Talia prancing at her side.

Back home, Talia raced around the small house joyously. Eager to explore the familiar surroundings, she barked at the back door to be let out. After letting her go, Skylar roamed her home, full of an aching kind of restlessness.

She wanted Matt. No, she *needed* Matt. But her phone never rang and she tried to tell herself—without success—that it was all for the best. For now.

For the rest of the week and through the weekend, she slept, she ate, she went through the motions, but she never felt truly herself. The combination of anticipation—she kept expecting the phone to ring—and sadness had her numb.

She wondered what had happened to José. She wondered where the ammunition had gone. But mostly, she wondered how Matt was, if he was holding up, if he needed her. She didn't know if he was still in custody or had been released.

Monday morning, her stomach in knots, she reported for work as normal. She hadn't been inside the building for five minutes when her intercom buzzed and she was instructed to go to David Northrup's office immediately.

Shoulders back, head held high, she did.

"Have a seat," he said. Unable to tell from his tone whether she was about to be berated or not, she sat.

"We've been named in a lawsuit," he told her. "Along with the ATF, you've been named personally."

Of anything he could have said, she hadn't expected this. "A…lawsuit?"

Expression drawn, he slid a paper across the desk toward her. "Matt Landeta. He's suing us for entrapment, illegal entry and theft of property, among other things. You're being named personally as the one who did the entrapping. You should expect to be served sometime today."

"Sued?" Though she knew she kept repeating his words, she didn't really know what else to say.

Lips tight, he nodded. "There's more. Landeta has also filed a restraining order. You're not to contact him or go within five hundred feet of him."

She couldn't speak. She felt sick. In fact, she suffered as if she'd been punched in the stomach. It took every bit of her willpower to keep from doubling over.

Back ramrod straight, she accepted the second sheet of paper he slid over to her.

"Read these at your leisure," David told her. "In fact, you might want to consult with an attorney. As of right now, you are officially on mandatory leave until notified. I'll have someone escort you to your desk so you can clean it out."

Horrified, she could only shake her head. "That's what you do when people have been fired. Everyone will think…"

He shrugged, clearly not caring. "I'll make sure they know that's not the case." Pressing his intercom button, he asked to have Agent Delvecchio sent in.

When he'd finished, he looked right at Skylar, expression blank, as if he didn't really see her. "That'll be all, Agent McLain. We'll call you if we need anything."

Skylar didn't move, even though the other agent stepped into the room. "I have a few questions. How long will I be on leave? I assume it's paid leave?"

"It is paid, and as I said, you'll be on leave until you're notified otherwise. Any more questions?"

Standing, praying her legs didn't give out from under her, she shook her head. Agent Delvecchio opened the door for her.

As she walked to her desk, accompanied by her silent escort, she felt the eyes of everyone on her. Heart pounding, she cleaned out her desk as quickly as she could, hating that she'd been made to feel like a criminal.

Worse, what the hell was up with Matt? She couldn't understand why he'd file a lawsuit to begin with. And to name her in it, as if she had replaced Diego Rodriguez as his enemy, defied comprehension.

Carrying her box of belongings to her car in the bright sunshine, she realized her life had just completely fallen apart and, once again, she was starting from scratch. On her own—and alone.

In the car on the way home, she resisted the urge to call Matt, even though she'd taken her cell phone out and placed it in the cup holder.

Curiously numb, she parked in her driveway, retrieved her stupid box and carried it into her house.

"We'll get to the bottom of this," she told Talia, earning a lick and a tail thump in return. "There must be some kind of mistake. Matt wouldn't sue me." After all, while there'd been no promises exchanged between them, she and Matt had developed the beginnings of a relationship.

Or so she'd thought.

What the hell? She'd already disobeyed one direct order. Picking up her home phone, she punched in the number. An unfamiliar male answered. "Landeta residence."

"Matt, please."

A pause and then, "May I ask who's calling?"

When she gave her name, she swore she could feel ice forming on the line.

"I'm sorry. Legal counsel has advised Mr. Landeta that due to the ongoing litigation, he should have nothing to do with you," the professional voice said with perfect diction. "Therefore, Mr. Landeta has requested that you not call him again."

Stunned, hurt and surprisingly furious, Skylar hung up the phone. So it was true. Matt wanted nothing else to do with her. "In a way, I guess I can't blame him," she told Talia, ruffling her pet's fur and resisting the urge to bury her face in her ruff and weep. "Ongoing litigation and a restraining order. I think it's safe to say that whatever we had between us is over. Or maybe I only imagined it."

Talia whined.

Feeling the prick of tears in her eyes, Skylar got up. "It's apparently possible I wasn't the only one playing a role," she said, heading into the bathroom to take a hot shower.

Only when she'd set her showerhead to the highest massage setting it had and the near-scalding water was pounding her body did she finally break down and let herself cry.

"The lawsuit has been filed." The high-priced lawyer in his expensive suit looked pleased. No doubt because of all the money he envisioned Matt shelling out to him and his firm. "The judge has ordered that you can legally return to your home."

When Matt didn't respond, the attorney handed him a manila folder as he continued, "Not only is it on file with the court, but we've had the ATF offices served, as well as Ms. McLain."

That got Matt's attention. "Skylar? What about her?"

"She's named in the lawsuit, of course. From what you told me the other day, there's no doubt she was the one who entrapped you."

Heart sinking, Matt began flipping through the folder, almost frantically. He stopped when he saw a paper marked Restraining Order Request. Narrowing his eyes, he looked up at the man he'd hired—and was now about to fire. "A restraining order? You filed a restraining order against her?"

Judging from the way he blanched, the lawyer realized at that moment that he might have overstepped his bounds. "Well, sir, it's common procedure in these kinds of situations. From what you've told me, the woman sounds like a stalker."

"That's it. I wanted the ATF to pay for what they did, but not her. Withdraw the lawsuit and remove the restraining order."

The other man's mouth fell open. "I believe if you stop and think this through, you'll realize that everything we did was in your best interests."

Coldly furious, Matt stood. "I want this handled today. Notify me once you're finished."

"But—"

Ignoring the beginning of what sounded like another protest, Matt held up his hand. "And when everything is completed, you're fired. Send your bill to my home address and I'll make sure you're paid."

Turning, he walked out the door.

Driving home, he cursed the law firm. Shortly after all the dust had settled from the Mexican gun battle and the ATF's pointless raid, which had been featured on the evening news—both local and national—Matt had taken to hiding out from reporters and photographers in his motel room. Though he'd despised feeling trapped in a place that wasn't even his own home, he hated dodging reporters and cameras even more. At least now he could return to the ranch. He'd once again take refuge in his home. The only time he would leave would be to visit José in the hospital.

Since his friend was still unconscious, Matt had yet to learn José's true story. Contrary to what he'd said earlier, Diego Rodriguez denied taking him captive. A prisoner of the state, Diego was lucky he hadn't been killed when La Familia had swooped down to exact revenge. He'd be held in a U.S. prison until he was extradited to Mexico. There, Matt had no doubt he'd be brutally tortured and killed. La Familia didn't forgive and forget.

Many of Diego's men had died, along with several of the Mexican nationals who worked for the big drug cartel. When the ATF had begun cleaning up the mess, they'd hauled all the wounded into the nearest hospital, and that was where Matt had found José.

His friend had a minor head injury and, judging from his blood workup, had been given some kind of heavy-duty tranquilizer. At least it wasn't heroin. For that, Matt counted his blessings. He didn't know if José would be up to kicking the drug a second time.

He looked forward to hearing José's explanation. Despite how everything looked, he still believed in his friend and would continue to do so unless José himself told him something different.

As luck would have it, he was there in the hospital when José opened his eyes.

"Matt?" Attempting a weak smile, José tried to sit up. Matt helped him, stuffing two pillows behind his back.

"How are you feeling?"

"Like hell," José answered, his voice gravelly from disuse. "Could you hand me a glass of water?"

Once his friend had taken a few sips, Matt leaned forward, about to question him. As he did, a nurse making her rounds entered the room, realized her patient was awake and called for the doctor. As she began making note of José's vitals, she turned to Matt and asked him to leave.

"You can see your friend later, once the doctor has taken a good look at him."

Which meant explanations would have to wait for another day. He went home, had supper and tried to think.

Restless, unable to sleep and missing Skylar, Matt wandered his ranch, ending up in the old barn with only his horses for company. This was where he missed Skylar the most. She'd loved it here as much as he did, he thought.

In the morning, Matt rose at his usual time and showered. After a brief ride to check his land, he grabbed some of the clean clothes José kept at the ranch, put them in a grocery bag and headed for the hospital.

From the look of the half-eaten breakfast on a tray, José had been up awhile and was feeling better. He eyed Matt cautiously, wincing a little, as if his head hurt.

Though he really wanted to know the truth, Matt wouldn't push for answers. He knew his friend would tell him when he was ready.

"How are you feeling this morning?" he asked.

"Okay, I guess." José looked down. "My head hurts."

"What'd the doctor say?"

"No major damage. I had a concussion." Shaking his head, José grimaced. "I wonder how long they're going to keep me here."

"You're in luck," a nurse said, strolling into the room. "The doctor has signed your discharge papers. All I need is your signature and you can go home."

When he'd finished and handed the clipboard back to her, she gave him his copies and pulled the curtain closed around his bed so he could get dressed.

"You know the Feds are going to want to talk to you," Matt said.

Slowly, José nodded. "Am I under arrest?"

"Nope. They'd love to have something concrete to pin on both of us, but they don't."

José nodded.

Matt handed his friend the bag of clothes he'd brought and went outside of the curtain to wait.

Finally, José emerged. Side by side, they walked outside to the pickup.

"Do you want to go to your house or the ranch?" Matt asked as they settled in their seats.

"Is it okay if I come to the ranch and stay for a few days?"

"Sure." Cuffing José lightly on the shoulder, Matt smiled. "You know you're always welcome."

José sniffed. "Thanks for believing in me. When those guys grabbed me, I really thought I could be strong and not tell them anything."

"Did you ever see Diego Rodriguez?"

"No." Frowning, José scratched his head. "Did he say I did?"

"Yep. He also wanted to trade you for Skylar."

"What?" Sitting up straight, José winced. "What the hell?"

"It was a diversion."

"Yeah, I guess. Matt, I'm sorry I told them about where the ammo was. They tied me to a chair and poured water down my throat until I nearly drowned. They did it over and over until I told them what they wanted to know."

"It's all right. Everything worked out in the end." He thought of something then. "What about the helicopter?" he asked. "We saw you waving."

Grimacing, José looked downcast, as though ashamed. "They had me doped up really good. One of the guys shoved me toward the window and lifted up my arm to make it look like I was along for the ride."

So far, Matt had accepted everything José told him at face value. But there was still one thing that needed to be explained.

Reaching the house, Matt parked the truck and helped José get out. His friend still seemed a bit unsteady on his feet.

They headed into the kitchen. Apparently, José was still in a confessing mood. "Right before all this, I told

La Familia about Diego, too," he said. "That guy is lucky he's still alive. The cartel don't play. That's why they decided to make their own grab for the ammo, so they could get to it before Diego did."

"He's still alive," Matt told him quietly. "He'll eventually be extradited back to Mexico."

"Where he's a dead man," José said.

"Exactly."

"Do you regret that you didn't get to kill him?"

This question, Matt considered seriously. "No."

"But you would have if you'd have gotten the chance?"

"No. I gave Skylar my word that I wouldn't. I promised her I'd let him be brought to justice."

José shook his head. "But I bet you hoped someone would get a bullet into him and do the job for you."

"Maybe. I'm not going to lie. I did want him dead."

"He will be soon enough." José swayed on his feet, reminding Matt that he needed to sit down.

"Level with me, bro," Matt said, pulling out a chair for José before taking his own seat at the kitchen table across from him. "The fifty thousand in your account? Where'd it come from? You were pretty pissed when I asked you that before."

Sitting heavily, José looked down, twisting his hands. "How'd you find out about that?"

"The ATF. Where'd you get it?"

José's olive complexion reddened, though he met Matt's gaze. "Chantal," he said. "She makes a lot of money modeling. She knew I wanted to buy land out on the other side of town, so she gave it to me."

"Fifty thousand won't even buy a residential lot," Matt pointed out. Never mind that the Chantal he'd dated had been so self-absorbed she wouldn't have willingly parted with even a fraction of that amount. Unless she had some sort of ulterior motive.

"It was enough for the down payment." A flash of pride lit up José's brown eyes. "I've already applied for a loan. I'm going to build a house there. And a barn. For a ranch of my own."

"Why didn't you ask me?" Matt asked quietly. "Money is the one thing I have plenty of. You know I'd do anything to help you."

Pushing back the chair violently, José stood. "I know and I appreciate it, but you do enough. Too much. Sometimes a man's gotta stand on his own two feet."

"True. But it bothers me that you'd rather accept help from someone like Chantal than me."

Instantly, José shot him a warning look. "Careful what you say, amigo. Chantal is going to be my wife."

Incredulous, Matt gaped at his friend, then belatedly shut his mouth and tried to look pleased. He didn't think he quite pulled it off. "I…I don't know what to say."

"*Congratulations* would be nice," José drawled.

"Of course. I'm happy for you. If this is what you really want."

"I do." For the first time since Chantal's name had come up, José looked uncertain. "As long as you have no problems with it. You don't still have…feelings for Chantal, do you?"

"No. Hell no." Realizing he had to be careful, Matt tried to tone down his vehemence. "I don't. Not at all."

"That's what I thought." Satisfaction colored his friend's voice. "After all, you have Skylar now."

Skylar. Even the mention of her name made Matt ache.

"You do have Skylar, don't you?" José eyed him, his brow wrinkled in confusion at Matt's silence.

"Not yet," Matt finally admitted. "There are a few things we have to clear up, if I can ever get her to talk to me."

"Uh-oh. What'd you do?

"Do you want a running list?" Matt shook his head and sighed. "First off, she got a lot of heat from ATF after the whole showdown. They wanted so badly to be able to justify their involvement, I think they were going to try to railroad me into a conviction, even without any evidence."

José grinned. "And Skylar wouldn't let them, would she?"

"Nope." Matt grinned back. "That's when they put her on mandatory leave. My private investigator found all this out for me."

"What? When was the last time you talked to her?"

Matt had to clear his throat in order to be able to speak past the lump. "The day all this went down."

José whistled. "Damn. So did the ATF drop all their charges?"

"They had to. Their case was flimsy at best. It's hard to levy a charge of selling ammunition illegally without proof."

"Yeah, I'll say. What the hell did you do with the ammo?"

"I took your advice and moved it." Pushing to his feet, Matt crossed to the fridge and grabbed a couple of sodas. Handing one to José, he popped the top of his and took a long swallow.

"Thanks." After a moment, José did the same. "What are you going to do with all those bullets?"

"I've already started the process to find law-enforcement organizations that need them. I'll be donating it to them."

"All of it?"

"Yep."

José looked impressed. "Does Skylar know any of this?"

"No. At least, I haven't been able to tell her."

"Oh, yeah." José took a swallow of cola. "You were telling me all the reasons the two of you haven't connected. There was her job and the fact that she hasn't called you—"

"Oh, she called. I was still barred from entering my own house. I don't know who talked to her or what she said, but her number shows on the caller ID."

Crossing his arms, José grimaced. "I'm guessing you tried to call her back."

"Of course." He grimaced. "I didn't leave a message, but I called several times."

"And she never called again? Any idea why?"

"Well, it might be because of the lawsuit." Matt tried not to wince as he told his friend what the law firm he'd hired had done. The only good thing they'd accomplished was getting him back the ability to return to his home.

By the time Matt had finished, José was shaking his head, looking dazed.

"That woman's got to think you hate her," he said.

"Probably. She's disappeared off the face of the earth." Matt gave a sheepish grin. "I paid a private detective to find her house, but she's not there. I don't know where she's disappeared to. No one at the ATF will tell me—I think they're actually worried I'm after revenge or something."

"Call her again."

"I've tried, believe me. Several times, actually, but she never answers. I went by her house, but her neighbor said she'd been gone over a week. I don't know where she's gone, and I don't have her cell-phone number. I hope she's all right." Despite his best efforts, he couldn't keep the worry and the longing out of his voice.

Eyeing him, José took a long drink of his cola before replying. "You got it bad, don't you?"

"Yeah," Matt admitted. "I do. Have a seat again, please. I really need you to help me figure out a way to get Skylar back."

Looking out the kitchen window, José grinned. "Looks like I won't have to. She's here."

Chapter 17

Not having a job to go to felt strange enough. But being without Matt filled Skylar with an emptiness and a sense of loss she hadn't felt since Robbie's and Bryan's deaths.

A hollow shell of herself, she drifted around her house like a ghost. The only thing that kept her grounded was Talia, who seemed to sense that her mistress was unhappy and went out of her way to be amusing in a doggy sort of way.

Finally, Skylar realized she'd had enough. It was time for a massive life change. Her time in law enforcement was over. She was ready to move on to the next big thing.

Since her mandatory leave was paid, she didn't hand in her resignation, not yet. David had called her two days after she'd been unceremoniously escorted from the office to tell her that Matt had dropped the lawsuit.

She supposed she should have been happy. Instead,

she just felt numb. She felt nothing, not even when David told her Matt had removed the restraining order, as well. Hanging up the phone, she told herself she didn't care. That part of her life had been brief and powerful, and damn near perfect, but clearly it was finished.

Unsurprised, she noted that David hadn't said a word about her coming back to work. She wouldn't actually be too shocked if he tried to pin the entire embarrassing fiasco on her. Once, she would have fought, but now she no longer had the energy.

Each day seemed to drag on longer than the last. Finally, even she'd had enough. Fed up with herself, she decided to make yet another change. Instead of allowing herself to wallow in self-pity, she used the time off to take a well-deserved vacation.

An online search, her credit card number and she was all set.

Packing Talia and a suitcase in her car, she drove to the Florida Keys. She'd rented a beachfront cabin for a week. There, she planned to try to relax and work on what she'd discovered she really loved— photography.

Before she left, she'd submitted the article she'd written along with the photographs she'd taken of Matt's Arabian horse-breeding operation to *Today's Arabian Horse* magazine. Since Matt was a well-respected breeder, part of the ATF's agreement with them had been, in addition to allowing her to use them as cover, that they'd actually consider publication if her stuff was worthy.

She truly believed it was. Time would tell, but she'd bet she'd see her first byline soon—and hopefully, deposit her first check.

In the meantime, she took photographs of everything

else. Dogs romping on the sandy beach, chasing waves, a fisherman silhouetted against the water and the setting sun. Talia loved the place and accompanied Skylar wherever she went. Skylar realized she was as close as she'd been in a long time—at least since she'd realized she'd loved Matt—to being happy. But while she found a deep satisfaction and a tentative sense of serene peace, she constantly ached for him. Despite everything. More proof she was a fool.

The days slipped by, and finally it was time to pack up and head back home. The ATF still had made no move to call her back to work, but as soon as they did, she had her resignation all typed up and ready to hand in. The life-insurance money from Robbie's policy had sat in her bank account untouched, and this would be what she'd use to live on while she tried to establish her new career.

And then there was Matt. Finally, she realized he was unfinished business. If she wanted to forget about him, she had to face him and hear from his own lips why he didn't want her.

He hadn't called—but then, she hadn't given him her cell-phone number and sure as hell no one at the ATF offices would give it out. He couldn't get in touch with her online because her presence in social media was all under other names. An undercover ATF agent didn't have the luxury of becoming a public figure.

He wouldn't come to her; therefore, she'd go to him.

If she wanted any sense of closure, apparently she'd have to initiate it herself. Which, she decided during the long drive back to Texas, she would do as soon as she got home.

Before she could take the first steps to her new life, she had to return to Matt's ranch and settle things with him. He might be able to go on with things unfinished, but she sure as hell couldn't.

Back at her house, she was surprised to see several calls on her caller ID from Matt's number. He hadn't left a message, but at least he'd tried to contact her. This gave her heart.

But she didn't want to hear him tell her goodbye over the phone. No, she wanted to look into his blue eyes one last time and hear his husky voice say the words that she'd know would be a lie.

Decision made, she didn't even unpack. In fact, she left her suitcase in the backseat of the car. It was three o'clock in the afternoon. She'd go now. Too much time had passed without her knowing the truth.

Whistling for Talia, she got into her vehicle. She needed her dog along for moral support—after all, Talia had been there with her through everything.

The drive went slower than she'd anticipated since she had to travel across Dallas, then southeast. Her dashboard clock showed it was nearly 5:00 p.m. when she turned down the long road toward his ranch. The gate was still open, which seemed odd, but she was glad since that meant she didn't have to push the call box and ask for permission to enter.

Pulling up in front of the house, heart pounding, she gripped the steering wheel. As before, the red-tiled roof gleamed softly in the afternoon sun, perfectly complementing the creamy stucco walls. As she had previously, she felt a sense of longing, a feeling of finally coming home. This time, she knew home was more than a place—people made a house a home. Corny, but true. This house felt like home because of Matt.

More proof she was forever destined to be a fool.

Though her legs felt as if they wouldn't support her, she made herself climb out of the car and clip on Talia's leash. Then, with her dog panting happily at her side, she started for the house.

At first, she headed toward the front. Then, realizing she'd never gone there, she reversed direction and walked toward the patio. She jumped as the back door opened and José came out.

"About time you got here," he said, winking as he brushed past her, though he paused long enough to pet Talia. Skylar stared. Winking?

Stunned, she made herself take another step forward, then nearly stumbled as Talia surged ahead toward the door, her tail wagging in delight.

Matt. Crouching down, he greeted her dog first, then raised his chiseled, beautiful face to hers.

Even the mere sight of him made her knees go weak.

She opened her mouth to speak, and her cell phone rang. Damn. "It's the ATF," she told Matt. "I'm sorry, but I've got to take this call."

"I'll be here when you've finished," he said and stepped back inside the house, Talia at his side, to give her privacy.

It was David, sounding jovial. His fake cheer grated on her nerves.

"How are you holding up?" he asked with pseudo concern.

She didn't bother with false pleasantries. "Fine. What do you want, David?"

He chuckled, no doubt to show her he didn't take her curtness personally. "I'm calling to let you know you can come back to work on Monday. Internal Affairs has cleared you of any wrongdoing."

"I had no doubt they would."

Clearing his throat, he made a sound that could have been either agreement or dissent. "Anyway, I'll see you on Monday?"

"Of course," she said smartly. "And I'll be there with bells on to give you my resignation."

"Resignation? But—"

Then, before he could say anything, she ended the call.

Surprised at herself, she realized she didn't even feel a single flutter of panic. She'd just quit her job. One roadblock on her path to happiness had been removed. Now she needed to talk to Matt and remove the other.

Watching Skylar pace as she talked on her phone, Matt felt a rush of love so strong he nearly staggered. While he wasn't sure she felt the same way, the fact that she'd come here counted for something.

It had to. He couldn't imagine life without her. Or, he thought, hands buried in Talia's fur, her dog.

Belatedly he realized he could use this opportunity to rehearse what he should say. He'd never been good with words—hell, most guys weren't—but if there had ever been a more important time for him to get them right, he didn't know of one.

Obviously finished with the call, she turned to make her way back to the house. Heart pounding, he stepped out onto the porch, meeting her halfway.

"I've missed you," he said. As far as openings went, it wasn't the best, but it was definitely the truth.

Skylar, however, appeared unimpressed. She crossed her arms and glared at him. "Did you? Then what was the deal with the restraining order? As if I'm some sort of psycho, stalking and threatening you."

"My lawyer did that. I didn't even know until he told me. As soon as I found out, I had it removed."

Gazing beyond him, as if it hurt her too much to look at him, she nodded. "I knew it was gone. I wouldn't have come out here otherwise."

He told her what the lawyers had done and how he'd fired them. Then, with his words running out and trailing off into silence, he said the one thing that was in his heart.

"Stay." His voice broke, but he continued, "Skylar, please don't leave me again."

At his words, she froze, going utterly still like a wild horse about to bolt. Swallowing hard, she raised her head and finally met his gaze, hers direct. He tried to throttle the dizzying rush of desire that ran through his blood.

"I need a reason, Matt. Give me a reason to stay." The combination of hope and sorrow in her beautiful green eyes felt like a dagger straight to his heart.

He pulled her close. Bent his head. Kissed her lips. Softly. So softly, moving his mouth over hers slowly, savoring her taste. "Is this not enough motivation?"

Though desire had darkened her eyes from emerald to sea-storm, she shook her head. "That's part of it, of course," she whispered. She stood so straight, so still, she might have been a glass statue, about to shatter into a hundred thousand pieces with the wrong touch.

He'd have to be careful to do this right. Nothing had ever been as important to him as this moment, this woman.

"You need more reason than this?" he asked, kissing her again, a slow stroking of his mouth across hers, deepening the slant, his tongue, and trying to convey his emotions—or at least some of them—with his kiss.

She sighed with her entire body, swaying against him. When he finally released her mouth, she held on to him as though her legs were too unsteady to stand, burrowing her face in his shoulder.

Overwhelmed, he held her close, breathing in the scent of her hair. He knew he never wanted to let her go.

"You're going to have to say it," she said, moving her mouth over the pulse that beat, steady and strong, at the base of his neck.

Say it? For a moment, he froze. All of him, from his breath to his vocal cords. And then, because he knew she was right, he nodded.

"I'm no poet," he began, cupping his hand under her chin and raising her face to his before releasing her. "But I'll try. You are everything to me—you're my sun and moon, as lovely to me as the most beautiful Arabian horse racing across the pasture."

As he tried to think of other words, she lowered her head and her shoulders began shaking. Was she crying? Horrified, he stopped, about to ask her if she was okay.

And then she snorted. Snorted? And then, and then, she began to laugh.

Startled, he watched her, a reluctant grin curving his mouth.

"I'm sorry," she managed between guffaws. "But I've never been compared to an Arabian horse before."

Hearing his own words, he couldn't help but smile. His smile widened into a grin as he realized what he'd said and then he joined her in laughing out loud.

"Try again, why don't you?" she suggested, wiping at her eyes and giving him what he guessed was an encouraging smile.

He winced. "No flowery words this time, okay?"

"No flowery words."

"All right, then." Eyeing her, her beautiful complexion porcelain and pink, her green eyes sparkling with happiness, he suddenly knew what he needed to say. He felt it, bubbling up from inside him, from his heart, from his soul, from his core.

"I love you, Skylar McLain. I want to spend the rest of my life with you and have children with you and grow old with you. Is that plain enough for you?"

Expression full of love, she nodded, moving toward him to embrace him. But he stopped her, holding up his hand.

"Wait," he said. "I'm not finished." Then, even though he had no ring, he got down on one knee and took her hand. "Will you do me the honor of becoming my wife?"

She gasped, her eyes widening. For one utterly horrifying, terrifying moment, he thought she might say no.

"I don't have a ring," he continued desperately, aware he was babbling again but unable to help himself. "But I thought we could choose one together. New York is nice this time of the year, or we could head to L.A. if you—"

She kissed him, effectively silencing him, for which he was grateful.

"Of course I'll marry you, Matt," she told him when they finally came up for air. "And now it's my turn to tell you how I feel."

Though he wanted to hear the words, he knew he'd have the rest of his life to hear her say them. He'd always been a man of action, rather than words, and right now, he wanted something else more.

"Sweetheart," he murmured, right before he claimed her lips with his, "why don't you show me instead?"

And, taking him by the hand, she led him into the house, to his bedroom, where she did.

Later, when they emerged, both deliriously happy, he grabbed her hand. "Let's go find José and give him the news."

Talia barked. They both turned, watching as a low-slung silver sports car pulled into the drive and parked behind Skylar.

"Chantal," Matt said, grimacing. "Apparently she and José are engaged. Do you mind waiting here while I go get him?"

"Not at all," she said. "I'll talk to her. I'm sure we have lots in common."

Though he wanted to tell her he doubted that, he kept silent. She'd figure it out on her own.

Hurrying down the back steps toward the barn, Matt shook his head. As far as he could tell, Skylar would have no way to relate to the bitter, self-absorbed woman his best friend wanted to marry. He could only hope for José's sake that she'd changed.

He found José in the barn, brushing down one of the mares.

"Chantal just pulled up," Matt said.

José's entire face lit up. "Great. I was gonna tell you, but things have been crazy. We have an appointment at city hall with the justice of the peace to get married this afternoon."

"Married?" Aware his mouth was open, Matt closed it. "Are you sure Chantal's okay with that type of ceremony?"

José shrugged. "She's the one who suggested it."

Would wonders never cease? Still, for his friend's sake, Matt felt he had to warn him. "Sometimes women say things and hope you'll understand that they don't mean them. Why don't you get married here, on the back patio or something? Give it a few days and I'm sure we can get the place looking nice."

"We're doing it today," José said stubbornly. "It's all planned. We got our marriage license last week. As a matter of fact, we were wondering if you—and Skylar, if she's interested—would be willing to be our witnesses."

"Of course." Clapping his friend on the back, Matt nodded. "It's the least I could do."

"Thanks." They started toward the house.

"I have news of my own," Matt said. "Skylar and I are getting married, too. I just asked her and she said yes."

Grinning, José high-fived him. "About time the two of you came to your senses. Hey, maybe we can make it a double ceremony."

"It's a seventy-two-hour waiting period once you get the marriage license." Matt was actually relieved. He didn't want to get married at city hall by a justice of the peace. He wanted to plan a ceremony Skylar would always remember.

When at first she'd seen Chantal strolling toward her with the unique confidence held only by the very beautiful, Skylar looked down at her faded jeans and scuffed boots and tried not to feel frumpy. But to her surprise, Chantal greeted her with a friendly smile.

"Matt went to get José," Skylar told her after introducing herself. "I hear congratulations are in order."

To her surprise, Chantal hugged her. "Thank you," she gushed, looking girlishly delighted. In fact, she glowed with happiness as she held out her hand so Skylar could examine the ring.

It was not the large rock Skylar would have expected a supermodel to wear. The small diamond winked brightly, the white gold or silver band adorned with flowers.

"It's beautiful," she said and meant it. It was exactly the sort of ring she herself would wear.

"Thank you. José picked it out. Say—" Chantal leaned in close "—José and I have an appointment at city hall to be married this afternoon. He plans to ask Matt to be his witness. I know we've just met, but I was going to ask a total stranger to be mine. Would you mind standing up for me?"

Touched, Skylar nodded. Evidently she wasn't the only one who walked the world alone. She had one question for the other woman. "It isn't weird for you?" she asked. "I mean, since you dated Matt and all?"

"Nope." Chantal didn't even hesitate. "We were never in love with each other. It was more like killing time. Though I never would have met José if not for Matt. The instant I saw José, I knew."

"Me, too." Skylar spoke without thinking. At the other woman's curious look, she hesitated, wondering if Matt would mind her sharing personal news with his ex. Since this woman was marrying his best friend and would forever be involved in their lives, she decided he wouldn't and smiled shyly. "Matt and I are also getting married. I don't have a ring yet—he just asked me a little while ago."

"Congratulations!" Chantal squealed, enveloping Skylar in another perfumed hug. "Maybe you and Matt can get married with José and me this afternoon."

Skylar shook her head. "We haven't gotten a marriage license and there's a waiting period. Plus, there's no ring."

Cocking her blond head, Chantal considered. "You

know, I wouldn't mind a ceremony here at the ranch. Would you consider making it a double?"

Staring at this woman that she'd just met, Skylar tried to think. Both she and Chantal had no one else, and since she'd lost Robbie and Bryan, she'd become more and more isolated and antisocial.

Right now, she was initiating sweeping changes in the way she lived her life. Starting over. Maybe the time had come to open herself up to the possibility of making new friends.

"I'm sorry. I don't mean to be pushy," Chantal said, glancing away. She must have believed Skylar's silence stemmed from disapproval. "Forget I said anything. I'll just go ahead with my wedding this afternoon with the justice of the peace."

"No, that's not it." Impulsively, Skylar reached out and touched the other woman's arm. "You deserve a better wedding than that. Actually, I love the idea. Matt and José are best buddies, after all. I think you and I might become friends, too." She shrugged, feeling a certainty and sense of rightness. "Let's see what the men think, all right?"

Chantal looked so relieved that Skylar knew she'd made the right decision. A wedding was another new beginning, too. Why not share it? After all, she would no longer be alone, nor would Chantal.

José agreed. Skylar got the impression he'd do anything Chantal asked him to do, even though it meant waiting to get married. Though Matt, she reflected happily, had also consented to the plan.

First, though, he said he had something to tell her. Taking her aside, he swallowed hard, letting her know whatever he had to say was important to him.

"After the gun battle, I took steps to have my name

legally changed back to what it was before. Miguel Lopez."

He sounded so worried about her reaction that she had to kiss his cheek. "I'm glad. What made you decide?"

Voice wickedly low, he nuzzled her neck, sending heat all through her body. "Because I wanted our son to carry on the family name. Do you mind being Mrs. Lopez instead of Mrs. Landeta?"

She tried to frown and look serious, but failed completely. The idea of having his son made her dizzy. "Of course not. But does that mean I have to call you Miguel instead of Matt?"

"Nope." Eyes full of warmth, the tenderness and heat of his gaze had her curling her toes. "I'm used to Matt."

"Then by all means, Mr. Lopez, let's go get the paperwork done."

He froze. "Do you have your birth certificate? I checked out the paperwork José had. In Texas, you need a certified copy of your birth certificate, among other things."

She grinned at his worried expression. "You know, I just got back from vacation. Because I'm a worrywart, I always have a certified copy with me. Along with my passport, my driver's license and anything else I might need."

On that note, they headed to town.

The morning of their wedding, Matt woke to the ominous rumble of thunder and the howl of the wind. Sliding out from under the sheets, careful not to wake Skylar, he padded to the window and peered outside.

Lightning flashed, illuminating rain blowing sideways in sheets.

Perfect, he thought ruefully. Their relationship had never been smooth. Of course it would storm.

He'd have to scrap their plans to have the ceremony on the back patio. Pacing, he stopped and smiled slowly as an idea struck him. Of course. He knew exactly where they'd be wed.

"Matt?" Awake now, Skylar sat up and rubbed her eyes. "Was that rain I heard?"

"And thunder and lightning. But no worries, I'll just move the location and we'll be fine."

Frowning, she ran her fingers through her tousled red hair. "Good thing my dress is satin instead of silk. Where are you thinking?"

Climbing back into the bed, he gave her a slow, suggestive kiss. "Leave that to me. I promise you'll love it."

When he went in to deepen the kiss, she pushed him away. "Move," she ordered, smiling slightly to take the sting from her words. "Not till after we're married, Mr. Lopez."

As she sauntered toward the bathroom for a shower, she gave him a saucy smile over her shoulder. "Tonight, I'll show you again how much I love you." Then she closed the door in his face.

He couldn't help it—he laughed. He couldn't wait.

Humming under his breath, Matt went to one of his other bathrooms and took his own shower. Afterward, he made a few phone calls and changed the location of the double wedding. He sent one of his ranch hands into town for umbrellas and got dressed in his Western suit. Through it all, Talia watched solemnly, as if she understood what was happening.

José arrived an hour before the ceremony. Chantal was already there, closeted in a guest room getting dressed, just as Skylar was in the master bedroom. Like Matt, José had been forbidden to see his bride until the ceremony.

When Matt told José where the wedding was to be held, José chuckled and agreed it was perfect. The two men played cards and hung out in the kitchen while they waited.

The justice of the peace arrived. He was given an umbrella and led away.

When Skylar and Chantal appeared on the stairs, both Matt and José sucked in their breath. Matt could hardly tear his gaze away from the beautiful woman who was to be his wife. She'd chosen a champagne-colored dress that fit her body lovingly. Her red hair had been piled on top of her head with corkscrew tendrils framing her face.

The wedding, attended only by the ranch hands, was tiny. Matt had no family and he'd learned neither did Skylar. José's remaining relatives were all in Mexico, and Chantal wasn't speaking to her parents. Talia's attendance, Skylar said, was more than enough for her. She'd make a new family here with him.

Everyone else was already in place, waiting. Matt took Skylar on his arm, his heart swelling with gratitude. Next to him, José did the same.

At the doorway, each man opened his huge black umbrella and walked outside, protecting his woman from the downpour.

Luckily, the wind had died down and the rain no longer came in sideways sheets. The steady deluge only drenched their feet. When they reached the old barn, Skylar squeezed his arm and grinned.

"Perfect," she said. "Our place."

His heart swelled. He'd known she'd understand.

Inside, among the horses and the scent of hay and manure and leather, the justice of the peace stood on a raised platform in front of the stallion stall. Talia had dashed ahead and was seated expectantly on the floor near him. Flowers decorated every stall door, and if a horse nibbled on them here and there, well, that was to be expected.

They'd all four chosen to embellish the traditional vows slightly with a few simple words.

"You are my heart and my life," Matt told Skylar when it was time for him to do so, "my shelter from the storm and my rainbow after the rain."

As Skylar repeated the words back to him, to his shock he felt his eyes fill. Not with tears of sorrow or pain, but with tears of joy at this new beginning. A life full of love and hope, rather than pain and regret. For both of them.

The justice of the peace turned to José and Chantal. Matt barely listened as they spoke their vows. He couldn't tear his now-blurry gaze from Skylar. His woman, his wife.

With trembling fingers, she reached up and wiped his eyes. Wonder and love and joy shone on her face, mirroring the emotions in his heart.

"I now pronounce you man and wife," the justice of the peace intoned. "Gentlemen, you may kiss your bride."

And so Matt did, gladly. Beside him, José did the same.

The ranch hands clapped and cheered. Talia barked. As Skylar gazed up at him, her green eyes went dark with passion and the promise of what was to come later.

Arm in arm, they turned to face their new future.

When they turned to exit the barn, they found the rain had stopped. Above them, in the still-gray sky, a rainbow glowed, transcendent.

* * * * *

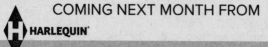

REQUEST YOUR FREE BOOKS!

2 FREE NOVELS PLUS 2 FREE GIFTS!

ROMANTIC suspense

Sparked by danger, fueled by passion

YES! Please send me 2 FREE Harlequin® Romantic Suspense novels and my 2 FREE gifts (gifts are worth about $10). After receiving them, if I don't wish to receive any more books, I can return the shipping statement marked "cancel." If I don't cancel, I will receive 4 brand-new novels every month and be billed just $4.74 per book in the U.S. or $5.24 per book in Canada. That's a savings of at least 14% off the cover price! It's quite a bargain! Shipping and handling is just 50¢ per book in the U.S. and 75¢ per book in Canada.* I understand that accepting the 2 free books and gifts places me under no obligation to buy anything. I can always return a shipment and cancel at any time. Even if I never buy another book, the two free books and gifts are mine to keep forever.

240/340 HDN F45N

Name	(PLEASE PRINT)	
Address		Apt. #
City	State/Prov.	Zip/Postal Code

Signature (if under 18, a parent or guardian must sign)

Mail to the **Harlequin® Reader Service**:
IN U.S.A.: P.O. Box 1867, Buffalo, NY 14240-1867
IN CANADA: P.O. Box 609, Fort Erie, Ontario L2A 5X3

Want to try two free books from another line?
Call 1-800-873-8635 or visit www.ReaderService.com.

* Terms and prices subject to change without notice. Prices do not include applicable taxes. Sales tax applicable in N.Y. Canadian residents will be charged applicable taxes. Offer not valid in Quebec. This offer is limited to one order per household. Not valid for current subscribers to Harlequin Romantic Suspense books. All orders subject to credit approval. Credit or debit balances in a customer's account(s) may be offset by any other outstanding balance owed by or to the customer. Please allow 4 to 6 weeks for delivery. Offer available while quantities last.

Your Privacy—The Harlequin® Reader Service is committed to protecting your privacy. Our Privacy Policy is available online at www.ReaderService.com or upon request from the Harlequin Reader Service.

We make a portion of our mailing list available to reputable third parties that offer products we believe may interest you. If you prefer that we not exchange your name with third parties, or if you wish to clarify or modify your communication preferences, please visit us at www.ReaderService.com/consumerschoice or write to us at Harlequin Reader Service Preference Service, P.O. Box 9062, Buffalo, NY 14269. Include your complete name and address.

HRS13R

Diego unbuckled her harness as Vanessa clutched the helicopter seat's armrests. "What are you doing?"

He pointed across her, out the door. "You have to jump, Vanessa."

Oh, no. Absolutely not.

Clutching the door frame so hard her fingernails ached, she shuffled her feet toward the edge and poked her head out the side to stare at the green water below. Over the roar of the rotor blades, she shouted, "Are you crazy? How high up are we?"

"Fifteen meters. It's as low as I can get with these trees."

Fifteen meters was fifty feet. A five-story building. Her stomach heaved. "There could be barracuda in there, or crocodiles. Leeches, even."

"That's a chance you have to take. There's nowhere else to land. The rain forest is too thick and we're out of fuel. You have to suck it up and jump."

"What about you?"

"I'm going to jump, too, but I have to wait until you're clear of the chopper. And there's a chance my jump won't go off as planned. We're running out of time."

She knew she needed to trust him not to leave her, but it was hard. She'd never been this far out of control of her life and she couldn't stop the questions, couldn't let go of the fear that he'd abandon her to fend for herself. "How do I know you're not going to dump me here and fly away?"

"I thought we went over this. Did you forget my speech already?"

"No." But promises were as fluid as water, she wanted to add. People made promises all the time that they didn't keep.

"You gotta hustle now. We don't have much time left in this bird."

She stood and faced the opening, then twisted to take one last look at Diego. What if he didn't make it? What if this was the last time she saw him? "Diego…"

"Jump into the damn water or I'm going to push you. Right now."

She whipped her head straight. Like everything else that had happened in the past couple hours, with this, she didn't have a choice. She sucked in a breath and flung herself over the edge.

**Don't miss
TEMPTED INTO DANGER
by Melissa Cutler**

**Available June 2013 from Harlequin Romantic
Suspense wherever books are sold.**

ROMANTIC suspense

CONFESSING TO THE COWBOY
by Carla Cassidy

Small town Grady Gulch has been held captive
by a serial killer targeting waitresses.

Mary Mathis may hold the secret to the killings,
but she risks losing it all if she confides in Sheriff
Cameron Evans, a man who has been captivated
by Mary. Will she confess to the hot sheriff
before the killer takes her as his final victim?

Look for *CONFESSING TO THE COWBOY*
by Carla Cassidy next month from
Harlequin® Romantic Suspense®!

Available wherever books and ebooks are sold.

Heart-racing romance, high-stakes suspense!

HRS278251